MW01169628

OATH OF OBEDIENCE

A DARK MAFIA ROMANCE

JANE HENRY

Copyright © 2021 by Jane Henry

All rights reserved.

No part of this book may be reproduced in any form or by any electronic or mechanical means, including information storage and retrieval systems, without written permission from the author, except for the use of brief quotations in a book review.

Photo by Wander Aguiar

Cover art by PopKitty

❀ Created with Vellum

SYNOPSIS

Oath of Obedience: A Dark Mafia Romance
Deviant Doms

Synopsis:

Marriage to a stranger is only the beginning.

She'll have my baby, too.

Many things have changed while I've been in prison.

The Family has been decimated.

Our enemies have gotten bolder.

My brother has taken the reins as the new Boss.

But one thing hasn't changed: my loyalty.

So when I'm released from prison only to be shackled to the daughter of our organization's biggest traitor, I agree.

My new wife has taken oaths to love, honor, and obey.

I don't want her affection.

I don't need her honor.

But I will gladly take pleasure in her body.

I will force her to carry my child.

And I *will* have her obedience.

But when the dark, dangerous secret she harbors threatens to destroy us, my unwilling bride will learn exactly how I mete out punishment to those who break their oaths...

CHAPTER 1

"My stars shine darkly over me." ~ *Twelfth Night, Shakespeare*

ORLANDO

I WAKE up at the crack of dawn. No one tells me what to do, most especially the roll call asshole who clangs an alarm at six in the morning. So my eyes snap open at five, every morning.

My roommate snores gently, but it doesn't bother me. I grew up with so many brothers and sisters, you just sort of ignore noises over time. They fade into the background like so much else. White noise.

There's a small window in here, a cell I earned for good behavior. The other cells are windowless when you're not locked into solitary.

I push myself out of bed, slide down the bunk, and hit the floor. Nothing like waking the body up with a morning plank. I drop into plank position, forearms on the floor, abs tight, welcoming the burn in my muscles. Give myself thirty seconds to rest the abs before I'm up again, pushing myself to the point of muscle fatigue. I'm panting and sweating by the time I'm done. I stand, stretch, then hit the floor for push-ups.

"When I get out of this hellhole, remind me to have you on speed dial, bro," Dario says, rolling over. He props himself up on one elbow and smiles, the flash of white against pink lips the only thing I see in the dark.

"Oh yeah? You startin' up a fuckin' bromance?" I say, panting, in between reps.

Dario chuckles and talks through a yawn. "Fuck that. You know if I wanted a bromance, would've hit on you when you were fresh outta the damn shower, not all sweaty and shit."

I smile but don't reply, my breath coming in short gasps, my muscles straining with the effort of doing push-ups. Last I checked, I hit a deuce and a half on the health office scale. Bulked up on purpose, but it's not easy to fucking push two hundred fifty pounds up, especially before I've had my coffee. You make do in a small cell, though. I've worked my body hard since I've been in here, and I won't stop.

Roll call comes and goes before the pay phone comes by, wheeled on a cart.

"Rossi. You're up."

The corrections officer shoves the call cart to me. I hear a murmur of voices from the next cell over and somebody mutters my name. Gotta be a new guy. Everyone else knows who the fuck I am.

"Don't need a call today," I tell him, turning my back on it before I grab the makeshift pull-up bar for another set of reps. He clears his throat. I ignore him.

"Nah, man. Incoming. Might 'make' that call today if I were you," he says.

I pull up and feel the lengthening of muscles in my abs and back and welcome it.

"Oh yeah?"

"Yeah."

He runs a hand through his hair, and I drop to the floor. I give him a sharp look. He knows something.

He takes a step back.

Good. Haven't lost my fuckin' touch in here. It's better for me when a look works as well as a fist.

The officer's young, thin, and ready to shit his pants. Never understood why guys like him didn't pick another fucking job. Why corrections officer? Why voluntarily put yourself into a prison with inmates that scare you shitless?

I take the phone, and he flinches. I sigh. "Bronson. Leave, man. Go cook some fuckin' books, will ya?

They pay better than this hellhole, and you'd sleep better at night." I shake my head and pick up the phone. Dario chuckles behind me.

I get a little knot in my throat when I hear Romeo. He'd been in Tuscany on business until last night. I've missed my older brother's voice.

"Got a surprise for you, Orlando."

I release a breath and run my fingers through my short, cropped hair. "Yeah? What's that?"

"Now if I tell you, wouldn't be a surprise, would it?"

I smile, warming at the sound of his voice, the familiarity of talking with him. Fuck, I miss my family. "Guess not."

"Be on the lookout, man. Around lunchtime."

"Alright, if you say so."

He chuckles, and I hear the whisper of a female voice in the background. Vittoria, his wife.

"Tell Vittoria I say hello. Any bambinos coming yet, man?"

He sighs. "Not yet," he says in a low voice. "Ain't for lack of trying."

I groan. "Rub it in, why don't you?" Still, I feel sorry for him. Rossi family tradition tells us that children are a king's crown jewels, and that life is incomplete without little ones running around underfoot. Some might even say the Rossi family views children as a commodity, and it's why my mother had so many.

I have other views, though. I think we helped her to not feel so lonely. Hell, maybe we still do.

Jesus, I miss them, all of them, even pain-in-the-ass Mario and bossy Rosa. Marialena, I miss most of all. My baby sister and I were always close and have grown even closer since my father's passing.

We chat a bit longer before I hang up the phone, curious about what he's got planned for me. Money, maybe, so I can pick shit up in the canteen. New books, even better. Already plowed through every damn thing he's sent and most of the books that interest me on the prison's library shelves. It won't be food, which sucks since I'd give fucking anything for a plate of Nonna's pasta or Mama's panzerotti. And it sure as fuck won't be a goddamn conjugal visit lined up for me, thanks to Boston's puritanical ways.

I slug down breakfast like medicine—tasteless oatmeal and burnt sausage—drink the swill they call coffee and toss down an orange for the hell of it. Suppose if they used oranges to fight scurvy back in the day when traveling by ship, couldn't hurt behind bars.

I do another workout after breakfast and check on deliveries. Nothing from Romeo. When I come back, nearby cellmates are yelling out chess moves. We can't play actual chess here, so the more astute yell out moves for a mental game.

"My bishop takes your bishop," Dario says, giving me a wink when I get back.

"You winning?"

"When am I not winning, man?" he asks. True.

I stand for the fourth damn roll call, wondering if Romeo was just blowing smoke up my ass. That's not who he is, though. Romeo's word is law, damn near carved into tablets like the commandments from Sinai.

I'm thinking. Mulling shit over. Finally, I clear my throat.

"Dario." I keep my voice low, so no one hears. "You know who I am, brother?"

He sobers and nods. "I do, man." His eyes shoot to the skulls inked on my knuckles, before looking at the rose on my forearm. "I do." There's fear in his eyes I didn't expect, and it dawns on me that he might think I'm threatening him. Wouldn't be the first time I bared my forearm as a claim to the Rossi brotherhood. Sometimes it helps to reference your status as an established brother of high rank in the most powerful organized crime ring in New England. Sometimes it doesn't.

I continue to keep my voice low. "When you get out of here," I say in a little whisper, "you come and find me. Do you know where to find me?"

He nods and swallows audibly. "I do."

"The fucking car theft landed you here. You come see me and I'll give you a better job than that."

We're always recruiting new men to our brother-hood, always swearing men in with vows of allegiance, obedience, fidelity, and honor. The original core of our ring is related by blood, but when we find someone worthy of the oath of Omertà, we're not above recruiting. And I know this man to be loyal, hard-working, and fucking ruthless.

It's time to hit the shower. I follow behind Dario, but when we get there, the usual guards are gone. My stomach clenches, my instincts primed. *Shit.*

Dario meets my eyes in a silent vote of confidence, and I give him a nod. Not a touch of fear in his gaze.

My eyes quickly linger on the scarred floors, marred by sharpened shanks. The shower is one of the most notorious places for a beatdown.

Someone overheard our conversation. Should've fucking known it.

"Orlando!" Dario shouts. I duck when I see him look over my shoulder, on instinct, and a fist flies through the air where my head just was. Adrenaline courses through me, excitement weaving its way through my limbs.

The brothers in my ring of men have been trained in many things. Interrogation, money laundering, intimidation tactics, among other things.

Me? I've been trained to fight.

I duck one blow, only to take one in the side. I elbow my attacker without a second thought and feel my elbow crack ribs. Dario has my second attacker in a headlock beside me, but the third barrels at me full force, knocking the wind out of me. While I'm heaving for breath, my attacker walks around me.

"You think because you're a Rossi, your shit don't stink?"

He circles me with a blade. I don't respond. There's no response to someone taunting me except to wipe this concrete floor with his face. I flex my fingers.

I don't have time to get away. He lunges for me, but I quickly dodge him. Not fast enough. His head rams into my solar plexus, winding me. I'm knocked on my ass. But I'm so furious, I come up swinging. He drives at me, slices along my arm. And then in one quick move I grab his wrist and go to snap it.

Dario shouts, "Orlando, no! You're out of here man. They're jealous. They don't want you out."

I knock one out cold and don't give him the beating he deserves. Dario sits on the second. The third I restrain with my own bare hands. Son of a bitch.

I have him at my mercy. I could beat the shit out of him. I could fucking kill him. At the thought, an image of the last man I beat, his head smashed against the concrete pavement outside of a dive bar in Southie, flashes in my mind. I'm serving time for involuntary manslaughter. I meant to give him a beating, teach him a lesson for bad-mouthing The

Family. I didn't know he was gonna hit his fucking head. Didn't know it would kill him.

And I don't want the blood of another man on my hands. Not now. Not over bullshit like this. I don't like spilling blood unless it's necessary.

It's why my father hated me. He did it for sport.

The alarm sounds, too late. Planned.

Guards come in, prepared to cuff and restrain. Dario speaks up. "Orlando was attacked, and he did nothing. Check the cameras. These guys came after him because they're jealous."

Goddamn it. If they fucked anything up...

A guard comes with a set of keys and shakes his head. "You're lucky you've got a friend in here," he says, shaking his head. "I'm here to let you out."

I blink. "Let me out?"

"Yeah, brother. You dodged a damn bullet, man. Dodged a fuckin' firing squad."

Dario grins at me. He called it.

"Remember, Dario," I tell him as I'm led out in cuffs. "Remember what I said."

"I will, brother," he says, nodding with a sad smile. He clears his throat and calls the next move out loud and clear. "Checkmate."

CHAPTER 2

"Many a good hanging prevents a bad marriage." ~
Twelfth Night, Shakespeare

Angelina

"LOOK WHAT I FOUND." Elise grins at me, surrounded by boxes and bags and hangers and clothes.

"I have literally no idea how you find anything in this mess," I say with a grimace. "Honestly, girl. You know I'm all about live and let live, but this takes the cake…"

Elise has a stack of boxes by the door, name brand designer shoes, and brown paper bags with embossed golden lettering, also name brand. Whenever we come to Italy, she stocks up. And that's saying something. At home, it's not exactly like she's conservative or moderate.

She pulls out a stack of paperback journals from behind her back. She sings in a singsong voice, "Do you remember these?"

I gasp. I was completely unaware that she still even had these.

"Of course I remember these!" How could I forget?

We called each other *gemella,* twin, when we were younger. We looked so much alike people would often mistake us for sisters, though these days I'm smaller than she is and she's the one with the designer clothes. We were inseparable.

These are the journals we wrote, lists to each other, letters that we shared from when we were younger. I was traveling abroad with my family, and she traveled abroad with hers. We were best friends from childhood but didn't get to spend anywhere near as much time together as we'd like, so we relied on writing to each other. Her nanny would mail the journal to me, and I would mail it back to her.

Those were such simple times. Times before we both had to grow up much too quickly. I reach for them. "Give them here!"

"Ah ah," she says, shaking her head. "Say please."

"Oh my God, you are the biggest bitch!" I tackle her onto a pile of bikinis she was trying on for our trip to the hot springs in Tuscany. She laughs and keeps them out of my reach, but I finally get her to cave when I yank on her bikini strap.

"Fine, here, *here!*" She tosses me one of the books. "I bookmarked where you listed the traits you want in a future husband." She giggles her head off.

"Oh my God." I don't know if I want to laugh or cry as I grab the journal and flip through the filled pages. A part of me already mourns the innocence of the girl who wrote in these pages.

I open the book to see hearts and flowers and swirls, Elise's name in thick black letters shaded as if they're blocks. I was always doodling, making artwork out of nothing. I still do, sometimes. We each have a bulleted, numbered list, one labeled *Elise's dream husband* and the other *Angelina's future mate*. Future mate? God!

I giggle and read in a high-pitched voice. "Elise." I laugh even harder. "Number one. HANDSOME. Underlined and asterisked and circled. Apparently, looks were top of your list."

She nods and absentmindedly twirls a piece of her hair. "Naturally. What else?"

"Is kind to animals, very, very smart, and doesn't mind how much money I spend shopping." I collapse into laughter at her list. It's so teenager, so juvenile. Yet so adorable and still... her.

"Oh, go ahead. Laugh at my list. Wait until we get to yours." She giggles uncontrollably. She grabs the book back; I reach for it, but she keeps it out of my reach, reading out loud. "Must have really, *really* nice eyes. Maybe blue, maybe purple." She gives a loud laugh. "Purple, Angelina? Are you serious?"

"Dude, I was like ten years old. Give me a break."

I still want a husband with nice eyes. I want to lose myself in them when he looks at me.

"Next."

She laughs uncontrollably. "Likes reading and poetry and good food. Empathetic, compassionate, feeling for others. Caring and concerned about their needs. Thoughtful, warm-hearted, forgiving, and sincere. Has big, huge muscles."

She falls onto the bed in helpless laughter. "Why didn't you add billionaire to the list? I think you put everything else on it."

A knock sounds at the door.

She squeals, quickly covering herself up.

"Oh my God, Angelina," she hisses. "If he sees me like this…" Her cheeks flush bright pink.

"You'll make his day," I say on a whisper.

Elise is hot for her bodyguard. Her very handsome, very protective, very much older bodyguard. She shakes her head and tips her head back, but not before she pinches her cheeks and purses her lips. I swear she even breathes a bit more heavily. "Come in!"

Piero, Elise's bodyguard, walks into the room. If there were a poster to be plastered in a travel agent's office to advertise for vacationing in Tuscany, Piero would be front and center with his classically Italian rugged looks.

"Your father called, Elise." He looks away, a muscle twitching in his jaw.

"Oh?" She's breathless, so obviously in love with this man that I don't know if she could hide it if she wanted. "And what did he say?"

"He wants you to pack your bags." I swear a vein pulses in his temple. "Now."

Elise pales. "What? I just got here," she says, a little furrow in her brow showing how perplexed she is. I know she comes here not just because she enjoys visiting Tuscany, but because this is where Piero is. She has bodyguards in the States as well, but they are older, kind of lumbering men. I'm not sure her father's ever seen this one, because if he did, he'd probably lock her up and shoot him.

"He wants you to pack up everything." He shakes his head and turns for the door. "And I can't tell you why." Something's terribly wrong. Elise looks at me in a panic.

He leaves. Elise is on her feet. My heartbeat quickens, and my hands feel clammy and damp. We ate panini at one of the little local restaurants for lunch, and I feel as if I'm going to lose it.

Elise has never told me who her family is, but I'm not stupid. I know who she is. I know who her father is. I can read a damn newspaper, or an online article. I never cared that her father was involved in organized crime. My own family doesn't lie on a bed of roses either.

My father's a drug dealer, and it's probably the only reason why I'm still friends with her. Any other parents would've ended our friendship long ago, but my dad doesn't give a shit what I do, and he never has. Probably even wants in with her dad.

We traveled the world, my school was paid for in full, anything and everything I wanted was mine... Except a dependable family. A relationship I could call my own.

I look at Elise. Just a minute ago we were laughing, enjoying reminiscing about old times in our child-hood, and now... now I don't know what to expect. I know that things change at the drop of a hat around here, that she's subjected to her father's whims and wishes whenever he feels like it. It's partly why we come here to Tuscany when he's in America and go back to America when he's in Tuscany. Just to escape him.

We've been attached at the hip since she saved my life... and I'll never forget it. I'll be indebted to her forever.

"We have to find out what this is about," I say to her. "We can't just accept that you have to pack your bags." My heart is hammering so loudly, there's a rush of blood in my ears. This could mean literally anything.

"Well, how are we going to find out what it is? I can't exactly call my dad. You know he's not going to say anything, and he's just going to get mad at me for even asking."

I bite my lip, thinking about it. I think I know what we have to do, but I have to choose my words precisely, so that I don't get her in worse trouble than she already is.

"I think you need to find a way to ask Piero. I think maybe you even have to seduce him to get that answer."

She blinks, wide-eyed and surprised. I'm not usually the one to suggest something dangerous, and I'm not quite sure why I'm doing so now, but somehow, I know what's going to happen next may change the course of her life forever. Something tells me there's no coming back from this.

She opens the door and yells his name. "Piero! Hey, can you come back here for a minute?" She twirls her hair seductively and shoves her breasts out to get his attention. What she doesn't know is that she doesn't have to even try, he's already completely enamored with her.

He walks back heavily, looking over his shoulder and from side to side, making sure no one knows he's coming back. She beckons for him to come into her bedroom.

When he enters, she shuts and locks the door behind her. Hands on her hips, all hint of flirtation gone, she skewers him with a look she likely inherited from her ruthless father. "Tell me everything."

He shakes his head. "I can't. Your father will..." He looks at me.

He doesn't want me to know what her father is capable of. But I already know. "Listen. Is it something serious?"

He doesn't answer but looks furtively at the door. "I don't care about me," he says. "I don't care if I lose my job or worse. But I don't want you to get in trouble."

Shit. This is worse than I thought.

Elise isn't even close to flirting anymore. She's gone pale and looks as if she might pass out. She doesn't have the strongest of constitutions. "What is it?" she asks.

"Elise." His voice is choked, and I don't know why. Fear or something else? "I can't tell you. He'll kill me." He looks back at me, and she looks back at me as well.

"For the love of God, you guys, I know who you are. Stop pretending I'm an idiot."

"I don't think you're an idiot, but sometimes it's better that you don't know things," Elise says.

"Exactly," Piero says. "Which is why I'm not telling you shit." He curses under his breath in Italian.

Elise draws in a breath. "If you tell me, they'll never find out. I'll make sure of it."

He curses again. "You can't promise that."

She nods. "I won't let them."

Neither of us says anything for long moments. We know that she has no power in this. We both know that she is a mafia daughter, and her life has never been her own. We know that it's only a matter of time before her father intervenes and chooses her future.

Piero looks around again and shakes his head. "I can't, Elise."

She pleads with him silently, giving him a look I'm not sure anyone could resist. He runs a hand through his short black hair and curses under his breath. When he does, a sleeve of his shirt pulls up and I can see ink on his arm I didn't notice before. If he's her bodyguard, is he one of them, then?

"I'll tell you," he says in a choked whisper. "But you didn't hear it from me. You never heard it from me, do you understand me?"

She nods. "Of course. Yes, of course."

I'm standing beside her, my hands clenched in fists. My heartbeat races, fearing the absolute worst. I don't know what happened or why, but I'm fucking scared.

"Your father made arrangements for marriage. You are supposed to marry one of the Rossi men. I don't know who. I know them, but I don't know who you're marrying, all I know is that it isn't Romeo because he got married last year."

"No," she whispers. "Piero... Tell me it isn't true."

In a bold move, he reaches for her and brings her closer to him. It's then I realize that the crush is mutual, but he doesn't kiss or embrace her. He shakes her shoulders. "It *is* true. They want you to pack your bags and go home tonight. They're taking you back to Boston on a red-eye flight. You'll be married as soon as you get there. They're wasting no time, not even planning a big wedding." His own voice chokes. "They'll kill me if they knew that I talked to you."

She looks at me in a panic, shaking her head. "What do I do?" she whispers. "What do I do?"

I turn to him. I feel as if I'm trapped in another time, when women weren't allowed a say. "Have they ever seen her?"

He nods his head. "I'm sure they have. I have no doubt. I mean, I'm sure Romeo has because he was the one that arranged this and he's the Rossi family Don. He wouldn't blindly pick a woman that wasn't..." his voice trails off and he looks at Elise. "Stunning."

She blinks, and a tear rolls down her cheek.

"Oh my God, will you two stop being so dramatic," I say, rolling my eyes. "We need a plan, none of this hand-to-brow dramatics."

Elise looks at me in shock. Piero looks to her.

"Take her. Get her out of here." I draw in a breath and release it slowly. "The man taking her home, the pilot, does he know why?"

Piero shakes his head. "No. We don't share any information, as little as possible." Smart.

"So if I go in her stead, they'll never know, will they?"

"Oh, no," Elise says, shaking her head. "No way. I can't let you do that, I *won't*."

"Do what?" I laugh, belying the roiling pit in my stomach and raw nerves that are going to kill me. "I'm not actually marrying anyone. I'll create a diversion only, then once you're gone, I'll escape." I've already lived a nomadic life. Why stop now?

She blinks and looks to Piero, then back to me. "What do you mean? What do you have in mind?"

"I'll get on the plane and distract them. And *you*." I stab my finger at him. "Get her out of here. Hide her. Safe house, family home, tiny little island in the South Pacific, I don't care. I'll get on the plane and head home and pretend to be her. Tell me you've got money."

He flushes. "Of course."

"And by the time they realize I'm the wrong one, it'll be too late. She'll already be sipping margaritas on a beach somewhere."

Elise shakes her head. "No, I can't let you do this."

"Oh yes you can." I take her hands and squeeze. "You saved my life once, Elise. And I won't ever forget it. I owe this to you. I'm only going to pretend to be you." I toss my hair. "And you know I have a degree in acting, girl. Let me actually get to use it, will you?"

She shakes her head. "Let her do it, Elise." Piero says. "You have to. She doesn't have to actually marry anyone."

"How will that work?"

He runs his hands through his hair. "She'll pretend she's you. Get on the plane. I'll call in a favor from a buddy, have her pretend to be taken, or the plane will crash or something. We'll get her out of there before she gets in the Rossis' hands, and we'll have to do it in a way that they never suspect."

"Wow. That's like evil genius."

He gives a modest shrug. Elise's eyes go wide.

"What will happen to my family?" she asks in a little voice. "I can't... I can't leave them in ruin."

"It depends on how the Rossis handle it," he says with a nod. "They may demand another type of payment but might be merciful if it's framed like an accident. I'll do what I can on my end to lessen the impact of all this."

He's putting his life on the line.

So am I.

"Elise..." his voice trails off. "I'm telling you this. I shouldn't be telling you any of this. But I've met the Rossis. I served time with Santo, one of their main core. The man is a fucking psychopath. I don't want you in that family. What if they marry you to Santo? I swear he has no conscience. I can't imagine you being with a guy like him..."

Oh God. I have to make sure I get away. I have to make sure I don't get captured by them or something.

I swallow hard. "Take her now. Here." I start stripping my clothes off right there. "Wear my clothes and walk out with him."

We don't look that much alike, but we both have the same length light brown hair. Though hers is often styled and mine is pulled into a messy bun, it will still serve the intended purpose.

"I owe you," Elise says, wrapping her arms around me and squeezing my neck. "I so owe you. And God, Angelina, I need you to stay safe..."

"I will, I promise. I'll escape as soon as I can." I've gotten this far with sheer tenacity and stubborn will. I can keep it up. Talk is cheap, though. My nerves are on fire.

Piero leaves us to quickly pack. Elise throws things in a small duffel bag to avoid attention, and helps me pack things that I can take with me. If Elise really was getting married tonight, she would have boxes and boxes of everything she owned, shoes and purses and clothes and jewelry. I decide to pack it all for the sake of appearances, but Piero comes back in and puts an end to that.

"No. Rossi said take only the essentials. He'll provide everything else."

Elise looks at me, pales, and hands me the journals.

She goes to give me a hug, but I shake my head. I don't want to make it look like we know that anything's happening, that we have any idea at all.

Piero looks at me and squeezes my hand. "Thank you," he whispers. "I'll pay you back for this, I promise."

He opens the door. "Angelina, they're waiting for you. Private jet will take you back to Boston. I'll carry your things."

"Go," I whisper in her ear. "I love you."

There's only a flight attendant and a pilot aboard this flight. "You ready, Miss?"

I nod as the door shuts and I can't see Elise or Piero anymore. I blow out a breath and feel as if I'm going to cry.

The plane takes off, while my heart, my hopes and dreams and anything I hoped to accomplish are back on the Tuscan earth.

CHAPTER 3

"Lady, you are the cruel'st she alive

If you will lead these graces to the grave

And leave the world no copy." ~ *Twelfth Night, Shakespeare*

ORLANDO

I BLINK in the bright overhead sun. The last time I came here, snow fell from the sky, just a couple days after Christmas. Now, the sun shines and green leaves are blossoming on trees. If I believed in signs, I'd feel as if this were a sign of new life. But I'm way too jaded to believe in shit like that.

Romeo stands next to me, dressed in one of his impeccable suits, and everyone around us gives him a wide berth. Even the corrections officers nod to him when he comes into the room. Most Dons wouldn't come themselves for a task like this but would send someone else in their place.

Romeo isn't like that. Romeo is as loyal as they come.

He hugs me so hard I lose my breath and smacks my back so hard it stings. But I welcome it. It's so fucking good to be out of there.

"Glad to have you out of there, man," he says, releasing me. His eyes quickly assess every inch of me, from the still fresh scar on my arm, to the bandaged elbow, to the laceration that's long since healed across my collarbone.

"Heart's still beating," he says. "You're still fucking alive. That's what matters."

Yeah.

Some guys don't survive prison. Some guys don't come out the way they went in. And I learned after my first stint in the big house, it was more important for me to have good mental stamina than anything else. If I could survive the torment of solitary confinement, I could survive anything.

Most men behind bars don't have the life experience I do. Most haven't suffered through what I have. So I guess one could say it's a fucking advantage.

The only one, maybe.

My heart warms when I see my brothers in the back of the Lamborghini SUV. Santo's in the driver's seat, grinning at me, never one to pass up a chance to drive when he can. We all have the option of drivers so we can conduct business when going places, but sometimes we like to drive ourselves. Santo never uses a driver. He owns six cars, and trades at least one of them out a quarter. Fuck, I missed the son of a bitch.

Tavi and Mario sit in the back.

"This is quite a fucking welcome home party," I say. Romeo smiles but doesn't reply. I wonder if he has something up his sleeve.

I notice pretty quickly that we're not taking the route to the highway that will take us to our family home, The Castle, in Gloucester. We're heading deep into the recesses of the City, where most of us own private residences in the high-end historical district of Beacon Hill.

"Decided it was best for you to have a night of total freedom," Romeo says. "We have family visiting from Tuscany, and The Castle's fucking bustling."

"We thought that maybe you'd like to have a little peace and quiet, is what he's saying," Mario, my youngest brother, says with a twinkle in his eye. "And maybe a little fucking tail." Always one to prioritize sex.

"Jesus, I love you guys," I say, putting my head on the back of my seat and exhaling. "What I really want right now is a cold one and some good damn food."

Santo laughs. "Told you." Romeo and Santo share a look I can't quite decipher.

"All right, what are you assholes up to? You got something up your sleeves, I know it." Mario hands me a plastic container, maybe to shut me up. He's like a modern-day James Dean with his rugged good looks and suave attitude. He melts panties when he walks down the street. "Eat, brother."

I open it up to see a flaky, crusty calzone, straight from our kitchen. My mouth waters. I keep my head over the box so I don't mess up the nice car, and shovel it in my mouth. I groan at the first bite. Oh God, it's so good. One of my favorite foods, and they know it. I like all kinds of food and will eat damn near anything, but nothing beats Nonna's spinach and sausage calzone. Pretty sure this one was meant to be shared as a family, but I polish the whole damn thing off in minutes while my brothers tell me about everything that's happened at home.

Mama has not seen the man that she was dating. Nonna and Mama have been fighting over which cookies to make for me upon my return. Marialena has gone to grad school, but still visits The Castle frequently. And Rosa... No one wants to talk about Rosa.

"What's going on?" I ask, concerned about my eldest sister whose husband died after my father ordered his murder after he cheated on her.

"She has her hands full with Natalia," Romeo says. "She's getting frustrated living here, and wants to

27

return permanently to Tuscany, but she's worried about what will happen there." And they don't have to tell me what they mean. I know what they do. If we sent Rosa back to Tuscany, we'd have to send a veritable army with her. She might not be safe from her ex's family. "She's back there with her bodyguards visiting for now, but left Natalia with us."

"How is Natalia?" I ask about my littlest niece, my only niece. Rosa's only daughter turned six years old.

Santo grins. "Perfect."

Romeo clears his throat. "Anything we need to know about what happened behind bars, brother?"

I shake my head. "No, man. Only thing I want you to know is that I'm recruiting my cellmate to be one of us." Romeo's face registers mild surprise, his eyebrows rising. He trusts me. I've never recruited anyone to our family before, and he likely knows that if I am now, it's for good reason.

"Anyone give you shit?"

"Of course. Why wouldn't they? I got it handled, though."

Romeo grins. "Of course you do."

We have a lot to catch up on. Romeo instructs Santo to take us to one of our restaurants in the North End. My family owns bakeries and restaurants, among other establishments. God, does it feel good to be back. The tension in my shoulders eases just with the smell of garlic, olive oil, and basil from one of our plants in the back.

"You getting sentimental in your old age, old man?" Mario says, smacking my back. I shrug. Maybe I am.

We feast on scallops, frutti di mare, parmigiana di melanzane, and fresh-baked focaccia bread dipped in olive oil imported from Italy while my brothers fill me in. They tell me everything that's happened. Who's gotten married, who's gotten divorced, who's had a baby, who's died. We have a large family from here to Italy.

It isn't until we're feasting on tiramisu and drinking espresso that Romeo clears his throat, and everyone goes silent. "I told you I had a surprise for you, Orlando."

I look at him and hold his gaze a moment. "This isn't it?"

He shakes his head. "No." He clears his throat. "Tavi's arranged marriage fell through."

Shit, I know where this is going.

"And you know stealing from The Family is a death sentence, unless you have something very, very good to trade."

"I do."

There's a pregnant pause before he continues. "The Regazza father stole from us, brother."

"And?"

"We accepted his bargain."

I already know what he's gonna tell me. I already know where this is going. But I want to hear him say the words. I want him to voice it.

"What's her name?"

He sighs. "Elise Regazza."

I've known for a very long time that when I marry and what I do with the rest of my life is not my choice, is beyond my control. It's no matter, I tell myself. Marriage for my family means nothing. A business arrangement, no more, no less.

Romeo clears his throat. "Youngest daughter. She's gorgeous, brother. Never saw her myself, but Rosa did. Swore she'd be a good fit."

"What about Mama?"

"What about her?" There's challenge in his eyes.

"You tell her?"

He shakes his head. "She'll want a big wedding, big to-do. This needs to happen fast. We need more solidification in our Family after what's happened in the past year." He sighs. It isn't just what happened when I was behind bars but my father's death as well. "The Family's weaker now, Orlando."

I look to Tavi. "What happened to the girl you were going to marry?"

He scowls. "Suicide."

Jesus.

"Did you know her?" I don't know why it matters to me.

He shakes his head.

Suicide. Jesus. She could've been married to my brother, a good man, one could argue. Mob, yeah, but loyal to the core. He'd have taken good care of her. But she took her own life in the face of marriage to a man she didn't know.

"When?"

Romeo draws in a breath and lets it out slowly. "Tonight. We've arranged for her to meet you in your townhouse, and Father Richard's ready to preside." He smiles. "Your welcome home present."

There's a reason I was released early. I don't know what Romeo did to make that happen. Not sure I want to know.

And then it dawns on me. If we need to marry rapidly, we need to replenish our soldiers. "Who, Romeo? Who died?"

He looks at the table. I'm fixated on the way his fingertips steeple.

"Nicolo. Matteo. Marcellus." His voice cracks. "We almost lost Leo, but he's in intensive care, and he's not going down that fucking easily."

God. *God.*

Nicolo, Matteo, Marcellus, all cousins.

The food I've eaten sits like a rock in my belly. If I'd been there...

Santo knows me well. "Don't beat yourself up, Orlando. You couldn't have helped us if you were there."

I shake my head. He knows it's a lie. He knows I'm the group heavy, I'm the one that battles to the death, that I never leave a brother in need and that I fight to kill.

"You said she's waiting for me?"

Romeo nods. "She will be, shortly."

I'll do what I have to for my brotherhood.

This is not going to be a wedding with a lot of ceremony. We haven't had a big wedding party in ages. Sometimes, a wedding is merely a quick affair.

I'm wearing faded civilian clothing. I need a shower and I'll be good. "Who's met her before? Just Rosa?"

Romeo nods.

I think about this, what the implications are for our family, what we need to do next. "You don't just need me to marry, do you?"

Romeo looks away. His own wife has been unable to bear him children. It's likely a sore point for him. But I know how The Family works, I know what's expected. I'll marry this woman I've never met. I'll have her as my wife, and give her everything that's expected, everything she needs. In turn, she'll learn what my expectations are, but as a mafia daughter, I expect she already knows much of it.

But I know what else I have to do. Now that my father's gone and Romeo and I are the only ones who'll be married, not only do I have to marry, but I'll have to have children. Fucking breed her.

"You said Rosa is in Tuscany. Does anybody have her number?" I don't have a cell phone. All of my belongings were taken from me when I was arraigned, and I sent my personal belongings home. Romeo takes out his cell phone, a sleek black number, hits a button on the side and hands it to me. "Call Rosa."

It's late there. She doesn't answer.

I hang up the call and hit the side button again. "Call Marialena."

The phone rings, and she picks it up on the third ring.

"Romeo? Do you have him? Did you bring him to his townhouse yet? Is she pretty?"

"For fuck's sake, Marialena."

There's a pause and then, "Oh my God, Orlando!"

"Yeah, it's me. How are you?"

"I heard what was happening, and I'm just worried is all. But Rosa says that she's really sweet. She likes to shop, but whatever, so do I. She really likes her fashion, but again, so do I. She's...maybe four, five years younger than you are. Um...I don't really know what else except that her dad probably kind of spoiled her, but you know, maybe she outgrew that."

I roll my eyes mentally. And maybe she didn't. Yeah, I can handle that. I won't have a spoiled wife.

"What does she look like?"

"I have no idea. But I know Romeo wouldn't arrange for a marriage to somebody who's ugly. She must be pretty."

I snort. It's all subjective.

"Alright, thanks. See you soon, kiddo."

I can deal with a brat. I practically raised Marialena. I can deal with someone who's cranky. I'm no walk in the park myself. I could even deal with a girl that wasn't pretty, since beauty's in the eye of the beholder and all that. But I can't deal with a nag or a bitch. I'm not gonna play games.

At this point, I don't fucking care. Men in my family often lay down their lives for us. The least I can do is marry.

We make it to my place in town.

God, it feels good to come home. I'm looking forward to getting up to The Castle, to eating Mama and Nonna's good food. Kicking back in front of a fire. Having a drink with my brothers. But not now.

We all own various homes throughout the world. We all have residences at The Castle and north of Boston, various locales in Boston proper, and

Tuscany as well. Romeo has a new place in Bora Bora too.

I was only twenty-one years old when I bought my first home. But this is the first time I see it through the eyes of a possible future wife. Will she like what she sees?

Do I care?

My parents had a loveless marriage, my grandparents as well. But Romeo... Romeo gives me hope.

Jesus. Apparently being in the big house has made me soft.

My marriage will be nothing more than a business transaction.

I've got what I need. A hot shower to soak my muscles after a hard workout. Refrigerator well-stocked with cold beer, wine from my family's vineyard, and food from my family's restaurants in the North End. I don't care about decorations, or subway tile, or whatever fucking granite countertops are the most recent. Marialena came with me and helped me pick out the decor and we paid plenty for it.

She said that my future wife is a shopper. I can handle shopping. My family has more money than they know what to do with, and my wife will be very well-off.

She'll earn it though. I have my expectations. We all do. In the Rossi family, men are the heads of their houses. And that doesn't change, no matter who we are.

I stand in the broad overhead lighting of my kitchen and stretch my arms up over my head. It's the first time I've been able to fucking do that. A prison cell is the worst type of punishment for a guy like me, big and tall and bulky. I got almost used to the daily backaches from the confined space and tiny beds.

I'll sleep like a fucking king tonight in my own bed.

Then I realize, I won't be alone.

Jesus, Romeo. Didn't give me a goddamn break. I know time's of the essence, though.

It feels fucking good to be out of there. I don't even know what I want to eat first, where I wanna go first, what I wanna do first. But a part of me wonders... Marrying so quickly after getting out of prison, will it be like being back in prison?

As I go through my home, like a stroll with a long-lost friend, I can tell someone's been here. Fresh bouquets of flowers sit on the kitchen counter, and in the bedroom on the nightstand. Candles are lined up on my dresser, high-end deals that look hand-made with varying heights, all cream colored and scented vanilla.

"Marialena?" I ask Romeo. He nods and smiles. He's always had a soft spot for her. "Of course. Who else?"

Marialena gets very excited about the prospect of a new sister in the family. She's become best friends with Romeo's Vittoria, and I have no doubt she'll try to befriend my new wife as well. While the men of our family rule the house, and handle the expectations of royalty, the women frequently buckle under the pressure of what's expected of them. Tavi's betrothed who ended her own life is a testament to this.

They are expected to marry, but never for love. It's a hard sacrifice to make, but we're expected to do the same. Not sure it's any easier for us.

The number one tenet of being a Rossi, as anyone who is raised in the mob knows, is that every life decision must benefit The Family.

As in everything we do, it must strengthen our ties.

Rosa married a man in Tuscany, who cheated on her. She's now single, with a daughter, and not as eligible to marry as is a single virgin.

That's one thing I have going for me. Any woman that I marry will be a virgin. Unsullied. I'll be the first man that ever touches her, if she's followed The Family's laws.

Maybe I can make this work. Maybe Romeo isn't the only Rossi brother that marries for love.

My brothers bring me into the bedroom, where a tux waits.

"Mama will kill you when she finds out."

He nods. "I can handle Mama." Yeah, we'll see about that.

I take a quick shower and enjoy every minute of the luxurious feel of soap on my skin, the hot water I let run and run.

In my mind, I'm still confined in that prison that smells like urine and hatred and despair. I don't know how long it will take me to forget any of that, or if I ever will.

Someone knocks on the door. I've been in here so long, my fingers are like raisins.

"Yeah?"

"Father Richard's here, man." Mario.

I close my eyes and let the steaming hot water pelt against my face.

"On my way."

CHAPTER 4

"It is too hard a knot for me t'untie." ~*Twelfth Night, Shakespeare*

"ELISE"

ELISE and I texted the entire flight. We didn't get into details about location or anything that might give either of us away if our phones were hacked, which they probably are. Her bodyguard kept her safe, bringing her all the way to the Switzerland border by car, and now here I am. God, I have no idea what will happen next, but I owe this to her. I can do this.

I'm so pumped on adrenaline I can hardly think straight. The pilot and flight attendant don't bat an eye when they see me. Either I look enough like Elise to pull off the ruse, or they just don't care.

"Get me a seltzer water. Please," I tack on as an afterthought. Elise can be bossy when it comes to hired help.

"Of course, Miss." The flight attendant gives me a tall glass with ice and a wedge of lime. "Just as you like it."

Is that a knowing look in her eye, or is that my imagination? I'm so nervous I can hardly swallow it, but I sit up straight and merely nod my thanks.

"How soon until we land?"

"Just under an hour." She smiles politely. I remember what Piero said about feigning "a crash or something." Now that I'm actually facing the possibility of a crash, I feel suddenly nauseous.

Will we crash? Is that what Piero planned?

The flight attendant's gone back to adjusting snacks and beverages at the front of the plane. I clear my throat to get her attention.

"Yes?"

"Um. Have you…" It's risky, asking for any information. I don't know if she's in league with the Regazzas or the Rossis or anyone. "Have you spoken to Piero?"

She holds my gaze a half a second too long for my comfort, and her smile seems a bit colder. "Not since we left. Why?"

"Oh," I say, feigning nonchalance. "No reason."

She goes back to her preparations without another word. My stomach plummets with the turbulence, before I realize we're heading downward, the nose of the plane tipping forward. I gasp.

"Nothing to worry about, Elise," she says casually. "Surely you're not afraid? You're the bravest flyer I've ever met. We're only preparing to land."

I breathe in deeply, then release a breath. My chest expands and deflates. I decide it's best not to reply, as I watch the clouds zoom past the windows like lightning, and my stomach hits my shoes.

I text Elise.

Me: Did you talk to Piero? What's his plan?

No response. I wait another half a minute and still, nothing.

Me: Hello? Yoo-hoo. Elise? Babe, we're about to land... or crash... and I don't know what's happening next.

Nothing.

My stomach clenches when we hit a particularly rough patch. I close my eyes and try to remember how to breathe through my nose. We're going to crash. I know it.

I text Elise again, but there's no response. Oh God, I hope she's okay. I don't know what her father is capable of and wouldn't put it past him to hurt her. I try to put my troubled mind at rest, but the next bout of turbulence makes me whimper out loud.

"Breathe," the flight attendant says. I didn't even

realize she's at my side. She leans in and murmurs in my ear. "The pilot doesn't know who you are. I do. I've escorted Elise on many flights, and you may look like her from afar, but you're not Elise."

Shit. I breathe in through my nose, too petrified of the looming crash to worry about what she's telling me.

"Piero paid me to help you escape, but then you're on your own. I've already gone above and beyond the call of duty."

I nod wordlessly, for if I open my mouth, I'm going to be sick, and throwing up on the only advocate I have is probably a terrible mistake.

"We're not going to really crash. It's too unpredictable. We're calling it a rocky landing, and it will cause enough distraction for you to get away." She lowers her voice to a whisper, as my heart beats faster. "But listen to me. You are on your own. You get me?"

I nod. "Of course."

"Good."

The plane dips again, and I realize for the first time I can actually see the ground below us. I close my eyes so I don't see and tell myself I'm just elevating, elevating, and no one will hurt me. I can get through this. I've gotten through so much more than this.

"When the plane hits, you get to the exit, and you *run.*"

I nod, but don't look at her, my eyes still closed tightly against the pounding in my ears.

She curses under her breath in Italian, and even though my Italian isn't the best, I swear I hear her say something about *stupid little girl*. But I don't have time to be affronted, because the next bit of turbulence rocks me to my very core.

"Hey!" she yells. "You don't have to make it so—" But she never completes her sentence. The plane's dragged down, then up, and we're both screaming as we're tossed about like ice in a blender. I grit my teeth, too scared to make a sound, and when we hit, something smacks my head. And everything comes to a stuttering halt.

"I GOT HER." A deep, masculine voice with an edge of a rasp in it. "She's over here."

"You got the pilot? Flight attendant?"

"Yeah, they're fine."

I try to open my eyes, but they're so heavy. I'm enveloped in the smell of leather and pine, warm in the back of—

I sit up, and my head hits the back of the seat. I wince on impact. Oh, God. I'm in someone's car and I'm being taken somewhere.

Shit. Shit, shit, shit.

I try to open my mouth, but it won't work. Something's wrapped up against my head. Whoever's driving this thing drives like a bat out of hell, every rock and divot in the road making us lurch and lunge.

"Stop, oh my God," I manage to mutter, and the driver almost crashes the car. He flinches as if struck.

"My God, when did you come to?"

My stomach quivers uneasily. "I… Just now, I guess. Where am I?"

This isn't how this was supposed to go. We were supposed to *fake* a crash, and I was going to escape.

"You're in the back of one of the Rossi family cars," he says. I can't see him, it's so dark in here, with hardly any lights on the road ahead of us.

"And who are you?"

He doesn't respond at first, just keeps driving like he's hiding something from me. This can't be the man I am supposed to marry, I reason. Men like him have drivers and servants and plenty of people to do their dirty work.

"What happened?"

"You crashed."

We crashed. Probably harder than we planned on or expected.

I don't reply, waiting for him to give me more answers, but he doesn't.

"And everyone's okay?"

He doesn't respond at first, but when he does it seems reluctant.

My phone. I was texting Elise. If anyone sees it, reads the texts, pretends they're me... I have to get out of here.

The car's roomy and luxurious but feels like a small prison on wheels as he careens forward.

"Where are we going now?"

Again, a pause before he answers. "I'm taking you to your husband."

My husband. *My husband!* I have to divert him, need to stall.

"I think you have to take me to a hospital first." Not that it'll be a cakewalk, but I have to find a way to escape without them knowing. And then it dawns on me.

God.

I can't just escape now, though, because if it looks like I escaped, Elise will pay. I was supposed to be abducted or hurt or *something*. This is a total shitshow.

I need to get in touch with Elise.

"Where's my phone?"

"I have no idea. Don't worry, we'll get you a new one."

And if they read my texts…

My mind races, but it's hard to connect thoughts when I'm so nervous about being found out, still injured from the crash. My mind feels jumbled and muddied, like a murky swamp after a hard rain.

"My contacts, though."

"They'll sync. We'll get a good one." *We'll*. Like this is all a nice family affair.

I know nothing about tech things, so I guess that's true but that's also *not my concern*.

I close my eyes and lean back against the seat, and for the first time since we heard about all this, I wonder… what would happen if *I married him? The stranger?*

I remember what Piero said about them. I imagine what they're like, bug-eyed monsters with rotting teeth. When I first figured out who Elise's family was, I did a deep dive down YouTube, watching everything I could about mafia life. Some of it seemed pretty normal, and the rest absolutely terrified me. There was this one guy with these eyes that looked empty and cold. I had nightmares about him coming for me for years.

Is it safer for Elise if I stay? Or safer for her if I flee?

I don't know. Oh, God, I don't know.

I never planned on actually staying, on actually *marrying* the guy.

But when we stop for traffic, I realize that I don't really *have* a choice.

In the light of the overhead streetlamps, I can see the huge shoulders of the man driving, his large height and girth, and he's focused totally on *me*. I can't just up and leave. A guy like him would probably follow me.

"Do you know my husband?"

"I do." Is that my imagination, or is he laughing to himself? Like this is a laughing matter?

I'm not going to ask him what he's like. I'm not gonna talk to him at all if he's going to laugh at me when I'm injured and being brought all the way here for…whatever's going to happen next.

We're in Boston, that much is clear. The traffic's congested, but the city excites me. There's a man playing a banjo on a street corner, small clusters of people dressed in designer clothes, high-heeled boots, wrapped in thick woolen scarves. It's a cool spring evening here in New England, and it looks as if most of the trees are starting to bud. I can't help but wonder if it symbolizes my future. Again, with the poet's mind. I can't help myself, I guess.

A frantic thought keeps pounding in my mind. I have to get away. I have to.

I look at the lock on the car door, and then almost shake my head to myself, but I don't want the driver to see. I can't just flop out of the car like a tumble-weed. I feel so desperate, though, as if I want to claw my own skin to get out of here. I don't know how to make this happen so that Elise doesn't get in trouble. I don't know how to make this happen so that I uphold my end of the bargain.

We're coming into an intersection with cars on every street. We crawl at a snail's pace because there's so much traffic, probably going two or three miles an hour at most.

"How's your head?" His voice is a deep rumble, almost a challenge, as if he's defying me to actually be hurt. I'm not going to buckle.

"Hurts a little, but otherwise fine," I lie. It kills.

He doesn't respond, just expertly weaves through the thick, heavy traffic down a street in Boston that looks as if it was lifted straight out of Italy, complete with cobblestone streets, antique streetlamps that look as if they're hand-painted, and small clusters of houses that might be apartments, or dorms, maybe both.

"You need to see a doctor. I won't take you to a hospital. My family has a doctor on-site."

Of course they do. Elise's family does, too. Probably helps to have someone that can repair bullet wounds and knife wounds without calling the police. Fantastic.

I lay my head on the back of the seat.

One thing I have going for me is the location. Even

though there are streetlamps everywhere, it's pretty dimly lit. If there's enough of a commotion or chaos, I just might be able to get away… or maybe I can delay things.

"I… don't know if you heard the plans for tonight?"

He doesn't respond, and I feel odd continuing to talk, but it's worth a shot.

"I was thinking maybe tonight's not the best night for a…wedding?" I grimace to myself. Surely, I could've come up with something better than that?

"We'll see what the doctor says."

My heart thunders in my chest. We'll see what the doctor says? What is that supposed to mean? What exactly do they have riding on this wedding, that they're prepared to marry me to someone I've never met, even after a dangerous crash and accident?

He pulls up to the curb, where there are men in uniforms waiting to take his car. It's the only space on the entire street where a car can fit, and I wonder to myself what we'll do next. Is it a valet? Someone that works for the guy that I'm supposed to marry? My eyes dart from side to side looking for a getaway, but I don't see one. The valet opens the driver's door first, and the man gets out of the car.

Holy shit. Seated, in the dark interior of the car, I couldn't see how big this guy is. He's huge. So huge I stifle a little gasp and crane my neck to look up at him, but I can't. His shoulders are enormous, his back bigger than three of me. His hands, oh *God*, his hands could span my waist and crush me.

He hands the uniformed man the keys, and then reaches for my door.

Instinctively I click the lock to keep him out, like an idiot.

He tries the handle, and of course it's locked. This is probably the most juvenile attempt at getting away I could think of, but I'm that desperate to get out of here.

He's unbothered. He simply takes the keys from the uniformed man, clicks the button, and the doors unlock. Before I can lock it again, he yanks it open so hard I fear he's going to rip it off its hinges.

"What the fuck are you playing it? You're injured and need to see a doctor. And you're expected inside that house. You're lucky you're hurt."

Is that a threat? That is definitely a threat. My heart beats faster.

I don't respond, I don't tell him it was an accident, because it wasn't. And I'm trying to reserve all my energy to figure out how to get away.

I can't trick him or run. He's way too big. And something tells me if we actually get in those doors, there are going to be way too many people for me to stage a getaway. I'll never make it.

I'll have to pretend to use the bathroom or something.

So I go with him. I let him lead me up the stairs. I pretend I don't like the way his hand feels on my elbow or on the small of my back. For a big, kinda angry guy, he's acting surprisingly gentle.

For the first time, I wonder... is this guy my husband? Because I don't know that much about Elise's family, but I do know the men are very possessive, and any man that was engaged to someone would probably chop off the hands of a guy that dared to touch his betrothed. Just *wham*, slice them right off. The Rossis are probably the same.

"Are you the guy I'm supposed to marry?" I can't imagine being married to a guy that big. He'll break me in two. He's like a fucking gorilla.

"What gives you that idea?" And I can't tell if he's smiling or frowning in the dark.

He opens the door, and just as I suspected, the entire front entryway is filled, and I mean *filled*, with huge, scary men all dressed in tuxedos, and *right* in the center is a man that looks like a priest.

Oh. My. God.

A man that looks a few years older than the man I'm with steps to the front. "Is she all right? We heard what happened."

"I think so. Think it was staged. Not sure why. We'll look into that."

Noooo.

He snorts. "She's well enough to try to lock the door so I couldn't get her out." They all kind of grunt.

God.

He looks mad as hell as he runs his fingers through his hair. "Bring her to the doctor. This has been the longest fucking day of my life, and I'm ready for it to end."

Why? Why was it such a long day? What else happened?

Why do I care?

This place is beautiful. I don't really have time to take in all the details, but this is definitely one of those high-end deals in Boston that cost several million dollars, I would swear to it. I've heard real estate here is extremely expensive due to the historic location, and this place is definitely one of those beautiful expensive places.

So that's a plus.

No! I can't be thinking of actually staying here, no matter if the guy's hot and rich and this is a nice place. Nothing is ever as it seems. Nothing. I, of all people, ought to know that. I have lived my entire life in a house of cards.

It's when I'm sitting on the couch, being looked over by someone with a stethoscope, that I realize the truth, though. *There is no easy getting out of this.* There's nowhere for me to go. If I try to escape now, these guys would maybe hurt me and Elise is *screwed*.

But I also realize, with a bit of surprise, these aren't really the mafia guys I've seen on YouTube. These guys are... definitely scary. Definitely dangerous. They all have scars, and tattoos, and those eyes... those blue-gray eyes that look cold and deadly.

But they're *hot*. The guy that brought me in here has a scruffy beard, dark brown-black hair, and eyes that look into your very soul. He stands right next to me during my inspection and grunts about medication as the doctor gives me some pain relievers and bandages up my wounds.

For someone who just crashed in a plane, I'm not really injured. I look like I was in a fender bender. Given the fact that the pilot and the flight attendant both escaped unscathed as well, I would think that maybe their plan actually worked. At least the part about crashing without killing us.

The part about me getting away? Not so much.

"Good. Take her upstairs, where she can get dressed. Keep it simple. I don't care what she looks like. She can wear fucking pajamas for all I care."

"Pajamas? Hey, maybe I don't want to get married in pajamas."

Uh, I don't want to get married at *all*. It's a pretty lame attempt at stalling.

He only stares at me like he has plans, and I'm not sure I'll like said plans.

My stomach churns because it's definitely him. It has to be.

I need to delay this. I need to get out of here. "I'd like to wait until tomorrow, please. Let's delay this just a few hours and then… well then your night is over like you wanted."

I swallow hard, my mouth suddenly dry. Because all of a sudden there's like ten pairs of very stern mob eyes on me.

God.

"No, I don't think so."

"You don't think so?"

"No. You tried to stage a plane crash. You tried to escape."

Uh, *barely.* But my heart thunders, because I know that the slapdash plans we made won't work, that they're either on to me or fully prepared to track me down and that if I don't go through with this, Elise is *dead.*

But I've been through shit. I've clawed my way through, fought unspeakable odds. I never backed down, not once, and I won't start now.

He can put a ring on my finger and go through this farce of a marriage, but he doesn't have my legal name or my consent. I'll muddle through this. For now. I have to.

"And we'll deal with you trying to escape later. But we're making sure this happens, now. If you need a few minutes to get yourself together I'll grant that. Then you get your ass down here." Is that a threat in his tone? He shoots me a hostile glare, and anything I thought about playing nice and maybe enjoying living in the lap of luxury quickly evaporates.

That's him. That's my future husband. He's furious, and fully prepared for me to try to escape, which means I'm definitely not getting out of here.

Shit.

CHAPTER 5

"Nothing that is so, is so." ~ *Twelfth Night, Shakespeare*

ORLANDO

ROMEO LOOKS at me sharply when Elise goes upstairs with staff. He keeps his voice low for privacy.

"She tried to get away?" His tone sounds as if he takes it as a personal affront against The Family, and for some reason that raises my hackles.

I shake my head. "Do *not* call Regazzo."

"I'm within my rights to do that, brother. You know that. He said he'd send her, and we have two expectations. First, that she come willingly without a fight. Second, that she's untouched."

I don't know why I'm defending her, why I don't want Romeo to be the one to bring down the fucking Rossi family hammer. She'll pay for what she tried to do, but at *my* hands, not his.

"She didn't really try to get away. She hit the lock on the car door when I tried to open it."

His brow furrows as if he's perplexed. "She tried to... lock you out? Like a child?" When Marialena knew she was in trouble, she'd always run to the pantry and lock the door from the inside, despite the fact that we had a key dangling from the hook right above the door. It was a childish move, like closing your eyes in the hopes of no one seeing you.

I shake my head. "I don't know what she was thinking, but she didn't get away with it. And whether or not that plane crash was intentional, there's no way of knowing."

Romeo shrugs. "Sure there is." I know exactly what he means. We get the pilot and the flight attendant and interrogate the shit out of them.

I don't wanna do it, though. Not now. Jesus, not now.

My childhood may have been brutal, my job may be savage, but I'd had a regular feast of violence in prison, and I want a fucking break. I'm sick of hurting people. I never liked it, I never will. I'll do what I have to, but this is not necessary. And I don't want to build my marriage on a foundation of violence and threats.

I exhale and hold his gaze. "Leave it up to me."

Romeo looks thoughtful, then finally nods. "Of course, Orlando. I trust you. You know what's at stake."

I do. It's within my power to solidify our family. I can do it. I just need to convince the little brat upstairs.

I don't know what is going on up there, but she's taking way too much time. I'm over it. I want this damn ceremony done.

I jerk my chin at nearby staff. "Get her, please. Bring her down." My brothers are the ones that rule with an iron fist. With my size and reputation, I rarely have to. Staff runs to obey.

Good. Now if only my wife would do the same.

We'll work on that.

Rings, vows, marriage.

Babies.

Obedience.

In that order.

I'm running out of patience. I'm so damn exhausted after everything that's happened.

Father Richard speaks gently. "Orlando, you've been through a lot." He's known me since he poured water over my head at my baptism. I eye him warily, wondering what he's got up his sleeve.

He smiles apologetically. "Perhaps you may consider... a gentle approach to your new wife."

I draw in a breath, and then I release it slowly. He witnessed the way my father was with my mother, how Leo is with his wife. My mother hated my father for his cruelty, and Leo, on the opposite end of things, has a wife who doesn't respect him because he's spoiled her.

I don't want to be rude to Father Richard, though. No matter who we are, I was raised to respect a man of the cloth. So I only nod my head. "Thank you, father, but the only thing you have to worry about is the ceremony."

He nods slowly.

Romeo mutters under his breath, "Gentle approach my ass. Let me know how that works out for you. You show her who's the fucking boss."

"I'll figure it out."

He chuckles softly beside me.

Finally, I hear footsteps. I look up, expecting to see her wearing maybe jeans, or just to be a wiseass the pajamas I suggested. But she isn't wearing either. The staff's got my future bride wrapped in a pretty, soft white gauzy gown, no evidence of any scratches or bruises or lacerations anywhere. It isn't a real wedding gown, maybe more suitable for a summer night affair. Her hair is done up in a gentle braid that sweeps to the side of her neck. She wears pearl earrings, a pearl necklace, and light makeup that accents her eyes and brings her lips full in pink. She's fucking stunning.

I swallow hard. I can't be soft on her, not yet, even if she's a goddamn supermodel.

"Get down here. Let's go."

Santo chuckles softly behind me. I don't fucking care.

She grits her teeth, sets her jaw, and clomps down the stairs.

I'm supposed to be making babies with this woman. But you know what? Not fucking tonight.

I meet her at the foot of the stairs, take her by the elbow, and half march her over to Father Richard. "Let's get this over with."

It's probably the least romantic ceremony on Earth, but I don't care. In a few minutes, she wears my ring, and tomorrow we'll make sure her name is legal. She balked at the word "obey" in our wedding vows, but I gave her a look that made her quickly take the vows.

They're only words, only words on a page.

My brothers open up champagne and pour it into flutes, but I'm so tired, so weary, I barely taste it. Elise sits beside me while Romeo hands out cigars, and waitstaff bring out elegant food on platters. But it isn't my mother's food, I'm not at home, and I don't want to eat anything.

I stand before we've even touched the cake from

Tavi's bakery in the North End. "I'm taking my bride upstairs," I say.

"Dude. It's that cream cake you like." I nearly groan. Tavi's bakery makes an Italian cream cake with vanilla, coconut, and pecans, laced with a whipped cream frosting, that melts in your mouth. People all over the country order it for their weddings. He knows how much I love his damn pastries.

"Alright. Cake only."

Elise looks stunned, and I wonder for a minute if it has something to do with her crash earlier. Maybe she didn't expect this so soon, or maybe she was hoping to get away. And now, here she's wed to a made man. I don't know why she looks so afraid or surprised, though. As a woman of the mob, she knew this was her lot in life since she was a little girl like my sisters, dressing up their Barbies in white wedding gowns.

I know what the rules are. I know that we're required to consummate this marriage immediately, within twenty-four hours. We've gone through the formalities. Now it's time to make this work.

"Everyone out," I announce when the last crumb of cake's been eaten. No one questions me. Even Romeo stands and nods. "See you tomorrow, Orlando?"

He knows after I've consummated the marriage, I'll need to bring her to The Castle where she'll meet the rest of my family.

Mario gives me a shit-eating grin and a wink, fist bumps me, and almost checks my bride out before I shove him out the door. "See you tomorrow."

Santo leaves without a word, and Tavi gives me a hard brotherly hug, complete with a stinging back-slap. "I'll bring more food tomorrow. I'm ready to arm wrestle you over the last damn lobster claw." Elise looks at me in surprise. She'll see what he means soon enough.

I kick everyone out of the house and promise Romeo I'll update him as soon as I have anything to share. He nods with a mischievous glint in his eyes. I make fluttering finger motions toward the door as if to sweep them all out. Romeo chuckles, but everyone follows his lead and exits, with lots of "we're so glad to have you home" and "we'll catch up soon."

I need to find out what makes her tick. I need to find out if she tried to escape and if so, why.

I try to bridge the silence between us.

"I hope you like it here."

She still doesn't respond, just walks beside me as if I'm leading her to prison. Does she really feel that way?

I should feel something being married now. It's the new stage of family life, the next step to being a made man, and I've just ascended into rank above Tavi. It doesn't matter. Tavi will be married soon, and he and I will join the ranks with Romeo as offi-ciating members of our family.

But tonight, I'm a high-ranking official. And after I have my first baby, our family will be even stronger.

Again, I think to myself that I should feel some-thing, anything, but I don't. All I feel is a dull ache in my chest. I figure I'm tired.

I wish my whole family was here. My mother, my Nana, Rosa, even my fucking father.

No, not my father. He hated me. But a part of me wonders, would he approve of me now?

This is our first night together. It should be special. My mind is reeling, and I'm exhausted.

I know I have a choice ahead of me. I could boss her around, tell her what to do. I could make her obey me and follow my rules. She could be the mafia wife that I need. She could learn her place by my side.

Or...maybe we could have something more. Just like Romeo. He told me that he decided long ago that when he married his wife, he was going to make something better than what he'd seen. And I know that I want that, too. Who wouldn't?

"Is this your primary residence?" she asks while she runs her fingers along the banister.

Something odd about this one.

"One of them. I also own property in Tuscany, and I spend a lot of time in my family's home, The Castle."

She looks at me and tips her head to the side. "The Castle?"

I nod. "I'll take you there tomorrow. I'm surprised that as a Regazza you haven't heard of The Castle. *Former* Regazza."

No emotional response. She only frowns and looks around as if trying to find an exit.

Maybe she'll like it at The Castle. Women dig that shit. Hell, so do I.

"Yeah, I did hear about that. I just forgot," she says, then quickly looks away. Embarrassed? "So will we stay here?" As she looks around, I wonder if she'll like it here.

"No. We come here on occasion. Sometimes we will stay in The Castle, sometimes in Tuscany. But you'll stay wherever I am." She won't be allowed a night away from me.

She looks away and worries her lip.

"I don't want to make small talk, Elise. We both know why we're here. We both know what we have to do." Any Regazza woman would know her duty, as well as I know mine. If she's at all curious, she doesn't show it but only looks away with a sigh.

We reach the landing. The house has been cleaned to within an inch of its life while I've been away. The hardwood floors gleam and shine like they've been newly polished. Flowers are on every little tabletop in the hallway, and from here we can see the living room, the entryway, and a small area where I keep the piano below. I don't play, but Mari-alena does. I like it here for her.

"I suppose we'll share a bedroom, too?"

"Of course."

We don't speak as we make our way to the bedroom. And for the first time since I saw her, a little part of me looks forward to what happens next. The blessed relief of letting myself go, and a good night's sleep after a good hard fuck. It's been way too damn long.

"You say that you're tired," she says, almost as if she's looking for an excuse not to do this. "Are you?"

"Why would I lie? I don't lie about anything."

My brothers and I have many faults, but dishonesty is not one of them.

We reach the landing, and she keeps up the small talk. "Why are you so tired? What happened?"

Doesn't she know anything about me? Does she have no clue where I came from?

"What did your father tell you about me?"

I open the door. I don't keep any of my bedrooms locked, even though we do at The Castle.

It looks as if the bedding is fresh and clean, the bed perfectly made. Again, flowers adorn the night-stands, and the blinds have been drawn. Velvet robes hang from hooks on the open bathroom door, and from here I can see the gleaming porcelain and white and silver accents. It feels like a fucking mansion after what I've been through, after what I've done and where I've been.

"My father told me nothing. I didn't even know your name." I can tell she's telling the truth this time. "He sent my bodyguard to get me. I was in Italy. He put me on a plane and sent me here. He said he'd send my belongings after me." She looks away. "You could say I was not prepared for this."

A normal person might feel sympathy.

Not me.

Her voice is higher, tighter, and I don't miss the tightening of her jaw or the way that her fingers clench into fists. "And I don't care if you say that I should have been prepared for this, because I knew that I would be put into an arranged marriage. *No one* is prepared for something like this."

Is she picking a fucking fight? She'd better not be, because that ain't something she's gonna win.

"I just spent six months in prison." I don't know why I say this with no prelude, or what I'm trying to prove to her. I guess a part of me wants to tell her a little bit about me, because it's not fair that she knows nothing. But I also want her to know that her life of luxury hasn't ended, and she may be pissed off that she's been married to a guy she's never met. Given what I know about mob life and the men she could've married, she's fucking lucky. Of all the assholes she could've been married to...

But I'm shit out of patience.

She freezes outside the door and braces herself against the doorframe. I don't know why I notice for the first time her short, rounded fingernails, or how her fingers are as tiny as a small child's. I could engulf both of her hands in one of mine.

"What for?" Her voice is a little breathy, shaky. Her knuckles whiten on the doorframe.

"I don't lie, Elise. So I'll tell you the truth. I served six months for involuntary manslaughter. I don't wanna talk about it, but that's the truth and you might as well know it."

I have no shame in who I am, what I do. I don't know why I have the feeling that some of this is new to her. It shouldn't be. Maybe she's lived a more sheltered life than I thought.

"You killed someone?" Her fingers grip the door-frame even tighter, and her second hand meets the first, both hands on the doorway, holding herself as if she's been trapped in a gust of wind and might blow away.

What is the surprise here? Everyone she knows lives by the code that I do.

"Get inside." I don't wanna justify myself to her. I don't want to tell her things she should already know. I'm not usually so short-tempered; goddamn if I don't just wanna do my job and go to bed.

"So that's it? You're not going to answer my question?"

I walk over to the chair by the bed and strip out of my suit coat. I lay it across the back of the chair and sit down. "Get in here."

I remember what Romeo said. I think it's good advice.

"I don't think it's right that you don't answer my questions, and you just... blurt out these orders or something. You just agreed to be my husband, not my father."

Something stirs in me. This woman needs a firm hand. She needs to know that I *am* the bottom line. She needs to know that I'm the one in charge of this relationship.

But the thought of mastering her... the thought of dominating her... it's more than duty.

My voice is thick with arousal when I reply to her. Now that we're in the dark, warm recesses of my bedroom, with a lingering smell of burnt candles and melted wax, fresh linen, and fresh flowers in the air, I look at the large bed in front of me and imagine the possibilities. Her tied to my bed, naked. Gagged and blindfolded, submitting to me with just enough fight to make it worth it.

"That what you need? A daddy?" She stands there staring at me.

"You're a kinky bastard," she whispers. "Aren't you?"

I don't answer at first. Of course I fucking am. "There's a tray next to the bed with chocolates and two glasses of wine." The newlyweds' reward. "You see them?"

She nods. "Of course I do." That tone.

I will enjoy every minute reddening her ass. "Drink it."

"And what if I don't drink?"

I slowly slip off my shoes, one at a time, and line them up beside my desk. She bends and straightens them.

I don't reply at first but hold her gaze when I reach for my necktie. I slowly slip the silky fabric from the knot, slide my tie off my neck and, still holding her gaze, wrap it around my fist. "You'd deny wine from my family's orchard?"

"Ah, well why didn't you say so?" She sashays past me as if she owns the place, lifts one of the glasses, and downs it. She sighs contentedly.

Well, that was a lot of to-do for shit.

"You do like wine, then."

"It's damn good wine."

I nod. "Thank you. Bring me mine, please."

She walks to me and hands me the glass, then backs away as if I'm going to bite her. I curse in Italian and shake my head. "You scared of me?"

She doesn't answer. She is but doesn't want to admit it.

Good.

A feeling of expectancy hangs in the air. It feels so good to breathe freely, to have the space to move, to know that if I wanted to take a fucking car ride to wherever, I can. Romeo pulled some magic.

"And what if I say...that I don't...like that." I watch when she swallows, her throat working.

I watch as her fingers flutter nervously in her hair and her gaze lingers on the tie wrapped around my fist. "Like what?"

"Kinky...stuff. What if I say I'm vanilla?"

Would a girl who is truly vanilla even know to call it that?

"I'd say it's my job to teach you."

"Teach me to like...kink? Isn't that like a nature or nurture thing?"

I don't know if she's intrigued or terrified. Maybe both.

I tighten the tie, smoothing my thumb over the silky silver fabric. I want to push her a little. See how she responds. "So you're one of those girls that overanalyze the shit out of everything?"

She doesn't flinch, or avert her eyes, or even look away. She just meets my gaze squarely. "I am. And are you just one of those guys that doesn't have patience for girls that can think for themselves?"

Oh, no. Oh no she doesn't. "Did you pay any attention to those vows you took downstairs?" I don't try to hide the tension in my voice.

"You thought those meant something? Vows are for people who choose to be married."

I stand, and for the first time since we came upstairs there's a little bit of fear in her eyes. Scratch that. She was afraid when I told her that I came from prison just now. She was afraid when I told her why. But now she's afraid for herself.

She takes a step back when I walk toward her, and I don't care that she's afraid. I want her to fear me.

We don't love one another. We don't even know one another. So she'll learn to obey me by fear.

"You vowed to honor and obey." And love, but that's a formality, and we both know it. At least she should since she's been raised in the mafia.

"I did. Did you really expect me to mean those words?" She flings the words at me as if she's trying to hurt me, and I have to admit it does sting. It shouldn't. I think of this as a business arrangement, no more, no less.

I don't know why I'm allowing her to unravel me. No one does that. I don't know why I should let her make me feel this way at all.

"The love part? That's neither here nor there. I'm sure you know your own parents got married for something else."

She doesn't respond, but then swallows again, betraying her nerves. Jesus, she's gorgeous, one of the most beautiful women I've seen in a long, long time. Curves in all the right places, an oval-shaped face with a little dimple in her cheek, sparkling eyes that probably light up when she screams. I bet her cheeks flush pink when she comes.

I go on. We need to talk about our vows. They were no fucking game. "The part about honoring and obeying, though? Those I intend to enforce."

"Enforce, obey. All these words as if you own me."

I walk to her. I want her close enough to touch, so I can drag her to me or quiet her with my hand on the back of her neck. I want to see how she yields, if she does at all.

She stands her ground, a full six feet between her and the doorway behind her where she could have backpedaled, but she didn't. She looks up at me. She's so small. I'm so much larger than her it would be funny, if not for the tension in this room. I grab her chin between my fingers and hold her there, looking into her eyes. "You tried to run away."

She shakes her head but doesn't say anything. "Do not lie to me, Elise. Talking back to me will get you punished but lying to me will get you a punishment that you've never had before, I can guarantee that."

I imagine her tied to my bed, naked, squirming and crying while she takes her punishment. *Jesus.*

"Oh, right. Is that part...of your kinky game?" Her voice is tainted with anger but husky, as if something I've done or said has aroused her.

I pinch her chin harder, and her eyes water. "This. Is. Not. A. Game."

How can she not know how dangerous this is? How vital it is that she does exactly what she's told without giving me shit? If she does something stupid and reckless, someone could hurt her. I'm a high-ranking member of one of the most powerful groups in all of Boston. That makes my wife a target.

"Your safety depends on you listening to me. Your safety depends on doing exactly what I say. As for the respect? I demand that."

"You can't demand respect," she says pointedly. "That's something you'll have to earn."

And with that, I've had it. I don't want to banter about this any longer. I have a job to do, I have a lesson to teach, and I wanna get some fucking sleep.

In one rapid motion I bend and pick her up, lifting her as if she weighs no more than a child. She's so little, but she's feisty. She kicks her legs and tries to slap at my shoulders, but I ignore her and march to the bed. My tie is still fisted in my left hand. I drop her unceremoniously, and she tries to get away, but I grab her by the ankle, yank her back to me, and slap her ass so hard she gasps. My palm tingles where I smacked her. Fuck, I like the feel of that. I like that she's fighting me.

I want her to fight me more. I want to own this woman.

The thin, gauzy dress she wears gives way like wrapping paper in my fingers as I tear it off of her. My goal is to tie her to my bed and punish her before I mark her.

But I pause when I bare her to me. She's so beautiful it makes me ache. My gorgeous, beautiful, unblemished bride.

I lower my body on top of her and I bring my mouth to her ear when she tips her head to the side. Her mouth parts as her eyes close quickly.

"Your father told me that you were a virgin, Elise." She knows what's on the line. She's not allowed to come to the marriage bed defiled. She knows that if her father promised her to me, I expect a virgin. "And you know that if I find that you're not..."

"You know I am." She says this without trying to hide the fear in her voice. It's evident in the way her voice trembles, and the way she shakes beneath me.

"I'll know."

She only nods her head slightly while I continue to tear off her clothes. She has a little freckle in the center of her back, right where it dimples and her ass swells. My mother always said there was an Italian tradition that freckles on a baby's body showed where the angels kissed. I bend my mouth to her lower back and give it a kiss. No angel better have kissed her there. This woman's mine.

She gently arches her back to me when I kiss her, and I love the way she rises to me, even as she groans as if she's fighting this, as if she hates me. I don't fucking care if she does.

All that she's wearing now are her bra and panties. They are simple white garments, which I quickly tear off of her. They fall to the floor in a heap with her dress. I spread her thighs open with my palms.

"Do you plan on destroying all of my clothing?"

"If it comes between me and you when I want you? Absolutely."

When I tear her panties off, I can see the pink bloom of my handprint where I smacked her ass. I want to do so much more than that, imagining her over my knee screaming for mercy while I brand her with my palm.

I want to test her. I want to see how she naturally responds to being dominated. And I want her to know that she has no choice in this.

"You're my wife, Elise," I say in her ear. "And you belong to me."

She pants, gently squirming, and her lips part.

How much of this does she like? We'll soon find out.

CHAPTER 6

"So full of shapes is fancy." ~ *Twelfth Night, Shakespeare*

"ELISE"

I WISH I could talk to Elise. I have so many questions for her, so many things to say. But she'd be horrified to know that I didn't escape, and that I am actually married to this guy. At least on paper.

Not for long, though. God, not for *long*. I can't believe I got tangled up in this.

I don't know what the legality of it is, and I also know it doesn't really matter if it's legal or not, because the mob gets what the mob wants.

I am naked, lying flat on my belly, my head swimming from that wine that I downed like it was water when I was parched and starving. It is strong damn stuff, even though it's good, but I'm not much of a drinker. So my head is all floaty and spinning. And I don't know what the hell's going on. But I do know that my husband... *so he says*... is pressing his huge, enormous, really sexy body on me, and he's got kink on his mind.

What does that mean? I've never had anything like this before. He's already smacked my ass. What else is he going to do?

I grab for the mattress, yanking the sheets between my fingers. They're nice sheets, silky and soft with probably like a three thousand thread count or something. But he's gonna ruin these sheets, I know it, just like he wrecked that gorgeous designer dress of mine, as if it were some kind of Halloween costume I bought on clearance. My God!

I am woozy and confused... and all kinds of aroused. I blame the wine. Maybe they make aphrodisiacal wine at his family vineyard. I wouldn't put it past them.

"You know you vowed to obey me. We've gone over that. But you also know what's expected of you, don't you?" He gets his rocks off on this whole "in charge" thing. Obey, submit, yada yada yada. It's the twenty-first century whether he wants to admit it or not.

I shake my head from side to side. "I mean, I'm starting to gather that you expect to be the head of the house and all that. Not exactly sure what that entails, but something tells me that you're going to fill me in."

"Did your father explain the expectation of children?"

Record screech.

What?

No.

My heart stands still. I don't move. I don't breathe. I swallow ice, it slithers into my chest and chills me. Children? *No. No no no.* I wouldn't have children with a normal guy, never mind with this monster.

I'm not supposed to be here. And when they find out that I am not the person I'm supposed to be, they're probably going to kill me. No, there's no "probably" about it. Every one of those made men I met were packing weapons and were fully capable of pulling a fucking trigger. I've seen the dark sides of men, between Elise's family and mine.

I can't get a *child* mixed in with that. No.

I'm not on birth control because the one thing I've got going for me, that's *not* gonna piss him off? I *am* a virgin. I don't do *sex*. Never have, anyway. Doesn't mean I've never been touched, or that I haven't experimented with a few things here or there. I'm not exactly a saint, but he'll find what he's looking for.

"Okay, so I'm not ready for babies yet," I say with what is probably the lamest comeback possible.

He's kneading my ass with his rough, thick palms, and I shiver. This should be at least fourth date status over here.

"We will not use protection. There will never be a barrier between me and you. Do you understand that?"

Whoa. He's certifiable. And yet… and yet, any woman this man really truly *did* love would be the very center of his whole world.

But still… "Never? How many kids do you wanna have?"

And what if I told him no, I don't want to consummate this marriage? No, I don't want sex?

Would he force himself on me?

The ice stabs my chest again, and a hopeless sort of panic clouds my mind.

"I don't know exactly how many children I want, but we'll talk about what we need to do when the time comes. Are you on any birth control? I know you're a virgin, but some women use it for medicinal reasons."

I shake my head from side to side, still stunned by how crazy and intense and new this all is, how unlike anything that I would have expected, or anything I ever experimented with or experienced before, it is. Or… *Anyone's* experience before?

"What do you mean, you know I'm a virgin?"

His hand tightens on my neck. "You have to ask me that?"

Uh, I just did, but I know it's probably stupid to snap at him, so I don't respond.

"Your father may be an idiot, but he isn't so stupid to break the code. A virgin daughter was his only playing card, wasn't it?"

I feel suddenly as if I'm going to cry. I feel so alone. So very, very alone. If I can't get away this very minute, at least I hope we do get to his castle soon, I hope we get to meet with his family, and I hope that there are some women there that I can talk with. I don't wanna be alone with him and his brothers with their scary eyes, their guns, their bodyguards and their rules. It's too much.

But I will not cry in front of him. Not now, not ever.

I should be braver than this. I'm mad at myself for even getting emotional. I was raised by a single father who did terrible things because my mother overdosed when I was an infant. Didn't stop him from selling that shit. But he never mistreated me. He did *stupid* things. He didn't take care of me, but he never abused me. He never really hurt me. Neglect, however...

"I'll ease you in," he says, taking me off guard. I don't know if I can trust the gentle side of him that shows itself when I least expect it. "I know that you're new to this."

Oh no he doesn't. Oh no he does not go all gentle on me. My husband, the made man whose shoulders barely fit inside the frame of this door, whose hands are as big as my entire head, cannot go all surprisingly gentle on me now. Because the only thing that's holding me back from crying is knowing that I'm doing this for my friend. If he shows any compassion at all...

He kisses my cheek. I blink, and a tear rolls down my cheek. *Fuck*.

He freezes; I feel his whole body tense over me. "Why are you crying?" I can't read the tone of his voice.

"I'm not crying," I lie.

He slaps my ass so hard that I come up onto my knees, and swear I feel like the sting went straight to my clit. What the hell is that all about?

"Ow! Are you trying to *make* me cry?"

"If I want to make you cry, I have other methods, Elise."

Shit. Of course he does. Visions of whips and chains and torture chambers flit through my mind. I squeeze my eyelids shut to compose myself.

"The air's dry in here and you're not the only one who's tired." I swipe up my cheeks, swallow, and make a vow right then and there that I will not cry another time.

"Good," he says. "There's no need to cry. I'll take care of you." He says it so matter-of-factly, like, "I'll pay for dinner."

"As long as I'm the perfect little wife, right?" My voice breaks on that last word. I hate that it does.

"Perfect? No." He shakes his head. "Sounds boring as fuck. I don't want you perfect. I like a little fight. I like the idea of teaching you what I want."

Oh, really, Mr. Bossy? Is that right?

Thankfully I've got the wherewithal to keep that in my head.

I want to fight him. If I could, I'd push back, shove him off the bed and fight him. Hurt him. I'm not a violent person, and I don't know why I'm tempted now.

We don't speak for long minutes. It's almost as if I can feel his heart beating along with mine, as if he's anticipating what's happening next, too.

But isn't he the one in charge here? I wonder why he's as expectant as I am.

He rests his huge, rough hand between my thighs. He braces himself above me with his left hand. For the first time, I realize that he has tattoos along his knuckles. Skulls.

Skulls.

Oh God, what have I gotten myself into? Skulls on his hand! Those symbols, do they symbolize every person he's killed? Do they mean something? I have so many questions, but I couldn't speak now if I wanted to, because his hand is between my legs, and all of my nerve endings are centered right above his fingers. The blood flow in my body concentrates below my pelvis. My entire world is centered... Right...There.

I stare at his hand in front of me, while my entire body focuses on the hand that's touching me. His skin is a little dark, olive-toned, with little wisps of dark hair. Nails are short, well-kept. He worked hard taking care of himself when he was in prison.

I wonder what's beneath the rest of that suit.

Maybe I don't have to leave tonight. I don't think I could if I wanted to, so might as well enjoy this first night with him. If that's...possible?

Not sure if "enjoy" is the operative word, but my body *throbs*. I've never felt anything like this before, and I can't tell if it's excitement or fear or both.

He bends down and whispers in my ear. "I want to perform a little test."

Oh, great. He's kinky, fancies himself in charge of me, and is obviously way bigger than I am. Not sure what the test is going to be, but I feel as if I'm not going to pass this one.

"Yeah? What test?" I try to keep my voice nonchalant, as if we're talking about maybe what to make for dinner. But I can't hide the little tremble in my voice.

"It's called the obedience test."

Obedience test. The guy sure is fixated on that word. Obsessed, really.

I nod, probably *obediently*. Maybe I'm passing the test already.

"And while we do this obedience test," he says in this silky, satin-covered voice that makes my body sing, goddamn him, "we're going to do another test."

I don't talk this time. Something tells me I need to focus right now, and he's going to tell me exactly what to expect.

And...I kinda like that.

Why?

"The test is to see how kinky you are. If it's your nature, your body will tell me. If it's nurture, as you like to tell yourself, then I fully intend on nurturing you into submission."

Whoa. *What?*

I don't even know what he's talking about, but I'm already panting. He gently presses the tops of his fingers to my pussy. I can feel him grazing the short hairs there, and I throb.

"If you disobey me, Elise, I will put you over my knee." He doesn't say anything else at first. My pulse races with an immediate vision of me sprawled out over his lap, and I imagine I'm getting a spanking.

Yeah, that's kind of hot. Somehow, I've forgotten it would also hurt.

And just like that, I'm wet. Without a word, he traces his finger between my thighs. His low chuckle's all man and all sex.

I don't know anything that's funny. To me, this is very, very serious.

He continues to talk and takes his perfect fingers away from where I need them.

This is, after all, an obedience test.

This is, after all, how I'm gonna get what I need.

My eyes are closed, so I can just focus on the feel of his hand between my legs. I feel his breath on my neck and I shiver, realizing too late that I've moved involuntarily closer to him.

His voice is in my ear again. "And when you're over my lap, I would spank you. I would slap your ass with my palm and redden it. The more you fought me, the more I'd punish you."

I want to push my thighs together, because something tells me that he is going to think I'm into that. Sure enough, he strokes his finger where I'm dying for him to touch. I don't breathe, the air in my lungs constricted and frozen, as he does his little test.

"When you go out in public, I'll have left my mark on you. Others may not see that mark, but everywhere you go I'll know that you're mine. Mine," he repeats. "Do you understand me?"

I nod. I do understand. I understand very well. I'm not sure what those marks are, but it's weirdly arousing thinking of going out in public while marked by my dark, big, dangerous, kinky...*husband*.

"I don't trust that you won't try to get away from me tonight." He rests his hand on my thigh. "So after we've consummated our marriage, I'm going to bind you to the bed. And you'll stay there until I give you permission to get up."

I don't know how I feel about that. I'm still panting, and I still like the feel of his hand *just there*, but what I really want is for him to touch me where I'm so desperate for release.

"You would keep me as you would a prisoner."

"No. If you were my prisoner, I would take you to The Castle and lock you in the dungeon." There's not a trace of humor in his voice. He's not joking.

"But what if something happens? What if there is a fire, or somebody breaks in, or you forget about me?"

"Elise," he says in my ear. "Those things are impossible. We have half a dozen men stationed outside my door." Oh my God. He really is one of America's most wanted.

"And there's one thing you need to know. You need to know this well." He pinches the inside of my thigh so hard that I scream and arch. It hurts much more than I would've thought it could. "You're my wife now. That means I put your safety above all others. I will punish you if you deserve it. I will dominate you because I like it. But I will never, never let you get hurt."

Yeah, that's not confusing at all.

I don't know what I like and what I don't anymore. I know that my head is swimming, that my hot husband, who smells really, really good, said scary things to make my heart beat faster. He's over me, with his hand between my legs, and no man has ever touched me there before.

"I don't know. I don't know anything right now."

"We'll see about that."

And with that, he removes his hand. I long for the feel of his warm, left hand pressed on my thigh again. I might make a little whimpering sound.

"Are you needy, Elise?" I nod. I'm not a robot.

"I have a hearty appetite, and I want you to know that. I like food, and lots of it. I like sex, and lots of it. And I will have you wherever and whenever I want you. Do you understand me?" I nod mutely because what's the response to something like that?

"Now we'll see about your punishment for what you've done tonight. I think it's important to start this relationship off on the right foot."

"Oh, I think that ship has sailed," I say before I can stop myself. His hand cracks down on my ass so hard and fast, I show I'm not prepared for the way it stings and burns in the way I yelp.

"You better watch that mouth." I swallow hard.

Oh fuck *off.*

"If you wanted a meek little submissive wife, you probably should've shopped around a little bit before you took this one."

That one, I thought about before I said it. I am ready to take whatever punishment he gives me, or so I think…

He kneels beside me, and I hear the sound of clinking metal. I look over my shoulder to see him unfastening his belt.

"You like telling me what I should do?" he says. I don't respond, because I'm completely fixated on the leather between his hands, that thick belt, and the way he fists his buckle and makes a strap.

"I know what I need. Hold onto the rails to keep your hands out of the way," he says and that's all the warning I get.

I grab for the headboard in a panic, just before there's a swish of leather, and his belt smacks my ass. I gasp in a breath and grip the headboard tighter.

He's standing beside the bed, his hand on my lower back. "I want you to know why you're being punished," he says. "You tried to escape tonight. You know that's not allowed. Your father sent you here, and you belong to me. Leaving would be like stealing from me. Do you understand me?"

I don't wanna answer at first, because I know as soon as I do, he's going to punish me again. But if I don't, he might, too, so… I nod my head, and that's both acquiescence and permission for him to strike me again.

The belt lands again, hard, but not as hard as I know he could strike me. I don't know if I want to ever find out how hard he could.

Still, my skin is on fire, and my fingers are sweaty on the wooden rails, slipping.

"Tell me the truth. Did you arrange for that plane to crash?" There's an edge in his voice I haven't heard before, steel that tells me who he is: the man that spent six months in prison for killing someone and isn't afraid to go back.

I shake my head from side to side, and I know it isn't exactly a lie, although it's not exactly the truth either. I wasn't the one that had anything to do with arranging an escape. Piero was.

He lashes me again, but I don't know why because I just told him the truth.

"Hey, why did you hit me again?"

"Because we've only just started this punishment. And I know that a part of you isn't telling me the whole truth."

How does he know? Is he skilled in interrogation?

Of course he is, I know he must be. The only thing I know about the mafia is that Elise's bodyguard stays with her at all times. But he doesn't tell her what to do, and he doesn't do scary shit, at least not *in front* of her. He's just a big tough guy, and her dad is scary as hell.

But this guy? This man who is not my husband? He's the scariest one I've ever met.

His hand presses more firmly into my lower back, and I have to rearrange my dampened fingers so I don't slip.

"Remember what I said about telling me the truth." I feel his hand pressed on my back. I feel the fabric against my bare skin. I feel my throbbing, aching skin, but most of all I feel my need for sex. I want him. I hate that I do, because a part of me feels like there's something wrong with me for wanting a man like this, a man I don't love, a man who's just whipped me.

"Tell me the answer to this question. I know what the answer is, but I want you to admit it."

"Then why ask?" I snap, even though I know he's going to spank me again for it. His belt comes down in three hard whaps, one after the other. Predictable, but still not something you can prepare for.

"Don't you ever raise your voice to me," he says. "Don't you ever snap at me."

"You heard what I said about wanting the perfect wife," I snap at him. It is the wrong thing to say.

I don't know what I expect him to do, but it's

not…this.

He drops the belt on the floor, and something tells me he isn't finished with me yet. We're high up on this huge, massive bed, so the metal buckle clatters to the floor with a bang.

He lifts me up and tosses me over his shoulder. Oh my God. Does he have, like…stocks, or chains, or some torture chamber here? Nothing would surprise me right about now.

Oh my God oh my God…

He slides me down his shoulder and plants me in front of a dresser with a huge, shiny mirror on top.

"Look right there," he says, his hands on either side of my face, holding me in place. "Tell me what you see."

I mumble with my cheeks pressed together. I glare at him to make him wonder which one of us he thinks I'm referring to. "A very angry newlywed."

Bending down, he kisses my shoulder, then sinks his teeth into the soft spot between my neck and shoulder.

"Mine," he says in a low growl before he looks in the mirror at me again. "*Mine.*"

It might sound nice and all? And I wish it were true, a part of me wishes that I was someone who mattered to him. But he's only staking ownership because of pride, not because of any sense of really wanting me to be his.

I can't find my voice. I don't know what to say as he takes my hands and plants them palms down on the dresser in front of me. My palms slide along the glossy top as he reaches for the fastening of his pants. My pulse races.

I've never had sex before. Ever. And if he thinks the best way to teach me whatever he wants to teach me is by taking me against this dresser...

My pulse quickens, and I stop breathing. I'm dizzy.

Stark blue eyes meet mine in the mirror. They skewer me in place, holding me in their thrall. "If this wasn't our wedding night, you'd be over my lap getting the spanking of your life for that mouth of yours. I'd redden your ass until you couldn't breathe. Do you understand me?"

His hot, swollen cock is between my legs. I've never done this before, but a part of me wants him, aches to be filled by him. I swallow and nod.

"But spanking you is only one way to punish you."

My logical brain is screaming at me as I bite back a retort. I have to stop mouthing off, or I might not survive this wedding night.

He believes I belong to him. He says that I'm his. What's to stop him from raping me? The thought terrifies me.

He drags his cock between my legs and teases my entrance, the hot head of his cock right where I'm longing for it.

"You'd take me like this?" I ask, staring into his eyes in the mirror, those beautiful, furious eyes of his. My voice wobbles, yet I hold his gaze. "My first time? You'd take my virginity with me pressed up against your dresser?" I bite back tears again. If he's thinking of raping me, maybe I could talk him out of it. "Why would you do that to me on our wedding night? Why would you take the only gift I've brought here to you and defile it like that?"

I don't know the woman staring at him in the mirror, logically arguing her way out of being violated. I feel as if I'm having an out-of-body experience. Angelina, the virgin who thought it wise to sacrifice for a friend of hers. And this woman here, naked and submitting to a hot but dangerous criminal.

Something shifts in his gaze. He blinks, as if waking from a dream. He still holds me up against the dresser with my breasts pressed to the edge, his body engulfing mine. Gathering my hair in his thick fist, he yanks it to the side and kisses my neck. Much to my chagrin, a shiver races down my spine. I wish I wasn't so easily manipulated.

He pulls my hair so hard I gasp. "Because I own you." He laps at my neck. My skin heats at the way he grips me, as if branding me with his touch will make it clear I'm his. "And because you like it."

I want to talk back to him, tell him he doesn't know what I like, but I can't because there's a tingling in the pit of my stomach and my lips won't work. He's so disturbing to me in every possible way, the maddening arrogance, the boiling anger, the rough heat of his skin, the way I know, *I know*, how he wants to unleash his full sadist on me.

But I'm no pawn in this. So I stand up straighter and arch my spine. I plant my hands on either side of his, despite the way he pushes me harder, grips me tighter, and growls.

"I don't believe you," I whisper in the darkness. I hold his ice-blue gaze. "Why don't you give me a wedding gift, big guy. I like it? Then show me."

A low growl fills the darkened room before he lifts me as if I'm a child, just slings me right up into his arms before he tosses me onto the bed. I barely bounce on the mattress before he pins me down. "Hands over your head," he orders, and when I don't obey fast enough, he claps his hand to my thigh. It stings and burns, but I do what he says and lift my hands up.

He bends and kisses me while he strips off his clothes.

I can barely think anymore, I'm so consumed by him. The smell of him, the feel of his lips on mine, the pounding of my heart. He grates in my ear, "Open your legs." His voice is husky, affected, and his cock is somehow hard and soft, silk-wrapped velvet.

My damp, slick arousal's all mingled with his pre-cum, and somehow the musky scent of sex makes my heart beat faster. I pant in anticipation, scared but excited.

95

"I told you I'd mark you." I nod, and my heartbeat spikes. Oh God. He nestles himself between my folds, dragging his cock through my slick, swollen pussy. It feels good. I want him to rub his cock over my clit until I come. It's exquisite, his hard cock teasing my entrance. He hasn't plunged into me yet.

"I want you wet when I take you. I want you to feel me, but I don't want you to hurt."

Yeah, achievement unlocked. I'm fucking sopping.

"This is the way I mark you."

He presses his cock to my entrance, and I hold my breath. My whole body shakes in anticipation. I want to feel this, but I'm terrified.

"Breathe," he demands. "I don't want to hurt you." I do what he says, taking in a deep breath, and as my lungs fill with air, he eases his way into me.

Vibrators don't prepare you for a thick, hard, dominant cock. Who knew?

At first, it hurts. It burns. "Breathe, Elise," he orders. "Do it."

I take another gasp of breath. He rocks his hips, and just like that, as if he's flipped a switch, the pain begins to fade to bliss.

Over and over again he moves in me. I'm moaning, consumed by him, drowning in the feel of him inside me. I'm so full I might burst, so full I want to cry from the utter perfection of it.

He's muttering something in Italian, and I don't know any of it, but I think he's cursing, or maybe praying, or both.

"You're so fucking tight. I'll mark you all right. When you walk tomorrow, you'll feel me with every step. Anyone that's near you will know that you've been well and properly fucked. You'll know that you belong to me. When I get you home alone again, I'll take you again."

Over and over he thrusts, and my body begins to heat even further. I don't even know this guy, but he's already mastered my body. And let's just say, that gives me mixed feelings.

I can't think anymore, as my body's consumed with heat, and fire, and need, and want. I'm moaning, pleading. *Begging*.

"Ask me for my cock," he says in my ear. "Fucking beg me."

I don't care anymore. I checked my humility at the door a long time ago.

"Please. I want you in me. Please. Don't stop." It hurts, but it hurts so fucking good. My hips begin to rise at the first spasm of pleasure that rips through my pelvis, as it flutters through my body like sprinkles of fairy dust.

"Thank me," he says into my ear. "Fucking thank me for taking your virginity."

"Thank you," I say on a scream as I shatter. He groans in my ear, and I feel him come inside me, hot and sticky and perfect. Somewhere at the damn back of my mind I'm aware that we haven't used protection, that he wants to impregnate me. He wants me to have his babies.

But I don't care right now. I want to live in this moment, I want to feel pleasure.

His forehead hits mine. "I told my men to tell everyone what happened tonight. They'll know I fucked you. They'll know my come marked your body and your cunt belongs to me. Everyone will fucking know who you are now."

I swallow, still riding the aftershocks. He kisses my cheek, my neck. And it's sultry and smooth and perfect, even the dark, dirty words he whispers in my ear. I only nod in a sort of sex-drugged bliss. I might speak, but I'm not aware of what I say if I do.

Everything kind of happens in a blur. I roll over on the bed while he walks to the bathroom. I hear fabric rustling, and realize he's tossed all the clothes to the corner of the room before he comes back to me. And then he's cleaning me up, lifting me up in one arm as he turns down the bedclothes with the other. Wow.

I'm so tired between the wine and the punishment and the sex, I quickly drift off to sleep. I wait to feel the heft of his body next to mine on this giant bed. I have a vague memory of him saying he'll restrain me. But I fall asleep before he returns.

CHAPTER 7

"Fate, show thy force; ourselves we do not owe; what is decreed must be, and be this so." ~ *Twelfth Night, Shakespeare*

ORLANDO

I DON'T SLEEP beside her. I don't want her to get used to me, to think I'll bring her comfort. If this is a business arrangement, I'll keep it this way.

I did my duty. And I won't lie, it was fucking months since I had a woman, and her tight, hot pussy was utter magic.

Now we'll sleep. Tomorrow, I'll go back to work and take her up to meet my family. Maybe have her meet my sister and mother while I get caught up with work. Then tomorrow night, I'll take her again.

And the night after that.

And the night after that.

There's only one way to put my baby in her.

One job I'll enjoy for once.

I won't leave her unsupervised, though. I briefly consider putting one of my men at the door, but then reject that idea. I want her to know that she's under my watch, and I don't want the eyes of any other man on her. Ever. She's mine, whether this is for business or not. She belongs to me.

So I lay on the sofa in the room beside her.

I'm so fucking tired, I can hardly settle down and sleep. The soft sounds of her whistling snores are like white noise, and slowly my eyelids close.

But my mind races.

My family's been demolished. Men have been killed. We're at war, and the only thing I can do is bring a baby into this world. I brought my wife into it, and now I have to keep the woman. I need to make sure she doesn't escape from me, either physically or mentally.

I need to make her mine, not just mine in name, with my ring on her finger and her body claimed by me...but mine in every way possible. My mind turns over every angle, everything that Romeo told me, and finally I fall to sleep, on a pull-out couch next to her dressed in nothing but my boxers.

The next morning I wake, not surprised to find I've got morning wood. Fucking hard as a rock. I have a vague thought that I had sex dreams featuring my new wife and her pretty mouth on my cock, but I can't remember details. I mean, I had sex for the first time in a year last night, and I'm nowhere near satisfied.

She's still snoring softly in the bed. Good. I didn't restrain her last night because my gut instinct said I didn't have to, that she wouldn't try to escape so soon, not surrounded by bodyguards and *me*.

I briefly consider taking her again, but she'll be sore, and even though I'll take her again soon, I wanna make sure she's ready for me.

So I adjust myself, groan, then walk to the bed and gently shake her shoulder. "Time to get up. I need a shower, and you're coming in with me."

"So I'm still your prisoner?" she asks. God, she's adorable when she wakes up, all tousled, her cheeks a little pink and her eyes half-lidded. I turn away because I don't want to soften myself toward her.

"Do you mean I still don't trust you not to run away? Of course. We have shit to do, and I don't want to waste any more time." I gave her ass a little swat over the bedclothes.

I peel down the sheets and blankets, not surprised to see she's got red marks across her ass and the tops of her thighs. She's not bruised or welted, though. We'll work up to that.

I ghost my fingers over her swollen, reddened flesh, gentle enough that I won't hurt her again. Enough that she'll feel me, though. "Are you sore?"

"Uh, yeah. You could say that." She rolls over and gives me a reproachful look.

"Don't give me that look," I warn her. "I don't care how sorry you are, you start that sass with me, and you'll end up right over my lap."

With a little pout that might mask arousal, she asks, "You're just dying to punish me, aren't you?"

"Honey, you have no idea." I stand up. "Shower. Now."

I don't give her a chance to disobey but pick her up and carry her to the bathroom.

"No morning sex?" She gives me a wry look and wriggles herself on me. "Looks like you're ready."

I groan. Fucking tease. "I'm always ready."

"Oh that's not arrogant at all."

"It isn't. It's the truth. I want to take my time, and we don't have that right now. I want to give you at least a couple hours to heal up."

"Very chivalrous of you."

I shrug and hold her with one arm while I turn the shower on. "If you're being passive-aggressive, you better knock that shit off."

She doesn't respond, only squirms a bit uncomfortably and changes the subject.

"Okay, Orlando. I really want to take a look at you. You've checked me out, and I briefly got a glimpse of you before you plucked me out of bed. I've noticed you like tossing me around like I'm spoils of war or something. But dude, you are not even winded carrying me with one arm. It's like you have superhuman strength."

Dude? Cute.

"Maybe it's my superpower."

"You say that as if it's normal."

I don't answer. In my line of work, it is.

Steam heats the bathroom, and it feels so good to be in here I want to stay all day, just lapping up the luxury of hot water, a huge bathroom, privacy. A fucking wife.

God, what I've taken for granted.

But I do what she asks and slide her to the tiled floor as I gather towels and check for toiletries. Of course someone's already thought of that, and the bathroom's well-stocked.

"Wow," she breathes. "Okay, so I've heard that it's pretty...common...for guys in prison to kind of work out a lot...like they've got not much else to do, but...*damn.*"

She likes what she sees. Cute. That pleases me.

I pick her up and place her at the end of the tub away from the hot water. "It sure as fuck passes the time and being strong helps me with my own job."

"So can you tell me what the job is now?"

"Your father really didn't tell you anything, did he?"

She shakes her head. "Like literally nothing."

Asshole. "I'm the group heavy. Enforcer."

"You're the one that breaks bones?"

"Yeah."

And beats the shit out of traitors, inflicts punishment on those that double-cross us, and kills anyone that rats us out. Among other things.

"Sounds...violent." Her voice is a bit raspy. Scared? "Do you like violence, Orlando?"

I don't answer as I lather up a washcloth and hand it to her. I'm hard as fuck watching her run it over her curves, her breasts, between her legs. I'm half jealous of her own hand that touches her. She watches me with a hooded gaze. Aroused, is she?

I don't know how to answer that question. I fucking hate violence, but I'm so used to it I barely think about it anymore. Violence is duty and survival, the only way. "Enough questions. You turned on, Elise?"

Her nipples are peaked, even in the warmth of the shower. She turns away from me, giving me the answer I want.

If I want to own this woman, I'll have to do it in more ways than one. And I do want this woman. *Fully*.

"Sit on the edge of that seat." I point to the tiled shower seat at the end of the massive shower. The steam clouds my vision for a minute, but she's walking away, obeying me. My cock throbs.

She's so small, she fits easily there. Her eyes hold mine, as she worries her lip. She's too small for me to fuck here, and I'm too big. She'll blow me, though. In time. And I'll make sure she fucking loves it.

"Brace yourself on either side." The way she obeys makes me harder than ever. The hot, steaming water pounds my back when I kneel in front of her.

"Orlando…" I can hear the fear in her voice.

"Quiet," I whisper. "Relax."

I bend and lick the inside of her thigh, so clean and fresh and slightly pink from the heat of the shower. We don't have much time. I have so much work to catch up on, but I can tell she's already aroused. I grip her thighs and open them wider, then bend and kiss the soft, short curls at her pussy. Her hands fly to my hair, gripping, but a quick slap to the thigh has her obeying me with her hands on either side of her once again.

"You want to come?" I ask, the heat of my breath on her pussy.

She nods eagerly, panting.

"Then do what I tell you or I'll take you to the edge of climax and leave you there. All. Day. Long."

"You wouldn't," she breathes, her voice choked.

"Try me."

I part her pussy and drag my tongue between her slick folds. Her soft, eager whimper and moan are worth every goddamn day I spent behind bars. My fucking reward.

I tease my finger at her entrance, but when she tenses, I know she's still sore. I part her legs, brace myself on her thighs, and suckle her clit as the water pounds on my back and my cock throbs.

"Oh God," she whispers, her body shaking with every stroke of my tongue. "What are you *doing?*"

"I told you," I whisper against her thighs, breathing hot air on her eager pussy. "Owning you."

I tease the tip of my tongue on her clit, then suckle before I lap again. Her head rests back against the tile, and water drips from her thighs. I shift and stroke my cock as I lick and suckle and consume every moan. "You taste so fucking good," I groan, stroking my cock while I lick her.

Her hips jerk and she says something incoherent. I grin against her naked, pink thighs, drag my tongue lower, and taste her entrance. Fuck, I can't wait to take her again. I drag my tongue from her entrance to her clit, then circle and suckle.

When I can tell she's on the edge, shaking with the first spasms, I take my mouth off her. She cries out, "No, no, *please.*"

"Ask permission."

"For—for what?" she stutters, whimpering.

"Ask me permission to come. If you come before I tell you, I'll punish you. Do you understand me? Right here, right now."

She gives a hoarse cry, lifting her hips as if that will bring my mouth back to where she wants it. I stroke my cock harder, faster, on the edge of coming myself.

"Now, Elise. Fucking now, or I come all over you before I whip you and leave you throbbing."

"Monster, you're a goddamn monster," she whimpers. "May I?"

Two of the most beautiful words in the English language. I nod my head.

"Come for me," I say before I bring my mouth back to her pussy. I come hard as I lap at her clit, groaning at the sweet taste of her as she comes on my tongue.

Jesus.

I kiss her pussy and finish stroking myself off. I come hard, welcoming the fucking release I needed.

I feel as if a weight's been lifted from me, and I have no idea what the fuck that's all about. I stand and arrange her in front of me so we can finish showering and head out. She's boneless when she slumps against me.

"So that's what that's like." I love that she knows nothing, that she's a perfect blank canvas for me to work on. *Love* it.

"Have you ever been with anyone at all?" I hate the question, hate the image it conjures up in my imagination. But I need to know. I put body wash on a pale pink loofah with a gold loop. Hers. I lather her back and hold her to my chest.

She shakes her head. "I kissed someone once… in college."

Rage burns in my chest so hard and savage it takes me by surprise. She notices the way I tense and looks up at me, her eyes still half-lidded from her climax. "Does that bother you?"

I speak through my fury, my voice tight.

"Bother me? What's his fucking name?"

She was promised as a child, was never free to share intimacy with another, and should have known better than to have kissed a man. She'll pay for that, and so will he, the fucking thief.

"Whoa, wait." Her palm hits the air as if to calm me down. Doesn't work. "I'm a virgin, but it doesn't mean I've never been touched by anyone."

"I want a list, Elise."

"What?" She blinks. "A list of…of what?"

"Men who touched you." I'll kill them, every last motherfucker.

"Orlando." She places her hands on my shoulders and holds my gaze. "You can't...you can't hurt like the two people I kissed under the bleachers in high school. Are you crazy?"

I sure as hell am crazy, and she ought to know that. "Any fucking moron who touched you should've known better. You were a Regazza. Off-limits."

"I was fourteen!"

"Doesn't fucking matter."

She shakes her head. Little droplets of water dot her bare breasts. "Uh uh. No. I'm not going to give you names. You can p-punish me or...whatever the hell it is you have in mind," she stutters, and she looks away for some reason as she says this. "But I'm not going to let you fuck up someone that didn't know any better."

"You're a fucking Regazza. He knew better."

Her eyes flare. "Did I tell you it was a guy?"

Wait, now. *Wait.*

My cock's hard again, that quick. "You mean it... wasn't a guy?"

She shrugs. "I maybe was a little curious is all. And anyway, I thought guys were into that...girl on girl and everything."

"Are you shittin' me?"

She shakes her head and laughs, a genuine laugh that makes my heart swell for reasons I don't understand. She gets up on her tiptoes to kiss my cheek.

"I was a virgin when I came to you," she says, holding my gaze. "You were the first man who ever made me come. You were the first *human* that made me come. I was undefiled." She rolls her eyes. "If that's what you want to call it. Is that good enough for you?"

"For now." I spin her around to rinse her off and rinse myself off, too. And I am momentarily mollified.

She's got stacks of clothes here waiting for her, since she's packed so little and hasn't had a chance to get her belongings yet. I don't want her to get much. She'll start anew as a Rossi.

I dress quickly. I've got so much work to do.

"So what am I supposed to do while you work?"

"Today, you'll work with me."

"Oh, God." She's slipping on a pair of shoes.

"What?"

"Orlando!" Her eyes are wide in surprise. I glance at the clock. I have to be at the restaurant in an hour. "I don't...I don't *hurt* people."

I blink, trying to understand, and when I do, I snort with laughter. "So you think the only job I have is beating people up? God, I'd fucking hang myself."

She winces but hides it as she looks in the mirror to wring out her hair. For a mafia princess, she's a little more sensitive than I'd expect.

"Okay, then, so what else do you do?" I'm mesmerized by the way her small fingers work through her hair, how she combs her fingers through it as she applies some foamy white product. It smells of lemon.

I shake my head to clear my brain. "My family owns ten restaurants in the North End. I oversee them."

"Oh, wow. Are you a chef?"

I continue dressing while I answer her questions. As my wife, she needs to know everything. "I can cook, yeah. Love to cook. Love to eat more. We have head chefs in every restaurant, though."

"Okay, so you don't just do mafia stuff, you do like actual work, too."

That makes me laugh again. It's like she's been totally sheltered. It's a little odd.

"Ah, that *is* mafia stuff. This isn't a movie. How much did your father shelter you?"

"Oh you have no idea," she says quickly. Too quickly. "I know *nothing* about the mafia."

It's an odd answer, but she doesn't meet my eyes as she's busy getting makeup out of a little silver bag.

"Nothing? You were raised by the Regazzas and you know nothing?"

She sighs and shakes her head. I'm mesmerized when she drags a little brush across her lips. They shine pink, then quickly brighten.

"Is that magic?"

She puckers her lips. "Magic?"

"Yeah, that stuff you put on your lips. It just… shifted color. How did it do that?"

Her eyes crinkle at me in the mirror. "It's a pH-color changing one. Changes color to match your body type." Her shoulders shake with laughter. "You know, I wouldn't call you *cute*, but when your brow's all puckered like that, you kind of are."

I grunt at her as my phone rings. "Fuckin' endorphins and shit." She only laughs harder. I glance at the screen. Romeo.

"Yeah?"

"You working on babies, brother?"

I turn my back to her. For some reason, talking about sex with Elise to anyone else feels like a betrayal. It's his job, though, to make sure I'm doing what I'm supposed to. "Yeah, on it. Did what we had to. What's going on?"

He sighs, and all humor fades from his tone. "Need you in sooner than later."

"Why?"

I adjust my tie and catch her gaze on instinct.

"Found a fucking traitor. Bringing him in now."

I flex my fingers and make a fist. Stifle a sigh.

Welcome home.

CHAPTER 8

"I have unclasp'd to thee the book even of my secret soul." ~ *Twelfth Night, Shakespeare*

"ELISE"

I HAVE SO many mixed emotions, I'm not even sure how to begin sorting them. I'm trying to compile a mental list of everything I've figured out about him and the questions I still have.

That list of questions is a hell of a lot longer than the list of answers.

I hate him, or at least I thought I did. All bossy and commanding and dominating, he steamrolled me like he's the king of the castle. He definitely thinks he is. And my attempts to take him down a peg or two...well, let's just say that was an epic fail.

He has decided he will show me who's boss, and he's pretty convincing. I have a feeling his need to control isn't just a kinky bedroom thing.

At least the punishment he promised me for trying to escape was *fairly* tame and ended in a climax, so…I dodged a bullet maybe?

He's got an insatiable appetite for sex, or at least it seems it. He didn't waste any time on our wedding night, jerked himself off in the shower, and already looks at me as if he wants to push me up against the wall and fuck me again.

But just now…someone called him, and whatever they said on the phone affected him. He's back to the brooding, angry monster of a man with tattooed knuckles and a mean palm. I can still feel the branding slap of his hand on my ass, and the promise of more to come if I didn't do what he said.

So I decide it's time to observe. Time to really understand him. If I'm going to escape, I'll really need to know what makes him tick.

It's all a bit surreal as we head to the North End. It's a cool spring day, with a bit of a breeze, but the sun still beats down optimistically. Warmer days are coming, for a little while anyway.

"Later, after I finish work, we'll head to The Castle. We'll spend the next few nights there." He's in the driver's seat of the car he used last night to pick me up.

"Don't you have a driver?" I know Elise's family does.

"Yeah, several, but sometimes I like to drive to work myself."

Huh. Interesting. Why?

I watch as his lips tip up, but it's barely noticeable. "Haven't you figured that out yet?"

"Ah. Control, then."

"Yeah. When shit goes down, I want the only blame to be on me."

Interesting.

"So what do I need to know about The Castle?"

"Marialena will be there, and Vittoria, Romeo's wife." Oh, God. So I'm not the first victim to be married to a made man. I hope I like them. Some of Elise's family...

I have a feeling I should know some of this, and I don't want to make it clear that I'm not Elise, so I decide it's better if I don't say anything.

"Rosa's in Italy for now. Unfortunately, she won't be back until the end of the month. I know you guys were friendly with each other. Maybe she'll FaceTime."

Shit.

There is no way on God's green earth I'm gonna FaceTime with someone who's supposed to know me. How much time did the Regazzas spend with the Rossis? From a distance I could pass for her, but face-to-face, I'm screwed.

"Hey, am I getting my phone back?"

"When I'm done with it, yeah."

Panic sweeps through my chest. "What do you mean, when you're done with it?"

Is he...checking it? Researching? What if he finds the texts I sent Elise? My mind races, trying to piece it all together. She isn't in my phone as *Elise* but *Bestie*. Thank God.

Our texts to each other though...we only talked about the Rossis, and that would be an obvious conversation to have the day before I'm supposed to be married to one of them. That's pretty normal stuff, too, I guess.

Oh God. Still. I need to look at my phone. I need to see if there's anything at all incriminating on it...

"Why'd you go all quiet?"

I look out the window and will my voice to remain steady. "Maybe I don't like the idea of you snooping on my phone."

He purses his lips as he takes a turn onto a main road. "Maybe I don't like your attitude."

Whatever. "Are you *always* looking for a way to dominate me?"

"No. I don't need to look for ways."

I manage to keep that mutter under wraps.

"As a Regazza woman, you ought to be used to being tapped. Why do you act like it's an invasion of your privacy? You've had no privacy since you were little."

He's genuinely confused, and I have to remind myself that I'm Elise Regazza, daughter to the Don. It's true, I know it. Elise hasn't had any privacy her whole life. Piero practically watches her pee.

"I just thought it might be different when I was actually, you know, *married*. I'm expected to have children with you, and I'm still being treated like a child." I look out the window as if affronted. But I'm not offended. I'm terrified. I squeeze my hands together, to hide the trembling.

I really should accept a bit more, at least ostensibly. Would Elise push back like this? No...she'd probably know better than to do that. I bite my lip. I have to find that one little, tiny, submissive bone in my body, wherever the hell it is.

The tension in the car is palpable, like muddied water and thick marsh. I feel as if I'm swimming for my life but only getting sucked down deeper into the murky pool.

We may have shared some tender moments together, but I can't let myself be fooled. If he ever finds out I'm not who he thinks I am, he'll kill me. Any of them would. It's the highest form of betrayal.

I'm not under any delusion that I'm safe with him. Not now, not ever.

He shakes his head, intent on driving through the congested streets of Boston before he takes a left down a private entrance to a parking lot right near the North End.

"You thought it'd be different than when you were a child," he repeats, as if mulling this over. Shaking his head, he sighs. "You seem to have forgotten last night...and this morning. Ain't nothing fucking childish about *that*."

My body tingles at the memory of him taking me, his thick cock marking me as his, his mouth between my legs, as I reached for his hair...

"Well...not *that*. I just mean the privacy. I don't get any now?"

"Absolutely not. I don't know what your father's restrictions were, but if he did his duty as the head of his family, he kept you safe, he kept you protected, and he kept you under his watchful eye."

I think back to waking up on Christmas Day with my father passed out on the couch, a used syringe on the floor. Christmas lights twinkled from the windows in the apartments across from us, and someone played music far in the distance. I put a blanket over him and poured myself a bowl of cereal.

I don't respond.

"Over time, we'll get to know each other. I'll find out more about you and you'll find out more about me. But for now, what's most important is that you know what I expect. You took those vows and signed away any promise of privacy. You'll be with me or a team of bodyguards at all times. Your Internet use and phone use will be monitored, completely, by me and my men. I'll give you anything you need."

I look out the window and don't respond. My hands shake harder, and I swallow the lump in my throat. I'll never get away. What a fool I am for thinking I could.

"We're here. And listen, I know you're new." It's a patronizing tone, so I'm not sure why I soften a little. He reaches for my hand and laces his fingers through mine. "I won't expect perfection from you. I'll ease you into this. I saw when my sister was brought into a new family after leaving ours, and I know there are growing pains." Again, the slight gentleness that lies below the rough, almost mean exterior gives me pause. I don't trust it. Did he take an edge off when he fucked me?

Or maybe it was the spanking.

Which is the real Orlando? The one who whipped me with his belt and promised more if I disobey him? Or the one who put a blanket over my shoulders and nearly tucked me into bed last night?

Both of them scare me. Both of them intrigue me.

And both of them hold me hostage.

"Growing pains," I say with a mirthless laugh. "Like spanking…"

The car glides to a stop as he parks it. His eyes darken. "Among other things."

Uniformed men wait outside the door. I wonder where they materialized from. I gasp when Orlando reaches for my neck, yanks me over to him, and kisses me. His tongue plunders my mouth, and he palms my breast. I'm shocked but my pulse races immediately as heat floods my core. Jesus, this guy knows how to manhandle me.

"What was that?" I breathe. "My God."

"First time my guards have met you as my wife. These are the men that oversee my business." He nips my ear, then withdraws, and my skin's on fire where his teeth and tongue touched. My heart begins to stutter. "I want them to know you're mine."

"So a ring and your last name aren't enough?" My voice is a little shaky.

He actually laughs at that and doesn't respond.

One of the uniformed men opens his door, but my attention's diverted when I hear my door open behind me. His men greet him in Italian. I remember that he was only just released from prison. Coming back to work is a sort of homecoming, I guess.

The guard who just opened my door reaches his hand to help me out.

"Touch her and fucking lose that hand, brother." Orlando's deep boom carries through the parking lot so loudly, I jump. The guard steps back and tucks his hands behind his back.

"I'm sorry, sir. So sorry. I only meant—"

"To touch what's fucking mine?" Orlando's walking around to my side of the car. Stalking, one could say. Whoa.

"Orlando," I say gently. "He was only—"

He shakes his head at me and narrows his eyes, a furious warning. I close my mouth. I guess you could say I'm learning.

"He was only on the verge of making a fatal mistake," Orlando corrects.

"I'm sorry, sir," the guard repeats.

Orlando takes out his phone and makes a call. I don't understand what he says, because he speaks in Italian. And for the first time since I got here, I realize that maybe I'm expected to know Italian, too. *Nooo.*

Oh my God, how will I do this? How?

I'm a quick study. I'll study Italian in my downtime and make up some excuse if he notices when he watches my Internet use.

The guard blanches as he talks, and I reason he must know Italian, too. Oh, God, *Elise.* What do I do now?

"Mi dispiace così tanto, signore," the guard says. He's apologizing. Why is he overreacting so strongly? I

wrap my arms around my chest to hide the sudden chill I feel, then gasp when Orlando drapes his arm around my shoulders.

"You cold?" The words are clipped. Angry. The storm rages within him again, simmering and volatile.

"A little." I'm shivering uncontrollably, but not just from cold.

On the other end of the phone, a deep voice responds to him. Orlando grunts. "Yeah. That works." He hangs up the phone and slides it into his pocket, no more formalities.

"You," he says to the guy that tried to help me out of the car. "Tuscany, tonight. You've got three hours to pack your bags. You come near her, I'll end you before you've left this country." I jump when he snaps his fingers at another uniformed attendant by a black car that's double-parked on the congested street. "Get him out of my fucking sight."

I walk beside him automatically, stunned and confused. I never would've suspected such a harmless gesture would be grounds for exile as it were. I watch the younger man hang his head in shame, before he opens the car door and leaves.

Does he have a family? A loved one? Connections here in the States that he's forfeiting now that he's been sent to another country for... trying to touch me?

I lose track of how many men greet Orlando, and a few women as well, as we walk the sunbathed streets of the North End. I haven't been here in years, but I love the North End. Abutting the Boston waterfront, on a sunny day like today, the salty air of the wharf smells like vacation and travel. Once, when I was a little girl, my school came to the aquarium at the wharf for a field trip. As we got our tickets, a large window into the aquarium showed penguins diving and doing tricks in front of us. It was the first time I'd ever seen them, and I fell in love.

Vendors sell cotton candy, popcorn, pretzels, and cheap touristy *Boston* T-shirts stretched on cardboard. And even though it's busy and bustling here, with commuters and college students, people riding on bikes, and heading into work, it's clear that Orlando is not a stranger. People look at him with respect and some with a little bit of fear. Some take a step back.

I understand that feeling.

"The restaurants are a little further off, aren't they?" I ask, as we cross a busy intersection and head away from the wharf and closer to where the smell of garlic and olive oil lingers in the air. My mouth waters.

"They are. I want to parade you a little."

Parade me. Jesus.

"Uh. What?"

"The Rossi family's well known here," he says in a low voice, as we cross the street. He quickly slides his way between me and the curb, an act of chivalry that doesn't really surprise me at all. I have a feeling I won't be lifting any heavy boxes or carrying any bags with him around. I definitely won't be splitting any dinner bills.

I wonder if Rossi men are deeply rooted in another place and time, when men were heads of the house and women were meant to be cared for.

I'm not sure how I feel about that. One could say mixed emotions sums it up quite well.

I practically raised myself. I met my own needs from a very young age, and by the time I was in high school, set out on my own. I value autonomy and hard work, and dislike the thought of riding anyone's damn coattails.

But it doesn't matter. Any of it.

I'm not here to stay.

So I can play along with this. For now. If I don't, he could suspect I'm not who I'm supposed to be, and I can't imagine what he'd do if he found out.

He slows his steps when we come to a narrow road lined with cars. The smell of roasting garlic, onions, and tomatoes lingers in the air. My mouth waters.

"Hungry, *piccolina?*"

I nod. I also really, really wish I knew Italian. When I look at him in bewilderment, his eyes crinkle around the edges. "What, you don't like my name for you?"

"Didn't say that," I mutter, trying to be vague. I need to learn Italian, *stat*.

He opens the door for me and gestures for me to enter. I wonder what he'd do if I tried to open it for myself. I decide it probably isn't worth finding out.

I have to step up to get inside. Once I do, the strong scent of good Italian food permeates the air. My mouth waters when a waitress walks past me with a tray of silver plates and bowls bearing cheesy, decadent dishes. At least I will eat well during all this.

We're instantly swarmed by people. Tall men in suits, some I recognize from the night before while others are new to me.

Romeo, the man in front, walks to me, bows, and reaches for my hand. I look quickly to Orlando to see how he'll react.

"Well done, wife," he says in a low voice. "Romeo is Don, the leader of all. He may touch your hand and even kiss it." He gives Romeo a warm smile. "And he knows I'll kick his ass if he does more than that, but as a happily married man himself, his wife would finish him off when he got home."

A younger man with suave looks reminiscent of James Dean's bad boy vibes, grins. He steps toward me and reaches for my hand as well. Orlando grunts his permission as one after the other takes my hand and kisses it. When each of the brothers has greeted me, Orlando stands up straighter and shoos them all away. "No more touching her. Romeo. You called me."

"Back room, brother." Romeo's eyes dart to me, then back to Orlando.

"Elise comes. She's been raised as a Regazza but seems sheltered. I won't shelter her anymore." Romeo nods. He may be head of The Family, but Orlando is clearly head of *me*.

Thanks?

Romeo talks in a low tone to a few of the men near us. Two station themselves at the door, an entrance to a back room at the very back of the restaurant. Two others come to me and flank my sides but are careful not to touch me.

"Look too long, Mario, I'll beat the fucking shit out of you," Orlando says with the glimmer of a smile on his lips. The ice in his eyes says he isn't joking.

The young, attractive brother smiles good-naturedly. "She only has eyes for you, man. You know that. She'll be a sister to me, no more, no less."

"Good," Orlando responds as they walk side by side. "Been working on my right hook in the big house."

Mario flinches but laughs it off. I, however, am not laughing.

To the right, the kitchen's in full swing. It's late morning, and I don't usually eat breakfast, but I'm starving. My stomach growls when one of the chefs pulls a pizza out of the oven, golden and sizzling hot. A waitress fills a basket with rolls so hot, she uses tongs to keep from burning her fingers. Another slices a thick slab of tiramisu and slides it onto a plate. For the first time, I hope he actually gets me pregnant so I have an excuse to eat my heart out.

Maybe he's bewitched me. Sex and food may be the hardest of appetites to tame.

But we don't head to the kitchen. Orlando opens the door, but this time gestures for me to stand behind him as Romeo and two of the other brothers, all dressed in impeccable suits, go in before him. Orlando takes my hand, and we enter the back room.

Boxes marked with food names in Italian line either side of the entrance. A few are open, revealing the round, silver tops of canned tomatoes, and others jars of olive oil. The only marking on the bottles are plum-colored stickers with *Rossi Family* emblazoned in gold.

I'm so taken by the food all around us that at first, I don't see the chair in the corner of the room, or the man strapped to it. I freeze when I do.

He's bloodied and bruised, but still an attractive man. Well-dressed, with the stunning good looks one might find in Hollywood. It looks like he's playing a scene in a movie, only this is all too real. Blood drips onto the floor from his mouth, his cheek, and multiple lacerations all over his body.

"Motherfucker," Orlando growls beside me. I let go of his hand. This isn't the man that lathered me in soap and held the door for me today. His eyes are cold and ruthless. This is the man who just spent time in prison for manslaughter and doesn't look afraid of going back.

"See that stool in the corner?" he asks, his eyes on the man in the chair.

Shaking, I look. I nod.

"Sit there."

I wouldn't think of doing anything but obeying right now. I've never looked into the eyes of a serial killer, but I imagine they'd look like his do now—cold, ruthless, detached. And very, very determined.

I'm not overly familiar with violence, but I'm not a stranger to it, either. Being raised the way I was, fending for myself in the face of depravity, I've seen my fair share of shit. So it isn't the brutalized man before me that scares me. It's the shift in Orlando's whole demeanor.

He paces in front of the half-conscious man, his expensive Italian leather shoes nearly noiseless on the concrete floor. His brothers stand behind him.

"Davis. You went after my wife."

What? His wife? I'm his wife. No one came after me. I've been under his protection from the minute the plane crashed.

I don't realize I'm holding my breath until I become a little dizzy. Mario walks to my side and speaks in a low voice. "You okay?" I notice his hands are in his pockets, as if to keep himself from touching me and maybe saving himself from a beating.

I nod. No one looks at us as we continue to talk in hushed voices. "Yeah. Fine. Nothing I haven't seen before." Lies. They're becoming easier. "I just don't understand why he's accusing him of what he just did. I've been with him the whole time."

"Ah," Mario whispers, nodding. He watches as Orlando paces around the man, who's begun to cry like a child. "You were picked up by Orlando when your plane crashed. Yeah?"

I nod silently. Romeo looks over at us, then back to Orlando. Overseeing all.

"This asshole heard of the marriage plans. Tried to make some extra dough, thought he'd prevent you from marrying Orlando. Guards caught him before he did, tapped his messages. Brought him here."

Oh, God. He's been in that chair, bleeding and half-conscious, since last night? It's late morning, almost afternoon.

Mario shrugs. "Didn't want to ruin your wedding night." He gives me a wink. I roll my eyes. They say Italians learn the language of flirtation right along with their native tongue. Mario is apparently fluent. "But we left him for Orlando to handle."

"Who...who hurt him? Who questioned him?"

Mario's jovial eyes grow serious. "You don't ask that, Elise. As mafia, you should know better than to ask that." Unlike Orlando, his tone doesn't seem corrective or chiding, but more surprised than anything.

Of course I should. *God.* How many times will I stumble before they find out the truth?

I shrug and continue to whisper. "Our families aren't the same. Our rules differed from yours. I'm sure there were similarities, but they aren't the same."

Mario nods. "True, true."

Romeo's gaze swings to us, and he puts a silent finger to his lips. I clamp my mouth shut. I do not need to be mafia to know that obeying the Don is a smart idea.

Orlando stands, his feet planted on either side of him like solid trees. Holding the gaze of his prisoner. "Everyone out," he snaps. Mario's eyes flare with surprise as he looks to Romeo, but Romeo only nods and beckons for the men to follow him out of the room. Shaking, I get off the stool, but Orlando's voice holds me in place.

"Except my wife. You stay right there."

No. *No.* He's going to kill this guy, and he wants me to be the only witness?

The door closes behind us, and when it's just the three of us remaining, Orlando walks to the door and throws the deadbolt in place.

"Elise," he snaps. Still not meeting my eyes, he shrugs out of his suit coat and begins to roll up his sleeves, revealing inked arms and strong, strong muscles. I swallow. "Strip."

I blink. "Strip?" I whisper.

Now I've got his attention. "You want to walk home today wearing clothes, or under my suit coat because I ruined yours ripping them off you?"

I blink at him.

"I won't tell you again. Strip."

CHAPTER 9

"Or I am mad, or else this is a dream." ~*Twelfth Night, Shakespeare*

ORLANDO

"YOU KNOW ME," I tell him, while I hold her gaze. "You look at her, and I'll cut your motherfucking eyes out before you die. Close them. I want you to hear me fuck her and know you lost before you go to hell."

I love the way she watches me, as if she's oblivious to the man in the corner whose eyes are squeezed shut. If she's horrified, she hides it well. This woman's made of steel, and I fucking love that.

I stalk over to her, rock-hard. She's shaking a little when I get to her. "Shhh, baby," I whisper in her ear before I kiss her cheek. I tuck her hair behind her

133

ear and flex my fingers on her neck. She lays her head on my shoulder as I lift her and wrap her legs around my waist.

"Orlando," she whispers. I silence her with a kiss, my fingers tangled in her hair, to hold her in place. I walk her to the wall right near him, where his lips mumble what better be prayers. I could kick my leg out and hit him. I push her up against the wall to hold her in place, her gorgeous, naked body flush up against mine, and I unbuckle my belt.

"Watch my eyes as I fuck you. Don't look at him. There's only me and you right now."

"Why?" she whispers.

"Because knowing I got the most beautiful woman in the fucking world as *mine* will make him rue the day he was born," I whisper in her ear. "Then I'll punish him for trying to hurt you."

My hands on her naked hips, I lift her slightly so I can keep her secured. I reach one hand to my waist and unbutton my fly. My rock-hard cock springs free.

I swing my gaze to my prisoner. His eyes are still squeezed shut.

Elise shivers. It's warm in here, so I'm thinking she might be scared. I hold her to my chest as I line my cock up at her entrance. She isn't wet enough, not yet.

So I tease her clit with the head of my cock and drag my tongue over her naked nipple. Her head falls back and she releases a gasp.

"Louder. I want him to hear you."

She whimpers only slightly louder than before. I slap her thigh hard, making her scream out loud, then bite her nipple. She screams my name in a hoarse voice.

"That's a girl. That's such a good girl," I say approvingly. "Very good, baby. Such a good girl."

I lick her nipples until she's dripping, then finger her clit while I guide my cock to her entrance. I know she'll still be sore, but I'll ease in, make the pain better. She moans when I drag my cock over her swollen clit. "Such a little slut you are," I whisper in her ear. "Call my name."

"Orlando!" she cries on a moan when I lave her nipple before I bite it. "Oh God!"

"That's right, baby. Just like that. Take my cock."

I ease into her hot, tight cunt. She squirms and shifts, but her pussy takes my cock with perfection. I lift her hips and gently thrust, groaning at her hot, sleek pussy taking my cock fully.

"So fucking gorgeous," I whisper to her. "Just like that, baby."

I begin to fuck her in earnest, easing up when she winces and quickening when she obviously enjoys it all. I love the feel of her taking me, her hot sex yielding to me. The way her head falls back on a moan.

I suckle and lick her nipples while I fondle her pussy and thrust into her. I watch our prisoner, but his eyes are closed, even though his whole body's rigid at the sound of our lovemaking. I mutter in Italian, words of adoration and praise. *"Piccolino mio."*

On the other side of the door, people laugh and talk amidst the clinking of glasses and sounds of forks and knives on plates. Our prisoner whimpers softly, but Elise only has eyes for me.

I thrust again and again. She takes me fully, panting with every thrust.

"Oh, God," she says loudly. "Oh, God, I love your cock. Yes. Yes!"

I don't know if she's saying that for my benefit or his, but I love her for it.

"Come, baby. I give you permission to come," I growl, just as she tosses her head back and screams. She rides her orgasm with perfection, squirming and crying out as she's wrapped in the throes of ecstasy. I come on the heels of her orgasm. In my peripheral vision, my prisoner flinches.

She pants, coming down from her orgasm, and drops her head to my shoulder. I hold her there, my cock still throbbing in the aftershocks. I hold her.

My possession. My reward. My wife.

I ready her and zip my fly.

"Get dressed," I tell her. "Everyone will know I marked you. Let's eat. Let the echoes of your screams ring in his ears while he waits for me to come back."

Her gaze travels to the back of the room. She blinks in surprise, as if just remembering our prisoner witnessed this.

"You still hungry, baby?"

"Starving."

And that's what I get for marrying a mafia princess. If she's bothered by this, it doesn't show. Either that, or she's lying.

I'll come back to our prisoner later.

Two hours later, I'm heading to The Castle. Tavi, Santo, and Mario are taking care of the prisoner's body. After I fucked her next to him, I made him sit waiting for his sentence while I ordered lunch.

I call Mama on the way. "Hey, Mama. I'm coming home."

"You're coming home?" Her voice is hopeful, and I can almost hear her smiling.

"I am. Rosa home yet?"

Elise sits stock-still and straight beside me.

"No, not yet. You bringing your new wife?"

"I am, of course."

"Ah, then. Maybe I'll wear something appropriate to meet my new daughter-in-law."

"Ohh, is he bringing the new girl?" someone questions in the background. Mama laughs.

"Yeah, Mama. I'm bringing the new girl."

When I hang up the phone, Elise is worrying her lip, a habit of hers.

"Who's there?" she asks.

"Marialena. Have you met her?"

"Uh, hmm. Not sure. I don't think so." She looks out the window. Why does she look like she's hiding something?

"Elise."

At the sharp tone of my voice, she swings her gaze back to mine. "Yes?"

"You hiding something from me?"

"No. Why would you think that?"

I shake my head. "No reason."

We drive in silence through traffic. I reach my hand to grab her knee. She lets me.

"When can I have my phone back?"

"Soon, maybe tonight. Why? You got something on there you don't want me to see?"

She only shakes her head.

"Jesus," I groan when we pull up to the house,

The Castle, the home I grew up in. The bright late afternoon sun glints against a cluster of pearly white balloons tied to the railing by the front door, and flowers line the path like a floral welcome mat.

"My sister sometimes goes overboard," I groan. She looks a little surprised but doesn't respond. I carry what few bags we brought, and when she reaches for hers, only need to narrow my eyes at her. She steps back. She's learning.

She ate a hearty lunch, even though she knew what I was going to do when we were done.

"Hope you're hungry again later," I say. "My Mama and Nonna will have cooked enough food for an army. Later." Our dogs walk quietly over to greet us, their thick, whip-like tails whizzing through the air when they see me. It's been a while.

"Ahh, here they are!" Marialena stands in the doorway entrance to the garage, her arms wide open. "The new bride and my jailbird brother!"

I grunt at her, but a second later she squeals when I swing her straight up into the air before I give her a bear hug.

"Oh my God, I'm glad you came home, too!" She reaches for my bride's hand. "Refresh my memory. Rosa hasn't told me much about you. Elise Regazza, yes?"

Elise nods, her cheeks a little pink. Embarrassed? Nervous? I watch carefully.

"Any siblings?" Marialena reaches for her hand and tugs her along into the house.

"No. I'm an only child."

"Oh, you poor child," Marialena says. "My brothers are major hard-asses, and Rosa's a bossy bitch, but I can't even imagine being the only one around for my Papa to harass." She quickly makes the sign of the cross. "May his soul rest in peace. Are your parents still with us?"

"Yes," Elise says, then she looks quickly my way with a silent plea for help.

"Marialena."

"What?" she asks over her shoulder. "Forgive me for wanting to get to know my new *sister!*" She squeals. "Oh, can I take her shopping, Lando? Please? Pretty please?"

Lando. I haven't heard her pet name for me in so long, my throat tightens.

"Marialena." A woman's voice comes from the steps. I look up to see Vittoria standing at the bottom landing of the spiral staircase that takes us to the second floor. "I of all people ought to know how hard it is to be swept right into the crazy Rossi family fold. Give her a little space, honey." She smiles softly at me. Romeo's bride. "Hi. I'm Vittoria, Romeo's wife."

Elise smiles shyly. "Hi."

"Ahh, here she is! The lovely bride!" Mama enters the room. "And my son! He's home!"

She walks to me on three-inch stilettos. She's colored her hair since I was gone and it looks like her cheeks are fuller, like she's gained a little of the weight she needed to. It seems life without the overbearing presence of Papa has suited her well. When she reaches me on tiptoes, even with her high-heeled shoes, I have to lean down to kiss her on each cheek.

"Happy to be home, Mama. Meet my wife, Elise."

She gives Elise the same warm greeting she gave me. Elise kisses her warmly. "Thank you so much."

"You two go up to your room and relax. Get freshened up if you need to, rest. We'll have dinner promptly at six tonight. You hungry?"

"No, Mama, we ate in town."

Mama winks at Marialena, then she turns to Elise. "My mother and I have been cooking up a storm. Later, Orlando can show you around The Castle." She smiles. "The girls like the tour."

Elise just nods her head, looking a bit stunned by everything. "Thank you."

I take our bags and swing them over my shoulder, when I realize my mother's eyes are focused on the collar of the white shirt I wear. The smile fades from her lips. "So soon, Orlando? You've been out less than a day, and so soon he has you doing your work?"

I look down to see drops of blood splattered on my collar. I won't lie to her. "He didn't get me out of prison early for a joyride, Mama." I lower my voice and give her shoulder a gentle squeeze. "We both know our family's in trouble. It's why I married that same night. You know that."

Her lips pinch together, and she stares at the blood on my collar. "Go change, son. Put on clean clothes, will you?" Her eyes quickly go to Elise. "The one blessing of being married to a woman raised like you." She sighs. "She won't be scarred by what she sees." Mama draws in a deep breath, then lets it out again. "Don't mind me. I'm growing softer in my old age." Her face melts into a soft, sad smile as she absentmindedly fingers the bare space on her finger where she once wore a wedding band.

Heavy footsteps approach, and Nonna fills the doorway. Shorter than all of us but pleasantly plump, Nonna's the very picture of an Italian grandmother. "Orlando! *Benvenuto a casa! E la tua sposa è bellissima. Un bambino, hmm?*"

"Nonna!" Marialena scolds. Vittoria bursts out laughing.

I smile at Elise moments before I'm accosted by Nonna. "You know what she says?" Nonna nearly bowls me over.

Elise's cheeks color. "My father doesn't like us to speak Italian. I did catch something about being home and... a baby?"

"Get her upstairs," Mama says, but her eyes are twinkling as she extricates Nonna from me. "Mama, leave them alone! My God, do you expect her to be pregnant on her wedding night? Give her a minute, will you?"

"Mama!" Now it's Marialena's turn to groan.

"Alright, alright, my pretty bride and I are going upstairs. We'll see you all at dinner and I'll give the tour then. Please reserve any more questions or comments until such time as I have a tall glass of wine in hand. And Nonna, tell me you made me my ravioli?"

Nonna's eyes twinkle.

I take Elise by the hand and bring her upstairs. It's hard to believe it's been only a day since I was released from prison and even less time since I took her as my wife. Vittoria always says that my family is on speed. It's the first time I really understand what she means.

CHAPTER 10

"Love's night is noon." ~*Twelfth Night, Shakespeare*

"Elise"

I DON'T KNOW what to make of the situation. I find myself almost liking Orlando, even after everything I've seen him do and say. I reason with myself that it's because he's so protective of me. He may hold me to high standards, but he's always by my side, always making sure my needs are met, and the sex... He's had me three times already, and I can tell he's nowhere near sated.

Neither am I.

But I know I don't belong here. I know that when he finds out who I am, it will be his duty to kill me. I know I have to escape before I'm in too deep.

Is it already too late?

His family's eccentric and intense, I know that already from the brief meeting I've had with his brothers, sister, mother, and grandmother. But it's a fierce kind of intensity I could grow to like.

I saw him do brutal things today. He fucked me in front of a prisoner, under the very real threat of removing the man's eyes if he looked at me. That should scare me. I think it does. But not as much as it should.

I should have my head examined.

I'm frantic to get to my phone. I'm nervous about what he'll find, and what he'll say when he does. But most of all, I'm nervous about getting out of here alive before anyone discovers my true identity.

Orlando's in the shower after stationing three guards outside our door. Even then, he's left the door to the bathroom open so he can keep an eye on me himself. "We have cameras on every floor, trained on every room and window. The walls themselves would report to me, Elise," he warned as he stripped out of his clothes.

I can't garner much control in any of this, but I could have a little fun anyway. I could try.

"Will the walls hear me when I scream when you make me come?"

Those vivid blue eyes of his narrowed on me, and he wagged a finger as he stripped off his white shirt. I saw what his mother did, the flecks of blood. He didn't make me watch when he ended his prisoner's life, but I knew exactly what he did on the other side of the wall at the restaurant.

Now I'm lying in bed, my mind racing, while my very hot husband takes a shower on the other side of that translucent glass.

For one brief, crazy moment I let myself wonder... what if I stay?

It's impossible. *Impossible.* He wants me to bear his children, like I'm an animal to be bred. And I know how brutal and unforgiving a mafia family like his really is. But the one thing Orlando can give me—undying protection—is the one thing I crave. The most glaring lack in my childhood above all else.

I took care of myself because I had to. Under his watch and protection, I could allow someone else to do it for once.

But it's a dream. Only a dream. And the price I'd pay is too hefty.

I look at the windows in this huge room. Like the other rooms in The Castle I've seen thus far, this one is large but not ostentatious, decorated with sturdy, hefty furniture that can bear the weight of a man like Orlando. I like the privacy of the town-house in Boston, but the charm of this house surpasses that.

And then I remember. Tuscany. He has a home in Tuscany as well. But no, I wouldn't be any safer there either, because his sister, the one who suppos-edly knows Elise, travels back and forth. And Elise's family might be there as well. I don't know why that thought even crosses my mind. I suppose it's born of a sort of desperation.

There's a knock at the door. Since Orlando's still in the shower, I push myself out of the bed and go to the door, still making sure I don't leave his vision when he looks through the shower glass.

I crack the door open a hair. "Yes?"

"So sorry to bother you, miss, but I have your phone."

I open the door so quickly, the soldier on the other side nearly jumps.

"Is Orlando here?" he asks.

"Oh, he's showering," I say with a smile. I snatch the phone right out of his hand. "Thank you for that."

"Ah...you might give that phone to your husband before you use it. He'll know you have it."

"And how would he know that?"

He frowns. "Because I'd tell him, obviously."

"Didn't ask for your input, douchebag," I say, as I slam the door in his face and spin around. *Ugh!* My heartbeat pounds as I look to the shower. He's still there. Still showering, even humming a little Italian tune to himself.

My hands shake so badly as I put the phone on, I almost drop it. I turn my back to him so he'll see me sitting right where he left me, but hopefully not see right away I'm using my phone. I quickly calculate how much phone use I could get if I ran out of this room and locked myself somewhere where he couldn't find me. Five minutes? And would it be worth the punishment that would surely earn me?

I check my texts. My heart sinks. I've got a few from some acquaintances and a few spam advertisements, but not a thing from Elise. Did she not send any to me? Or were they erased?

I dial her number. I'm not surprised when it goes to voice mail. I shoot her a text.

ME: *Hey bestie! I'm here at The Castle with my new husband. Need to chat when we can. How are you?*

NO RESPONSE, of course. Nothing. I'm shaking with nerves when the shower turns off. What will happen to her if he finds out? What will happen to me?

Is she okay? I don't even know if she and Piero made it alive and safe. I want to cry.

I slide the phone in the bedside table and lay back on the bed.

An hour later, we're dressed for dinner and heading downstairs. He has no idea about the phone. I haven't said anything, and he didn't ask, so I feel no need to offer that information. He'll find out soon enough, and it will be on him to prove I did anything wrong.

I go through the motions at dinner, my mind racing with everything I fear, but everyone is nothing but charming. The other brothers have arrived, everyone dressed formally. Marialena's lent me a dress and shoes, until I can furnish myself a wardrobe.

The food is delicious, and I find it a bit amusing how Orlando and his brothers pack it away.

"Here," Mario says, handing the tray with the last chicken cutlet on it to Orlando. "I'll even let you have the last one tonight."

"Pfft, last one," his mother says, rising. "As if I only made one tray."

"Hope you were paying attention," Marialena says, sipping a glass of wine. "That is the one and only time my brothers actually didn't fight over food."

The only one that doesn't talk throughout the whole meal is the brother just older than Orlando, named Tavi. When I thank them for a delicious dinner, he eyes me seriously, sipping his wine with a look that makes me squirm. Does he know something about me? Does he suspect something?

But when I go to leave with Orlando, he rises with the rest of them out of respect, then presses a shiny white package into Orlando's hand. It's then that I remember. Tavi was the one who was supposed to be married before Orlando. His betrothed took her own life. I bet seeing me with Orlando is bitter-sweet for him.

Soon, Orlando and I are heading upstairs. All I can think about is that phone in the drawer and my friend, when Romeo pulls Orlando to the side.

"Just a minute, Orlando. I'll let you go, have to fill you in."

Every conversation they have feels like it could be the one that reveals all. I jump when I hear a low chuckle right behind me.

I spin around to see Nonna standing in the doorway, a dishtowel slung over her shoulder. She's looking at me as if she caught me sneaking out past curfew to a forbidden party. I give her a tight smile.

"Italiano," she says with another chuckle. She's really amused. My heartbeat quickens, and I swallow hard. I feel a little dizzy.

"Italiano?" I repeat.

"Si, si." Her lips curve upward. "*You?*" Then she bursts out laughing and shakes her head, muttering under her breath as she walks away.

Oh God. *Oh God.* How does she know I'm not Italian? She might be the only one under this roof that knows I'm not Elise. She also might be the only one under this roof that just doesn't care.

I briefly consider confiding in Vittoria or Marialena. They aren't like the men. There's an almost unspoken solidarity with them as women of The

Family. But I'm too new here. I don't know who to trust.

I have to get to the phone.

"Orlando, I'm going upstairs," I say, risking interrupting his conversation with Romeo. Romeo blinks at me in surprise before he scowls at me, and Orlando shakes his head.

There's a thread of authority in his voice when he responds, obviously displeased at the interruption. "You'll wait for me."

"I don't feel well," I lie. I hate lying to him. It's the one thing he hasn't done to me. "I'm going upstairs."

I know immediately it's the wrong thing to say. Romeo's brows rise in surprise, as if he's shocked I dare talk back to my new husband. And Orlando's bright blue eyes darken. "You heard me, Elise."

I consider going anyway, but instead I wait, dread growing with every minute that passes. I wonder what he'll do when he has me alone, but for long minutes he's silent.

I'm preoccupied, though. I can't fully pay attention to anything, and Orlando knows. When his mother, who I've since learned is named Tosca, brings out trays of chocolate mousse in elegant cups, he walks over to me and whispers in my ear, "Are you overwhelmed? You're very quiet. You're also in hot fucking water."

Overwhelmed is an understatement.

I nod.

"We'll take ours upstairs," Orlando says. He reaches for my hand, and Mario catcalls.

"Course you will," Mario says with a smirk.

"Someone's gonna get his ass kicked," Orlando says with a smile in a singsong voice.

"Boys," Tosca warns.

Mario's undeterred. He shoots Orlando a lascivious wink. "Go, go. Bambinos, bambinos!"

Nonna smacks him across the back of his head and takes him by surprise. "Hey! Nonna!"

She curses him out in Italian, much to Orlando's amusement. Orlando still gives him a warning look. "One more word, Mario. One more word, it's your last warning."

Mario finally holds his hands up in concession. "Alright, alright. Jesus, settle down. You said you want—"

Orlando's hand swings out so fast, I gasp. He's got Mario by the throat, pinned up against the wall. Mario's eyes bulge but he's still grinning, his palms up in the air in surrender.

Romeo rolls his eyes and gestures for staff to refill his wineglass. The man called Santo checks his phone. Tosca rolls her eyes, and Marialena says something to Vittoria that makes her laugh.

"Sorry," Mario sputters, his face reddening. "Jesus, man."

Orlando drops him to the floor. Mario hasn't stopped grinning.

When we get upstairs, we undress in silence. I'm fixated on the drawer that holds my phone, but also nervous about the air of expectancy between us.

Orlando sits wearily by the bed. He's wearing nothing but boxers, and I'm dressed in a small camisole and panties. I yawn, exaggerating it.

Orlando faces me, all dark and brooding and serious.

"Come here, Elise." He pats his knee.

I walk over to him, wondering what he has in mind. I don't know how to get him out of the room so I can get to the phone. Did anyone tell him that they'd returned it?

When I reach him, he tugs me onto his knee. I sit heavily. He's so big, so strong, he barely shifts when I sit. "Downstairs just now, you asked me if you could come up here. And what did I tell you?"

I bite my lip. "You asked me to wait for you."

"Yes. And did you obey me and show respect in front of my brother? My Don?"

Shit. I swallow hard and shake my head. "No."

He grips my chin and tugs my gaze to his, deadly sober. My heart races faster. Is that a buzzing in the bedside table? Did I forget to silence my phone?

"What did you do, Elise?"

"I—I talked back to you. But I really wanted to come up here."

He holds up a finger to stop me. "Do you think I'll allow you to talk back to me? In front of my brothers?"

I shake my head, and I begin to tremble. A part of me actually hopes he'll punish me. I feel such pent-up guilt from the lies and betrayal, maybe it would alleviate my guilt.

"No. No, and I'm sorry."

Soberly, he nods, then gently pushes me to standing. "Go to the bedside table."

My heartbeat races. I feel dizzy.

"The table?" Blood pounds in my ears so hard I can barely hear him.

"Yes. The bedside table. When you get there, I'll tell you what to get me."

Does he know about the phone?

I walk, shaking. I don't even know how I get there. It's sheer muscle memory, one foot in front of the other, as I walk to the table. With a shaking hand, I open the drawer. How did I not notice that I put my phone beside a small black box?

With my back to him, I bend over. Do I risk looking at the phone?

"Do you see the black box, *piccolino*?"

Shaking, I nod. "I do."

"Bring it here."

I reach for the box with my left hand while I tap the phone on with my right. It's buried so deep in the drawer, he can't see.

"Now, Elise. What's taking you so long?"

No messages. No calls.

I shove it down further into the drawer and take out the black box. I turn to face him. He crooks one finger at me while I fight tears.

Elise, where are you?

Are you okay?

It doesn't matter if I had that phone in my hand right this minute. If she hasn't returned my messages or calls, something's wrong. I know it.

Logically, I know she might be in a place where she has no cell reception, but I can't really believe that. In my heart, I'm afraid something's terribly wrong.

I walk over to him and hand him the black box. I'm so overcome with emotion, I don't care what he's got in there or what he has planned for me. I need something to help me get over my panic and fear... something to ground me.

With a slight frown, he lays the box across his knees and lifts the lid. I'm mesmerized by the skull tats on his knuckles, the thick, masculine fingers capable of so much. He killed a man with those hands today, without remorse. After fucking me in front of him.

I shiver as the lid drops open. I'm not surprised to see he has an arsenal of tools, mostly things I don't recognize or couldn't name.

"What are those?" I ask.

He lifts something small and metal, fingers it, then shakes his head and nestles it back in the box. Something jeweled and wicked, something wrapped in black leather. "Your wedding gift."

I lace my fingers together in front of me to keep them from shaking when he removes something black, soft, and silky, lays it on the table, then closes the box and puts it beside the black silk. "I'll take it easy on you tonight, though."

"Yeah?" My voice shakes.

He holds up his hand. That huge, massive hand that's twice the size of my own. "This is all I need."

Oh, yeah, I bet that's all he needs. I bite my lip.

"Come here."

I stand between his legs. Without a word he lifts me so I straddle his lap, my legs on either side of him and my pussy pressed up to his crotch. His thick, heavy cock strains for release beneath me. I swallow hard.

I did that to him. I'm the one that made him hard.

He wants me.

And he might be angry and wicked and have a crazy intense concept of love and marriage that defies all modern logic... but I like that he wants me. I like it a lot.

There's a certain power a woman holds when a man desires her, a certain thrilling knowledge that she's the object of his attention. And I've got that in spades right now. He's utterly focused on *me*.

I love the way his warm, hot hands wrap around my lower back as if to anchor me in place while he draws me closer to him, so he can kiss my cheek, my chin, my forehead. My mouth is slightly parted, waiting for his kiss.

"You're mine," he whispers in my ear.

I feel a smile spread across my face. "Thought we covered that."

That earns me a pinch to my ass. "We have. What we haven't covered is what I expect from you as mine." His mouth is at my ear, hot and insistent, before he laps the shell and nips the lobe. "You took your vow to me."

I nod. "Yep."

His grip on my waist tightens. "You vowed to obey me."

"Right, about that..." I gasp when he tugs my hair.

"Don't you ever talk back to me in front of my brothers again. Do you understand me?"

I nod. "But why...why is it so important to you?" I don't understand his archaic adherence to these tenets.

He massages my ass with hard, firm strokes. Priming me? I shift on his lap, and he groans.

"Every single fucking day you're with me, you're in danger. Do you understand that?"

I nod. I do. I really do. I don't miss the guards stationed at every door and entrance, the harnesses they wear laden with heavy weapons, and I saw what happened today. But he's the man who walks with near impunity, who does what he thinks no matter what anyone else says to him. He's the most dangerous of all.

"Yeah," I breathe. I want his mouth on me again. My body remembers the feel of him on me, *in* me. I'm already starting to crave his possessive grip, the firm feel of ownership. In the dark corners of my mind, a warning bell clangs.

I shut the door on it and revel in this.

"When I give you a command, I want you obeying on fucking instinct. I want you to do exactly what I say, because a split second could mean the difference between life and death." His voice grows deeper, heated. "And if you can't obey me in the smallest things, how can I expect you to obey me when it really matters?"

I don't respond. My mouth is dry, and something tells me this is a rhetorical question anyway.

"In the presence of my men, you are the first and primary example of submission and duty. If I don't have the respect of my wife, why would they respect me?"

I nod. Alright, that makes sense. Again, a rhetorical question.

"That's the only explanation you'll get." He grips my hair and pulls it, painfully. My mouth falls open on a gasp when his eyes narrow on me, his voice a low growl of warning. "Don't you ever fucking do that again."

"Yep," I say, and my ass clenches because I know I'm toast. I'm married to an overbearing beast of a man and can only hope after he does whatever he's going to do, he might make it better.

But the truth is, I don't care what he does. I don't care what happens next. I want to know where my friend is, if she's okay. I need the assurance. Everything else fades in the face of what matters most. I'll grin and bear it or grimace and bear it as the case may be.

I have to get in touch with Elise.

Holding me to his chest with one hand, he lifts the silk tie with his free hand.

"Open up, buttercup," he says without a trace of humor. I blink, then part my lips. What is he doing?

With a fierce look of concentration, he winds the tie around my mouth, the fabric silky on my lips and tongue. When he leans in to tie it at the back of my head, I'm momentarily consumed with the masculine scent of raw spice and a hint of vanilla, and something else I can't put my finger on. It smells of luxury, whiskey, and cigars, the scent one might find in the recesses of a man's study. My pulse races.

His mouth at my ear, he commands, "Close your eyes."

I do what he says, closing my eyes, and in the next second I'm plunged into darkness with the same silky fabric.

"Hands, *piccola*."

I'd ask him what that meant, but I can't talk. Obediently, I offer him my wrists.

The phone buzzes insistently in the bedside table.

I go completely still. I don't breathe or move. Even my heartbeats seem to still.

"You hear that?"

I shake my head.

"That buzzing sound."

I shrug and gesture to the box, as if to remind him he has a bunch of things in that box that could be going haywire. I feel like a total jerk. I don't like lying. I've never been one to lie before, and now it feels as if my very being is a lie.

With his hands under my arms, he hoists me up, spins me around, then yanks me over his knee. I can't see what I'm doing but feel myself upended bodily. I try to flail my arms in front of me, but I can't with my wrists secured.

I wait for the first stinging slap of his palm, but none comes. Instead, I feel his hand between my legs, and they part on instinct, craving more of his touch, craving more pressure.

"Such a responsive girl you are," he whispers in my ear.

The buzzing's stopped. I close my eyes and feel as if I've dodged a bullet.

"I could spank you for what you did."

I nod, dizzy from the fear of him finding the phone, and nervous about what may happen to Elise. Where is she? Is she okay?

But he distracts me the next minute with his hand between my legs again, stroking me over my clothes.

"I should tame that mouth of yours," he says in a low whisper in my ear, with another stroke between my legs. Slowly he removes my clothes and palms my ass. Again, I wait for the stinging slap of his palm, but there's no spanking. It seems he means to punish me in another way.

"On your knees," he says, and I blink in surprise behind the blindfold before he parts his legs and guides me to the floor. I swallow when I feel his swollen cock still trapped in his pants. My mouth waters. He's so fucking hot I want to see what I could do if I had a chance to please him. I crave an ounce of the control he gives me when he wants me.

I want him to want me.

The gag and blindfold fall to the floor with two flicks of his fingers, and he unzips his pants. I lick my lips when his cock springs free, thick and hard. I lean forward and stroke my tongue along the length.

He groans. I grin and take him fully between my lips, holding his gaze. I love the way his eyes go half-lidded. I love his groans of pleasure and how he jerks his hips. I love the salty, masculine taste of him, his powerful hips on either side, and the way we're irrevocably entwined in the heat of this moment. I've had more passion and pleasure with him in the space of a few days than I've had in my entire lifetime.

The more I please him, the louder he groans, and the wetter I get. And for the first time since he dragged me here, the first time since he put a ring on my finger and made me his... I don't want to leave.

CHAPTER 11

"For women are as roses, whose fair flower, Being once display'd, doth fall that very hour." ~*Twelfth Night, Shakespeare*

Orlando

SHE SLEEPS beside me like a little angel with her hands tucked under her chin. Her soft little whiffling sighs make my heart swell. I've never felt this way about a woman.

I ease myself out of bed and tuck the blanket up around her shoulders. She sighs and rolls over onto her stomach.

I revel in the way she submitted to me, the wonder in her eyes when I brought out the vulnerable part of her. I'm honored that she's revealed parts of herself to me I'd be willing to bet she's never shown anyone before.

Raised in a mafia family, she's known since infancy that she'd never wed for love, that she was nothing more than a pawn her father would use for his ultimate endgame. In the end, he saved his own ass with his daughter. It's not uncommon.

Doesn't make it easy or right, but none of this is. And a part of me wonders if maybe I shouldn't even hope for a glimpse of something good in this.

But Romeo... Romeo found love. And there's hope for the rest of us.

I pour myself a shot of whiskey and stare out the window into the gloomy darkness. Moonlight glints on the water behind The Castle. It ripples with a gust of wind, like folds of silk, smooth and calming. I squint ahead of me and tilt my head to the side. Is that a ship coming into harbor? So late? But we have men that man the border and harbors, contacts with law enforcement, and a dirty cop that'd give his left nut for a seat at our table. This isn't my job. It isn't my watch.

So I turn my back to the ocean and stare at my bride.

I wonder when she'll have my child. I wonder if I've impregnated her yet. A part of me hopes we'll have to try a little longer.

I only just got out of the big house. I only just met Elise and have barely begun to scratch the surface on what it will take to get to know her. We're so new.

A buzz sounds near her side of the bed, and I wonder what it is. She looked that way earlier today when I went to restrain her, but I didn't want to investigate. Now, however, I'm curious.

I walk to the side of the bed, softly so I don't wake her, and go to open the drawer. But when I reach for the handle to gently ease it open, she stirs on the bed.

"It's so cold in here without you," she whispers without opening her eyes. "I need my hot water bottle back in bed."

I bend down and brush a stray piece of hair behind her ear. "You want to cuddle?"

She snorts. "You say it like it's a bad word. I'm not a cuddler. I just need your big, manly body to warm me up."

I've been hard on her, and she's taken it. The least I can do is lay beside her so she falls back asleep. I walk back to my side of the bed and slide in beside her. The sheets are warm and silky, and I adore the feel of her small body molded to mine, warm and comforting. She wriggles her butt, and I give it a teasing slap. She moans. Jesus, she's perfect.

"Don't," I groan. "You'll make me hard, and I need to fuckin' sleep."

She settles down but I swear I can hear a smile in her voice. "That attracted to me, are you?"

"Fuck yes I'm attracted to you. Tomorrow, you'll thank me for the wardrobe I'm about to buy you with a blow job. Got it?"

"Are you seducing me?"

"Now why the hell would I need to seduce a woman I am already married to?"

"It's blackmail, then, isn't it? It is."

"Nah, baby. It's what I want."

She nestles her back against my front. I wrap my arm around her, and she sighs in contentment. "Good night, husband."

A few seconds later, she's gently snoring again. I close my eyes, and sleep pulls me under.

CHAPTER 12

"Pleasure will be paid one time or another."
~*Twelfth Night, Shakespeare*

"*Elise*"

I pretend I'm asleep. I inhale and exhale, mimicking his breathing until I'm confident he's asleep beside me.

I don't dare get out of bed and get my phone. He'd wake, see me, and the thought of doing anything even remotely disobedient, or something that might earn me punishment, terrifies me. I can't do that. I won't.

Tomorrow, when he's working, I'll find a way to get to my phone. I have to.

The ruse is up or close to it. I suspect that Tavi knows I'm not who I say I am, and Nonna sure as fuck does. The question is, how much longer can I keep this up? And am I better off staying longer and hoping he falls for me, that I survive whatever his family inflicts on me...or is it better that I find a means of escape now?

My mind's a jumble of thoughts and fears as I finally drift off to sleep.

I wake to his mouth between my legs. I squeeze my thighs together, reveling in the feel of his coarse hair on my inner thighs.

"Orlando," I breathe, still half asleep as he licks and sucks my clit and teases my entrance with his fingers.

"Awake, baby?"

"Ohhh, yeah," I whisper. "I so am."

I squirm and whimper when he pulls his mouth away. "On my face," he groans. "Sit on my fucking face before I blow my load. I want your mouth on me, *now*."

He doesn't make it hard to do, as he quickly falls back on the bed, arranges his head on a pillow, then places my pussy right at his mouth. Straddling him, I eye the way his hardened cock bobs in front of me. A glinting drop of precum glistens at the tip. I swallow, stick my tongue out, and lick it off. His pleasure-filled groan consumes me just has he grips my hips and tongues my pussy.

"Oh God." My hips jerk on their own as he licks and sucks. I take his whole cock in my mouth and suckle hard.

"Fuuuuuuck," he groans, giving me a hard, punishing slap to the ass. "Fuck, baby, that feels so fucking good."

I'm squirming on his face as his tongue works its magic, eager to blow him well, because I *love* what he's doing to me right this very minute. I whimper and groan, and we continue to pleasure each other with our mouths until he slaps my ass to tell me to stop. It's too late, I'm already sailing toward perfection when my hips jerk over his face. He grips my hips, forcing me to stay still as his tongue glides through my center, and a spasm of perfect bliss washes over me. He licks me to climax, rolls me over, then glides his swollen cock in my sopping wet folds. I'm sore, but already adapting to the frequency of lovemaking with him. My pussy milks him, as he comes with a guttural groan I feel deep in my belly.

We lay in a sex-hazed bliss for long moments before we clean up. I lay on his large, muscled chest.

"Damn," I breathe, and for that one moment in time, I give in to the fantasy. I may not be Elise, but he really does want me. Maybe I'm more than a commodity. Maybe I'm not just a notch in his belt, a woman he was forced to marry. Maybe I could mean something and maybe, just maybe...this will work out.

But how could it? I'm not the woman I'm supposed to be, and I can't keep this farce up forever.

"I need to take a shower," he says. My pulse spikes. I need him occupied so I can see if Elise tried to get in touch with me.

I nod and yawn. "Go ahead. If you don't mind, I'm going to rest a bit more. Your sister said she'd take me shopping today, and I'm exhausted after everything that's happened."

The little grin he gives me is almost boyish, almost teasing. I haven't seen many glimpses of his playful side, but for one second, I feel I can actually see the boy beneath the tough exterior. He isn't just a man who served time, or a guy who killed a man yesterday. There are layers to my barbarian of a husband.

I pretend to be asleep, my eyes closed, as he goes to the shower. Like yesterday, he leaves the door open, but it's all I need. I yawn, stretch, and lean over so I can open the drawer next to the bed.

The phone isn't there. My heart races as I feverishly push everything aside, including the black box with the instruments of torture he used last night. I didn't hear him take anything. I didn't miss anything, did I?

My fingers brush something cold and solid. The phone. It fell deeper into the drawer and is still there. With a choked sob, I take it out. I didn't realize how attached I am to this phone, to getting in touch with Elise, until that moment. I look frantically at the shower. He's still in there, lathering up.

I flick it on.

Bestie: OMG are you okay? Are you? I haven't had reception in so long, I couldn't call you.

Me: It's me! I'm okay! BUT OMG I'M MARRIED

No response. I want to cry. I've had four missed calls and two texts.

I swipe the phone back on.

We have to talk. Things didn't work as planned. But are you okay? Tell me you're okay.

No response. I fall face-first onto the bed and stifle the sobs that want to pull me under. I feel so desperate to talk to her, I've begun to panic, half-frantic to know she's okay. But these messages are recent. She's okay.

I dial her number. It rings and rings. On the sixth ring, there's a click and a pause. My heartbeat soars.

"Hello?"

"Oh my God," I whisper into the phone. "Are you okay?" In a panic, I hiss, "Do not use my name in this call."

"Well…" her voice trails off. "We're okay so far. We made it over the border, and Piero has some family friends that are putting us up. But his friends have been trying to get in touch with him, and my father flies into Tuscany tonight. He knows I'm not there, that I'm supposedly where you are, but Piero thinks…this could get ugly."

It could. She isn't exaggerating.

It's going to, I know it.

"What do you mean you're married?" she hisses, just as the shower turns off. *Shit*. "Does he have any idea at all who you are?"

I cringe. "I have to go," I hiss. "Let me go. I'll text you."

Bestie: You didn't escape. My god, what do we do? What can we do?

Me: The most important thing is that YOU'RE safe.

Bestie: No, YOU!

I don't respond at first, because I have no idea what else to say and I have no time.

I shut off the phone and slide it in the drawer, just as he enters the room. I close my eyes, having a hard time breathing. That was too close. *Too close.*

"Sleep well, *piccola?*"

I nod. "What's that mean?"

I gulp as he removes his towel, his perfect ass and thick cock on full display. I stand to head to the shower myself, as he twists the towel into a rope and snaps it at my ass.

"Hey!"

"It means little one."

Little one. I think I melt a little. "I like that. It reminds me of *The Little Prince*."

He gives me a quizzical look. "Okay, tell me you know what that is."

"Of course. I might be a violent asshole, but I'm not uneducated," he says, affronted. "In fact, my French teacher made me read it *en français*. Should punish you for that, you little brat."

"Your moods swing like a saloon door, you know that?"

He snaps the folded towel at my ass again.

"Ow!" It hurts like the crack of a whip.

"I'll give you mood swings."

"Apparently you will!"

I narrowly dodge another whipping slash of his towel.

"So what is it about *The Little Prince*?"

"Oh, just the whole *piccollino* thing. It's cute." I reach for the sheets, navy blue with small stars on them. "I used to read that book when my father was —" I stop myself mid-sentence, clear my throat, then continue. "Occupied."

Damn it. That was too close for comfort. Way too close for comfort. I almost told him about my real father, *Angelina's* father, the drug dealer who neglected me and left me to my own devices, not the mafia lord that ruled the real Elise's family with an iron fist. "All stars are a riot of flowers," I say softly.

"That from *The Little Prince*?"

"It is."

"I like that. You hungry?"

"Starving."

"Go, take your shower, then we'll head downstairs."

I take a quick shower, the entire time turning over every possibility. I'll get Marialena to take me shopping and sneak out when the guards aren't looking.

Yeah, no. Orlando will likely insist on coming with us.

I could...go for a walk by the garden and sneak away? Or...cause a distraction and run?

I can't call the police, that much I know. I can't call Elise, she's overseas and I can't have her worry.

Or maybe I could...maybe I could make him fall in love with me. If he fell in love with me, he wouldn't hurt me.

Would he?

He's distracted on the phone when I finish getting ready. I reach for the drawer as he turns to me.

"Something in there you want, Elise? Did you see something that interests you?"

I swallow hard. "Uh, yeah. I saw lots of things that interest me, but they kind of scare me, too."

He takes my hand and with his other, squeezes my ass. "I know. But we have a baby to make. We'll have lots of chances to try everything you want, and maybe a few things you don't know you want yet."

"And if I don't like something?"

"I'll be the judge of that."

Right. This is hardly a consensual little foray into BDSM.

Why does that appeal to me? To lose total control to a man like Orlando? He's got a mean, steely edge to him that scares the shit out of me. But underneath that hard, toughened exterior...my fingers trace the skulls on his knuckles as we go downstairs.

"What do they mean?"

"What?"

"Those tats."

"Initiations," he says without hesitating.

"What...kinds of initiations?" I wonder at Mario's earlier admonition not to ask questions, and I wonder how close I'm skirting to the edge of what's allowed, what I should know if I am who they think I am.

"Things I did to earn my rank. I don't want to talk about it, *piccola*." His features darken, and he frowns as we walk down the spiral staircase to the dining room. "Not now."

I drop the subject.

If I were to make him fall in love with me, what would that look like?

The dining room's positively bustling with activity. Servants bring in trays of baked goods that make my mouth water, and Tavi's pouring tea from a carafe into delicate espresso cups.

"May I have one?" I ask timidly, because for some reason I feel as if he's suspicious of me.

"If your husband allows it," he says. I laugh, but he doesn't even smile.

"And…why would my husband not allow it?"

His lips thin ever so slightly, as if barely annoyed at my pestering questions. "In case you're pregnant."

My jaw drops. "We were married two nights ago."

He shrugs, and his scowl deepens. "Yeah, it only takes one."

Ew. Crass. I give him a hard stare and think about what to say, then remember I ended up over Orlando's knee for disrespecting him in front of his Don.

Probably not a good idea to challenge Tavi right now either. Still. Jerk.

Marialena waves me over. "Come, sit with the girls and let the men plot world domination," she says pleasantly, but with such ease, I wonder if she's only half-joking. She's sitting beside Vittoria, and a little girl about six or seven years old sits beside her.

"You're pretty," she says, as she butters a scone.

"Ah, thank you. My name is—" Oh my God. I almost said my real name. I laugh to cover my fumble.

"Elise. And what's yours?" Marialena turns her head to the side and talks to Vittoria. I think she may not have heard my blunder.

That was too close. *Too close.*

"Natalia. My Mama is Rosa. I think I've seen you before?"

My heart races, and I grip my coffee cup harder.

"Oh. Yes, yes of course! How could I forget? You were so much littler."

She smacks her lips. "Yup. I've sprouted up, Nonna says."

"Is your mother here?"

"Soon," Natalia says. "She's in Italy but I'm here with my nanny. I didn't want to be in Tuscany." She rolls her eyes. "It's so *boring*. Plus, I like being here. I like the food and I don't have to go to school."

Marialena tweaks her nose. "She has a tutor, don't you, baby? You coming with us shopping today?" She shakes her head and pushes her chair out when she sees Orlando. "Uncle Orlando!" she screams from her seat. She jumps up so fast she knocks over her chair and almost takes out Nonna, who's standing behind her with a large, beautiful platter of fruit salad which drops to the floor.

Nonna mutters in Italian and waves her off. I bend to help her, and when we're both cleaning up the mess, she leans close to me to whisper, "Bring these your husband." She holds a small paper bag folded over at the top. "His favorite. He like. Men ruled by the belly."

She stands, and I grip the bag in surprise, but she only leaves the room, tidying as she goes.

Natalia does a running leap at Orlando, who swings her up into his arms and gives her a big kiss on the cheek. I forget they haven't seen him in a while. "Ah, Natalia. You look so grown up. I see you've met my lovely wife, your new aunt?"

Ugh, it feels so wrong deceiving a child.

She nods. "You did good, Uncle. She's so pretty."

His eyes twinkle at me from across the room.

"Thank you. But you be careful jumping up from the chair, Natalia. You almost knocked Nonna over. You must not do that again."

She nods her head eagerly.

I can't help but notice how natural he looks with her in his arms, how the way he corrects her is firm but gentle. She's obviously close to him and happy to have him home. My heart gives a little squeeze.

"He was always the gentlest, you know," Marialena says thoughtfully, as she plunks a sugar cube into her espresso and gives it a little stir.

"Orlando?"

She nods. "Yeah. He hated violence and gory things. Would hide his face during violent movies. And believe it or not he was always the one that kept me out of trouble."

I nod, imagining a younger Orlando. "He's so serious now. So stern, isn't he?"

She looks at him thoughtfully as she sips her coffee. "He is. But he's been through a lot." With a sigh, she looks over my shoulder. "We all have. It's changed us, really."

"I understand." But do I, really? I decide to go for broke. "Marialena, can I ask you a question?"

Vittoria looks at both of us curiously.

"Actually, both of you."

They both focus on me. "Go on," Vittoria says. "Now's a good time."

"Maybe you'd know best," I say to her. "If you were...arranged to be married to a man you'd never met." I sigh. "How would you...get him to...like you?"

Marialena folds her hands on the table, leans across it, and speaks frankly. "You mean, how do you get him to fall in love when he hardly knows you?"

Vittoria laughs. "Ah. The million-dollar question, isn't it?"

"Maybe literally for you," Marialena snorts.

"Hey!" Vittoria playfully swats at her.

"Okay, you two need to fill me in on that one."

"You'll find out soon enough," Vittoria says with a smile. "So how do you get him to love you? Well, that's simple. First, have you noticed how much these men love food?"

I look over to see Orlando's loaded a platter of pastries, eggs, and sausage on his plate, and as I watch he slaps at Mario's hand when Mario goes to take the last piece of bacon. Mario gives him a good-natured grin, gestures for Orlando to take the bacon, then ducks and swipes a sausage from Orlando's plate before he runs at full speed for the door. Doesn't stop Orlando, though. Orlando pushes up from the table, and in two large strides gets Mario by the back of the shirt, shakes him down to get his sausage, then slams him up against the wall to dismiss him.

Tosca mutters in Italian and throws up her hands. I watch them both in wide-eyed wonder.

"Ah, yes. I see what you mean. But I don't really cook." For once, I wish I *was* Elise. The girl can cook.

Vittoria shrugs. "No matter. You don't have to. Just *feed* the man."

Why would that matter? He already has people that do.

Marialena nods. "Yes, I agree. And, you know. Just be yourself. Don't try to be someone you're not."

The words hit harder than I expect.

Don't try to be someone you're not.

I know she means them metaphorically, but the truth of my situation sinks deep in my belly. I've suddenly lost my appetite.

Other than pretending to literally be someone I'm not…I've been myself.

Still, I can go with this. It may be my one opportunity. "And what if he…what if he doesn't like who I really am?" The lump in my throat's the size of my fist.

"Oh, honey," Marialena says with a charming grin. "What's not to like about you? He will love you." Her eyes soften, as she looks over her shoulder. "We all dream of marrying for love, Elise. All of us." With a sigh, she looks into the distance. "But very few of us manage it. Romeo and Vittoria have, though, haven't they? Wasn't right away, though."

It will take time, the one thing I don't have.

Nonna walks by me and winks. Marialena sips her coffee and puts it down on the table. "That was a conspiratorial wink if ever I saw one." She shakes her head. "Wonder what she knows."

Tosca comes to our table and sits. "So tell me about your family," she says. "Rosa really enjoyed the time she's spent with you."

I slip my hands under the table to hide their trembling, and smile. I stifle an inward groan.

"Ah, my family's a little crazy. I'm not close with any of them. My mother doesn't live with us, my father is pretty much only focused on the business, and I've spent most of my time with tutors and part of my time in Tuscany. I was sheltered, though. My father didn't tell me much about what he did..." This is all true so far, if I am indeed Elise.

"Ah, I know all about the sheltered life," Marialena says with an eye roll. "Though I will admit it's gotten better since Papa is gone." Tosca only nods. We talk for a while, and I look around for Orlando. He's still with his brothers, likely catching up. With a close-knit family like this, I imagine it's been hard for him to be apart from everyone for so long.

I don't know why I care. I shouldn't. I don't know why it matters at all. He leaves me with his sisters to talk with his brothers, but they're only the next room over. I sit back, tired but comfortable, while my mind races about all that has to happen. All that I have to do.

I can't get comfortable here. I can't let any of this make me grow complacent. I have to figure out where I'm going and what I'm doing. I look around me for an exit and wonder what I'd even do at this point if I were able to get away.

I wonder again...what would he do if he knew who I truly am?

I can't keep this up forever. I'm surprised I've been able to keep it up as long as I have.

I'm leaning back against a leather chair, my eyes closed, when I *feel* him come up to me. I can smell his signature scent and feel his heat. I smile to myself when his hands come to my shoulders.

"You look tired, *piccola*."

"Oh, God, you don't let him call you that, do you? Ew," Marialena groans. "That means little one. Don't let him belittle you!"

It doesn't feel belittling...

"You keep your nose in your relationship, and I'll keep mine in mine," Orlando says with a reproving look that's a little amused.

"Yeah, like you keep your nose out of any relationship." She snorts and rolls her eyes. "Are you for real?"

I can't imagine talking to him like that, but she just spouts off apparently whatever's on her mind. I don't ask her any questions.

"Have dinner with me tomorrow, Elise. I have business to do tonight, or I'd take you tonight."

"Here at The Castle?"

He shakes his head. "No. We'll go into town and have dinner at a regular restaurant." He brings his mouth to my ear. "Before I bring you back here for the rest of our honeymoon."

"I think you like having the duty of making a baby," I tell him, as my cheeks heat at the very thought.

I can't get pregnant. I can't have any more ties here than necessary.

But God, the way I crave him, the way I feel when he's near me. I even crave the way he looks at me, like he wants to consume me mind, body, and soul. I like the way we fit together, the push and pull we have. He's smart and witty.

But he's mafia.

I bat the inner protest away. My best friend was raised in the mafia and my dad is a drug dealer. Maybe I know how to handle people like them.

He'll never let you go.

Is that a bad thing?

Or maybe I'm sex-crazed and horny and a little lonely.

"Let her come out with us," Marialena says to Orlando. "I want to get her new things, buy her a 'congratulations for being married to my literally insane family' gift. Maybe get her Tarot cards read."

Orlando scowls. "No."

"No to what?" I ask. I'd love to pick their brains about anything and everything it means to be a woman in this family.

"Everything. No leaving my side, no congrats and welcome to my insane family gifts, and definitely no Tarot."

Marialena pouts with her arms crossed on her chest. Her dark brown hair falls into her eyes and her lower lip sticks out. "Aw. Lando, c'mon."

His eyes gentle at her. "Don't," he warns. "You know I can't say no to you when you call me that." I watch his fingers drum on the table beside him. "Listen, I want Elise with me today. You'll have plenty of time to kidnap her and take her for yourself later, got it?"

She sighs dramatically, but he doesn't seem to care.

"No, Lena. Not today."

With a labored sigh, she pushes up from the table, walks to him, and gives him a hug from behind. "Missed your overbearing, bossy ways," she says on a sigh. "Wasn't the same here without you. Take care of her, Lando. She's special."

Special? What makes her think that? I open my mouth to protest when he responds.

"I know."

Okay, so that's not fair. I'm supposed to be finding a way to escape, not allowing him to endear himself to me. *Great.*

CHAPTER 13

"Love thoughts lie rich when canopied with bowers." ~ *Twelfth Night, Shakespeare*

ORLANDO

I THROW MYSELF INTO WORK, getting accustomed to everything that waited for me when I was away. But I hate the minutes and hours that pass when I'm away from Elise.

She is the one I never knew I needed, and now that she's mine, I can't be without her. I crave her like an addict craves his next hit, every thought consumed with thoughts of her when we're not together.

"You fucking lovebird," Santo says a few days after we've returned to The Castle. Elise has occupied herself with my sisters and mother, quickly adapting to life at The Castle. She's a natural with Natalia, too.

When I'm here, I like her near me, close enough to reach. When I'm not, she's got guards that flank her every side.

Santo caught me smiling like a lovesick fool just thinking about her earlier.

"Fuck off, Santo."

He rubs his hand along the stubble on his chin.

"You're falling for her."

I tap the stack of papers I was reviewing and slide them into a manila folder. Property rights to another restaurant space we're buying in Boston, and I'm the one that oversees real estate.

"Of course I'm fucking falling for her. We're married." He shakes his head and takes a smoke out. "You light that up in here, I'll shove it up your ass," I warn him.

He chews the end of the smoke and leans back in his chair.

Santo is the only made man in the inner circle not related by blood, the only one my mother ever let my father fully corrupt. He taught us many things, but Santo he took under his wing. Santo got the full effect of my father's true depravity.

It shows.

"She may be your wife, but you can't go fucking soft on her," he says with a grimace. "Jesus, man, I thought the big house toughened you up. Seems it didn't have the effect on you I thought it would."

I lean back in my chair, the one I had custom-built to accommodate my frame. It swivels back. I steeple my fingers and look at him. "Maybe I like a woman to come home to, brother. Doesn't mean I've gone soft." Whereas Romeo has always viewed women as a duty, as it was his job to marry first, and Mario sees women as his playthings, Santo sees women in a very different light. The day a woman thaws his icy, sadistic heart pigs will fucking fly.

His lips turn downward in a sardonic smile. "Women are useful for two fucking things and you know it."

"Yeah?" God, I've missed this asshole. He's ruthless as fuck but there's no one I'd want at my back in a fight more than Santo. Loyal to the damn core, he'd lay down his life for any one of us. "Let's hear it."

He rolls his eyes. "As if you don't know."

"I wanna hear what you think."

"Fucking and feeding. She can suck my cock and give me her hot, tight cunt, after she brings me dinner and pours me a cold drink."

I can't help but snort. "What, you don't want her to rub your feet by an open fire and call you 'My Lord'?"

He shrugs. "That's a given."

"Jesus."

Someone knocks at the door as I tap out a message to Elise. She has a burner phone, a child-safety version that's *only* used to text me. She can't text anyone else, and can't access the internet. I won't give her access to her own phone, not yet.

Me: You ready for dinner tonight?

Elise: Wait, that's tonight?

OF ALL THE GODDAMN... I blow out an angry breath and text her again.

ME: You mean to tell me after all the to-do finding something to wear and getting your hair cut and giving me shit about manners at a high-end restaurant and you fucking forgot it's tonight?

I GLANCE at the clock and groan. We leave in thirty minutes.

My phone buzzes with another text, but it's a picture message. I tap it and see Elise sitting primly by the window seat in my—*our*—room. She's wearing a stunning ivory dress with a plunging neckline, just low-cut enough to be salacious without showing too much skin. Enough to make any man jealous of me for the woman I've got on my arm tonight.

Her hair hangs loose, gently tousled and styled, her eyes shining bright, as if lit by magic, her lips full and pink. My dick gets hard just staring at her.

ME: *Sorry you forgot. Looks like you're ready for bed. I'll put my yoga pants on, too.*

As if I own yoga pants.

ELISE: *hahaha. Sorry but they don't make men's yoga pants in jumbo size.*

I SEND her a text with the waving hand three times in a row, and hope she gets the right message of that palm across her ass while she flails over my knee. It's been a couple of days since she's been taken in hand, and goddamn the girl needs a tight leash.

I adjust myself. Doesn't take much to make me hard when it comes to her.

Not that I'm complaining.

Doesn't mean I haven't fucked her, though. I'm determined to put my baby in her and coming home to her at night's the highlight of my goddamn day.

ELISE: *Does that mean you plan on punishing me, sir?*

. . .

ANOTHER PICTURE, this time with her covering her mouth with her hand in wide-eyed shock, and the next, with her bent over a chair in our room with her dress-covered ass fully ready for me.

Jesus.

"Go," Santo says, a note of bitterness in his tone I didn't expect. "Go take your pretty wife out to eat and wine and dine her or whatever the fuck you do to someone you're already married to. You hear from Rosa lately?"

I shake my head. "No, I haven't. You?"

"Yeah. She wants to come home and see you but still has some work to do. Might surprise you, though. Wait and see."

"Would be nice to see her. Elise would like it, too, I'd think. They know each other."

The sound of heated voices outside my door catches me by surprise. Is that Mario? I look to Santo expectantly. He stands and silently goes to the door, then puts his ear up against it.

"Mario," he breathes, then shrugs. He doesn't know who the woman is.

I stand and stretch, then walk to the door and yank it open. Mario stands in the hallway and to my shock, Natalia's nanny stands in the doorway of Mario's office, her face beet red.

"Everything alright here?" I ask, shoving my hands in my pockets to make it seem less like an interrogation and more like a friendly question. I can tell by the way the nanny—whose name I don't even know —responds, it's not exactly friendly. She flinches and looks away.

"Oh, it's fine," Mario says with uncharacteristic anger in his voice. "We were just having a little chat. Weren't we?"

She nods, flushing a pretty shade of pink, before she scurries off.

"Jesus, brother, she's a decade younger than you," Santo mutters with a grimace. "She ain't even legal. What is she, a fucking high school freshman? I knew you liked to rob the cradle, but..."

Mario shoves his hands in his pockets and leans up against the wall. "I like to rob the cradle, shake the cradle, and flip that cradle upside fucking down," he says with a shrug. "But I'm not after her. She's way too young. She only pissed me off because she let Natalia go through my things."

Santo scowls. "Let her go through your things? Like what?" I have an immediate visual of his weapons and porno mags.

Mario curses under his breath. "She was in my office, coloring on my calendar with sharpies."

"Oh," Santo says, unable to stifle his smirk, or maybe he didn't even try. "Sounds like we should let her go."

"*And* the wall. And the desk."

I wince. That desk is a hand-me-down from Nonna, and worth more money than the rest of us make in a week.

"Natalia's old enough to know better," Santo says, shaking his head. "I'll talk with her." Of all the uncles, he's the one she's closest to. "Probably misses her mama. Good thing she's coming home soon."

"YEAH," Mario says. "I don't give a fuck if she wants to use permanent markers in my office because she misses her mama or she wanted attention or her fucking fish died, I don't want that to happen again."

"Got it," Santo says. "I'll make that clear. Now calm yourself the fuck down."

Mario grumbles and grunts but finally leaves, but not before he kicks his office door shut behind him. It's unlike him to be so damn grumpy.

"What's his problem?" I ask.

"You ate the last damn scone," Romeo says as he walks down the hall. "Tell Tavi to bring more from town."

I roll my eyes.

"Also, his flavor of the week broke up with him."

"Since when is he even in a position where anyone will 'break up' with him?" I ask, shaking my head.

"Thought he only did hookups and one-night stands?"

Tavi joins us, a cup of steaming hot cappuccino in hand. "Yeah, until you two have to go show off and get married."

I shake my head at them. "We've got dinner tonight. You guys let me know if Rosa's in town, will you?"

"Will do," Santo says.

A thrill of excitement rushes through me at the knowledge that I get to see Elise again, that she's dolling herself up just for me. And then I know.

Santo's right. We did have to go show off and get married. We're the only ones in our family that actually made it work. Or in my case, seem to have anyway.

I feel like we've got a ways to go before we get there.

Bright beams of sun break through the stained glass window in the hall, casting a rainbow of color on the carpet before me. I feel whimsical, as if I'm walking down an enchanted hallway toward my bride.

"Oh, mamma mia."

She sits on a window seat at the end of the hall. Each landing has something special and unique to mark it—a little table with framed prints, an octagonal stained glass window, a small table with vibrant flowering plants. This floor houses a window seat with a tufted pillow.

"Mamma mia yourself." I tease her, but I feel my face break out into a smile. "Why mamma mia?"

She stands and pretends to fan herself. "You're turning me on," she whispers. "You're just... you look amazing."

I reach her and slide my hand along her lower back. I bend my mouth to her ear and nibble. "Thought that was my line."

"We can share it."

I lace my fingers through hers and inhale her provocative scent. I'm getting turned on just touching her, just smelling her.

"Where are we going?"

At this point, she's been to several of our restaurants in the North End. Now, I'd like to take her someplace she's never been before.

"It's a surprise, *piccola*."

When we arrive, our driver brings us to the main entrance. My bodyguards and hers discreetly walk behind us, dressed like normal civilians but armed to the teeth. "Do people know who they are?" she asks quietly. I shake my head.

"Do they know who you are?" She laughs to herself. "Actually, scratch that. I know the answer."

The doors open for us as if they open by themselves, uniformed servers escorting us to our table. I pull a chair out for her, and she drapes herself in it with an elegance befitting a queen. My heart swells. She doesn't know I've brought a surprise for her tonight.

I think I might love this woman. We have so much life to live together yet, but since the Rossi family's on speed, breaking through modern conventions, forcing us together in an arranged marriage may have been the easiest way to bring us together even quicker.

"My God, this is amazing," she says of the grilled olives and chorizo skewers. She eagerly tastes every bite of the sampler platter I order at the tapas restaurant. I wanted to bring her here, to sample the small plates in a leisurely way since this is our makeshift honeymoon.

I finish everything she doesn't eat.

"You guys are hysterical the way you inhale food, for real."

"It's not funny at all," I say, giving her a pointed look. "We take it very, very seriously."

"Oh, I know." She looks pleased with herself.

"You hiding something?"

"Oh, nothing."

"Elise," I say, warningly. She only smirks at me, the little brat. "If you're holding something back from me…"

The waiter comes to our table to take our order. I order for both of us. She sits back in her seat, her hands folded gently on her lap, and watches with shining eyes. I order mini chicken croquettes, empanadas, and spring rolls. This place boasts an unparalleled multicultural menu.

"God, that sounds incredible." The wine flows as if our glasses are enchanted, as the waiter brings plate after plate of small plates.

"Orlando," she says with a gentle smile. "I want to know so many more things about you."

I swallow a bite of food and nod. "Go ahead. I'll answer anything you ask."

Her face registers surprise before she controls her features. "Anything?"

"Of course. You're my wife. Why would I hide anything from you?"

I watch as she picks at her salad plate, her little fork swirling through parsley and thinly diced pear. When she bites her lip, I know she's nervous. I reach my hand to hers and rest it on top.

"Hey. Look at me."

My heart somersaults when her eyes meet mine.

"Don't be nervous. It's me. We've got a long way to go, but babe, you're doing amazing."

She nods. "Thank you. I'm just...I'm wondering something that I've been meaning to ask you."

"Go for it."

She lowers her voice. Whether she wants to make sure no one overhears her, or she's afraid that she'll show too much emotion, I'm not entirely sure. I give her another reassuring squeeze.

"My family...doesn't believe in fidelity. Marriage is only a convenience." She blinks, and there's challenge in her eyes when she looks at me. "I want to know the truth. Will you have a mistress?"

So that's what's been worrying her? I know Romeo's faithful to Vittoria, but he's the only one who ever has been. Even my Uncle Leo had a side girl in Tuscany when his wife was in America. He never even tried to hide it. Mario fucks anything with legs, and Tavi's too broody and stern to consider marrying right now. Santo...no one ever knows what's going through that guy's head.

I lean forward and take both her hands in mine. My voice is low, but a direct command she's been taught to obey. "Look at me, babe."

Tentatively, she raises her eyes to mine. And like a good girl, she holds my gaze. "Yes?"

"I don't ever want anyone else between us. Ever. I will not take a mistress." I lean across the table. "And you already know any man that touches you would lose limbs before I'd allow that."

"You wouldn't even let them help me out of the car," she says in a breathy voice, as if surprised.

"Of course not. That's my job."

After a few long moments, she finally nods. "Okay, alright. You won't have a mistress." She exhales, sagging with obvious relief. "And I for sure will only be touched by *you*. Well, that's a relief."

"Which part of that?"

She sighs. "All of it. Another question."

"Yes."

"Are women in your...family...allowed to go to college?"

Jesus, really?

"Of course. Why would you even ask such a thing?"

Her hands grow clammy in mine. "Also a question stemming from my family."

The waiter brings over a charcuterie board, a mid-meal appetizer, as it were, and we release hands long enough to fill our plates. I watch as she takes a small sampling of everything.

"You like all of those things?"

"Oh," she says with a gentle flush. "I have no idea. But I'm willing to try anything."

I take a bite of Manchego cheese with a rustic cracker and groan. God, I love food almost as much as sex. "I love that about you."

"What?"

"Your sense of adventure."

She shoots me a wicked grin. "Any woman married to you would have to have a sense of adventure. Wouldn't she?"

Why do her eyes grow wistful when she looks at me like that? We're already married. She's already mine. We're committed to each other and nothing short of death would tear us apart.

"I guess you could say that. Hey, listen." The black velvet box in my pocket burns like a hot coal. It's time. "I got a little something for you. We've done shit so backwards, I guess it makes sense I got this for you *after* our wedding, and not during the engagement like every other asshole does."

I watch her eyes widen, and her lips part adorably.

"You bought me something?" she says, as if I just told her she'd sprouted fairy wings and could soar into the night sky.

"I did. Open it." I hand her the velvet box, but she only stares.

"But I didn't get you anything, Orlando. I didn't know…that was expected."

"It isn't. I wanted to get you something, and so I did. I don't want or expect you to reciprocate. Now are you gonna take this, or will I have to spend the rest of this meal holding a velvet box in my palm?"

Gingerly, her fingers clasp it. "It's heavy," she whispers.

Better be heavy. Fifteen carats is nothing to sneeze at.

"Do I…?"

"Open it? Of course."

She does that thing where she bites her lip as she raises the lid to the velvet box, but I don't expect the tears that shine in her eyes. "Oh my God," she says in a trembling whisper. "Oh, God, Orlando. This is… this is too much." Yet she traces her index finger along the first twinkling diamond. "I can't…"

"Take it? You'd goddamn better." I look at the dainty gold chain studded with star-shaped diamonds in the box.

"It's like fairy-spun gossamer," she whispers and swallows. "Oh, it's so lovely." When she lifts it from the box, she gasps again. "Orlando. You didn't."

Against the black velvet backdrop, a little silver tag reads *A Riot of Flowers*.

"Come here," I say softly, as she swipes at her eyes. I rise and walk to her. She'd have a fit if she knew this string of precious gems cost a cool five mil at a Christie's auction in Hong Kong. She doesn't need to know that. She's worth it. "It's your wedding gift. Get over here, and I'll put it on you. There are rubies and diamonds set in white gold and precious platinum, whatever the fuck that means."

"You're so romantic." She sticks her tongue out at me and I give her chin a little squeeze. She flushes pink but doesn't take her eyes off the string of diamonds the entire time. "It's so rare to see *one* star-shaped diamond like that," she whispers, clearly an expert. "I can't imagine how…how much…all those diamonds…"

I stifle a chuckle. I love that I've bought her a gift that's rendered her speechless.

"I'm not telling you how much this cost."

"It's more than anything I've ever touched before in my life."

I open my mouth to retort, but she holds a palm out. "If you want to talk about your gold-plated dick, save it. We're in the middle of high society and there's no place for your utter maleness."

I lean down and whisper in her ear, even as I'm grinning. "Watch that tone, woman." I love the way she shivers and flushes a deeper shade of red, the way her eyes go all sleepy and sexy with the threat.

We eat the rest of our meal in comfort, laughing, talking, and joking until it's time for us to go. "I want to see you wearing nothing but this tonight," I tell her, already imagining those diamonds sparkling on her naked skin when I fuck her. We haven't had a single night we've missed together, not one, since we married.

My phone buzzes when the waiter brings us dessert. I lift it to see a text from Romeo. I'm high from just being with her, her obvious pleasure at my gift, and her company. I kinda want to pinch myself, because I can't believe I get to spend the rest of my life with this fucking masterpiece of a woman.

ROMEO: You still at dinner? Don't want to bother you.

Me: Yeah, but wrapping it up. Everything okay?

Romeo: Tavi's been tapping Elise's phone. We need to talk.

I LOOK across the table at her. She's fingering the necklace, her small, delicate fingers tracing each star-shaped diamond.

ME: She has her phone?

Romeo: She didn't tell you?

Me: No.

I PUT my phone in my pocket and signal to the waiter.

She's in so much goddamn trouble.

"Check please."

CHAPTER 14

"I do remember." ~*Twelfth Night, Shakespeare*

"ELISE"

MY FINGERS SKIM my neck where the necklace lies, like actual stars in the sky. I can't believe he got this for me. I didn't even know he was paying attention to me, that he knew something like this would mean so much.

No one's ever bought me jewelry, and no one's ever bought me anything expensive. I can tell just by looking at this it's worth more than I even want to think about.

"Everything okay?" For some reason, just looking at the way he's staring at his phone, the way his gaze has cooled to ice, makes the food I just ate sit like a rock in my stomach.

"Why would you think something's wrong?"

Tonight at dinner, there was an almost...light-hearted air about him. Almost jovial. *Almost*. He still carries himself with utter seriousness almost all of the time, but every once in a while, I get a glimpse of the man who was once a boy. I can see the laughter behind his eyes, the softness in his jaw, the whimsical twinkle in his eye. But then he blinks, and it's gone, like scattered dandelion seeds in a gust of wind. I reach for them, hoping to touch the filament like fairy dust, but too soon the moment's over. And now, after the most delicious meal I've ever eaten, he has that look in his eyes again. The look that tells me he's troubled. Something's on his mind.

I've learned not to ask questions. Or...to time the questions right, anyway. I walk beside him and reach for his hand. His grip is almost painful. I wish he could speak to me more freely, but in our current situation, I'm sure he needs privacy before we talk. At least that's what I tell myself.

When we get to the car, our driver pulls up to the curb. As usual, Orlando opens the door for me and I slide in, my finger still tracing the twinkling edges of the necklace he gave me. He follows behind me and slams the door hard. My heart jumps.

I wouldn't really say Orlando has a temper. But I also wouldn't call him a temperate sort of guy. He burns hot, like embers in a fire, pretty much all the time. Even when he's sleeping, he's physically warm to the touch, and that might just be my body responding to his on instinct, but I don't think so.

But even in the privacy of the recesses of the back of the car, he doesn't speak. He offers no information at all. He drums his fingers on his leg and looks out the window distractedly.

"Orlando."

He looks to me silently.

"We had such a nice dinner in there. And then you sort of just…closed off. What happened? If it's something you can't tell me, I understand."

"We'll talk about it back at The Castle."

I don't question it. And it isn't just because he's taught me to obey him, but also because I've learned to be a little more patient. When he has something to say to me, he always tells me. He doesn't hide anything from me, at least I don't think so. So I sit back in the seat, and I close my eyes. I enjoy the feel of the necklace on my skin. I'll never forget the way his eyes shone at me when he put it on me. He likes making me happy.

Then why the anger?

It doesn't take us long to arrive at The Castle, and I've managed to convince myself that him being troubled is all in my mind. But this doesn't feel like the sort of erotic expectation I get before he punishes me. This feels like something else.

A car I haven't seen before sits in the driveway. I don't think much about it because people are always visiting The Castle. It's a large house, with many occupants, and the Rossi family is wealthy and popular. This could be the President of the United States for all I know. Doubtful, but still.

I've checked in with Elise, and I know her father and the rest of her family are still in Italy. Still...it wouldn't take much for the ruse to be up. I've maybe grown complacent knowing that he cares for me, told myself that even if he did find out who I am, he'll forgive it.

But maybe I'm lying to myself.

So I don't ask him who's here. He opens the car door, gets out, and then reaches for my hand. The chilly wind kicks up as I step outside of the car.

"Looks like she might've arrived early. I was saving that as a surprise for you."

Surprise? Trepidation builds in my belly. I don't know if any surprises are good right now.

"I'd like to take you on another tour of The Castle, this one showing you many more rooms we haven't seen before," he says. There's a knife-edged tone to his voice, sharp and alarming to me. He's angry.

Is he angry at me?

Does he know I'm not Elise?

"As far as our guests, we don't have any. I think Rosa may have come home. Santo said that she might. And as much as I miss her, I'm not in the mood to visit tonight. I'd like to show you around The Castle, and then take you upstairs. We'll meet Rosa in the morning."

Oh no. Oh no *oh no*. Rosa will know I'm not Elise. Maybe I should tell him. Maybe I should tell him everything...

"This right here is the entryway." His voice is a little aloof, detached, refined. It's as if he's giving a tour of The Castle to a stranger. I reach for his hand, but he doesn't take it. Instead he takes my elbow roughly and helps me up the stairs so I don't stumble, then releases me when we get to the top.

Something is gravely wrong. Has Rosa already seen me? Does she know that I'm not Elise?

When we enter the front door, I hear laughter from the other room. Voices rise and fall, and glasses clink together. The family's rejoicing that Rosa's come home. Rosa, Elise's friend. I don't know how I ever thought I'd get away with this, that I'd escape his wrath.

Thankfully, the noise of the family chatting and eating fades into the background as he takes my hand in his much larger, rougher one, and escorts me out of the foyer. There's a sort of gleam in his eye I don't miss.

"Everything alright?"

"Mm," he says distractedly. "We usually eat in the dining room, but last night we convened in the Great Hall."

"The room with the huge ceilings and flags?"

He nods. "Beyond the Hall is a courtyard. It's a family favorite in the warmer months because of the indoor pool."

What? No way. "You have an indoor pool?"

He nods again, still distracted, as if he's mulling something over. I imagine there are lots of things on his mind.

"I'll show you that later. Right now, I want to show you the back of the house."

Taking my hand, he shows me everything. I feel as if I've stepped back in time when I see the magnificent home, and at the back of my mind I wonder where we're going next. His steps are quicker than I'm used to, and I find myself walking faster to keep up with him.

"Is everything okay?" I ask.

He doesn't respond. "This is the pantry," he says, gesturing to a large room that looks like a small office, laden with every food item one could imagine. "Next to the kitchen and behind here is the war room where my father used to work."

"You haven't told me much about your father," I say softly. The war room looks like a study, lined with shelves and books and a heavy desk.

"My father was not a good man," he says softly, running his hand thoughtfully along the doorframe as he gazes inside the room.

"No?"

Shaking his head, he clears his throat. "He hated me because I didn't like doing my job. I didn't like hurting people."

I wonder if he really means that in the past tense.

I come closer and sidle up next to him, my side flush against his. "You sure like hurting people now," I tease.

He actually chuckles a bit at that. "Maybe *you*."

I put my head on his shoulder and think about what it was like to have a father who disliked you for being good. My stomach clenches with the thought.

"My father neglected me," I say, then I bite my lip so I can thoughtfully pick out the right words. I have to be careful that anything I say is generic enough it could be Elise's father, and not so mean that Orlando will hunt him down to seek revenge. And that's absolutely something he would do.

I want him. I don't want to let him go. I love that he's so possessive, so protective. I love this man.

I twirl a piece of my hair thoughtfully as I think about my words. "His friends mattered to him, his work. But not me. I was only an accessory." I close my mouth so I don't say much more.

"Why do you speak in the past tense? Your father's

still with us." As he talks, he gently places his arm around my shoulders and pulls me to him. I lay my head against him. It's a soothing sort of feeling, one that brings surprising tears to my eyes.

"I just meant that it was like that when I was a child. Now, we live our separate lives..." I don't look at him when I say this. I have to be careful not to slip up like that again. I have to change the subject. "Do you still meet here?"

"Yeah, Romeo holds inner circle meetings here sometimes." He's brushing his thumb across his lower lip when his phone dings with a text. It startles me when his eyes go dark after reading it.

"Everything okay?"

Again, he doesn't answer. "Let's finish this tour."

We head to another section of the house. Everything's decorated in ornate decorations, some imported directly from Italy. Heavy drapes hang by windows, but they don't look stuffy. It's elegant in here, refined, with the taste of old-world culture and a flavor of the modern. And I love it. I love it so much.

"Downstairs is the secret wine cellar," he says. "Or was. The bottles in the dining room line an entire wall. They're straight from our vineyards in Tuscany."

"Wow, so that's not over-the-top at all."

That earns me a stinging pinch to the ass.

I hold my breath when he opens the entrance to the wine cellar, a hidden doorway marked only with the outline of a doorway.

"Okay, so, tell me this is how you get to the dungeon," I say with a forced laugh. "You and your knights imprison your captives until they're brought to the presence of the king, eh?"

"Very good. That's exactly how it goes."

There isn't a hint of humor in his voice. I clear my throat.

"Uh, Orlando. This is kind of, like, scaring me."

No response, just a tug to my hand that makes me quicken my step.

"Orlando..."

"We're almost there."

He leads me down to the dungeon. It looks exactly the way I'd expect a dungeon to look—dark and dank, with chains on the wall and a cement floor that's dark enough to hide whatever stains it.

"You weren't lying," I breathe while I cringe.

"I was not."

I gulp, and he threads his fingers through mine as he leads me in. "This is the dungeon. We interrogate our prisoners here, and it's a useful place to put someone if they've broken a rule and need to be punished."

I'm sick to my stomach. I can almost hear the

echoes of pleas for mercy, the screams of the damned.

"Got it." My heart's beating faster, my mouth all dry. I squirm when he leads me to the middle of the room where chains are dangling from the ceiling.

"These chains here," he says softly, as he hefts one of the manacles, "work really well for keeping prisoners in place."

Without a word, he lifts my wrist. "Orlando, I—"

The click makes me squirm. I tug my wrist to find it secure in the cuff. My heart races faster. He takes my second wrist and lifts it, then slides the other cuff in place. "There you go," he says softly. Is the man a psychopath? He just put me in chains in the dungeon. "Now we can have the talk we need to have."

I can't see him when he paces behind me, but I can hear the soft treading of his feet. "Orlando..."

"Elise..."

Does he know who I am? Does he know I'm an imposter? What did he bring me here to do? I'm shivering uncontrollably from the fear. I'm secured so high up, I'm on my tiptoes. In my peripheral vision, he takes something out of his pocket.

"What are you doing?" I whisper, terrified. I stifle a whimper. "Orlando..."

If he's brought me here to punish me for lying to him...

A strip of leather skates around my neck, making me shiver and squirm. "Got a text from Romeo."

I gulp. *Shit*. He holds the leather something in his hand, a cluster of leather strips dangling from a sturdy handle. I stifle a cry when he gives it a little flick on my neck, the leather kissing my skin.

"Did you?" I whisper. "And what did he say?"

"That you were given your phone a few nights ago. He was quite surprised you hadn't told me."

Walking around me, he traces my body with the little leather tassels. "What is that thing?"

"A flogger."

"Flogger?"

"Yeah, baby. Flogger. And the little leather strips are called falls." I close my eyes when he brings his mouth to my ear. "Usually a flogger can be a very tame tool for punishment. I didn't bring you here to punish you but to ask you some questions. They're gentler than some other implements, unless I use a cat on you. But that could damage your skin." It tickles as he lays it across my shoulders. "The thicker the falls, the more thud it brings. This will sting but not damage you."

I nod, a little overwhelmed. My head swims.

"I have questions for you."

I whimper. "Go for it."

"Did you make any calls?"

When I don't answer right away, the leather smacks against my ass, once, twice, three times, each lash leaving a little burst of pain. It's nothing like his belt, though. It's hardly even like his hand. It hurts, no doubt, but it's a quick flare of erotic heat. The thought of him taking it to me, though, is intimidating as hell.

"Yeah. I did," I choke out. "I called my friend. Told her we were married. That's it."

"But you didn't think you had to tell me." He whips me again with the flogger, harder than he did last time. It burns.

"No! I... I wanted a little privacy." It's not a lie.

"Didn't you know I'd find out? I told you we'd tap your phone."

I didn't say anything to her that would get us in trouble. I knew there's only an illusion of privacy here at all. I knew he'd find out but figured it was worth the risk.

I nod and close my eyes when the falls land across my ass once, twice, three more times. It brings a sting with a sensual heat unlike anything I've ever felt before. I look over my shoulder and see him standing behind me, his eyes dark little pools in a sea of darkness. He holds the flogger in his hand upright, then flicks his wrist before he snaps it again.

"You have no privacy here. You know that. As a daughter of mafia, you should know that."

I should tell him. I have to. If I don't tell him now, we'll only end up here again, only it will be so much worse for me. Maybe for both of us.

I can't do it. I open my mouth, and all that comes out is a strangled cry when he lets loose another lash of the flogger. It hurts, but nothing like what I've experienced before. This is almost a warning, and he's told me he doesn't want to punish me.

"What did your friend say when you told her that you were married?"

He doesn't know, not yet.

"She isn't happy."

It's true. She isn't. She wants me to get away from him.

"And what then? What was your plan on telling me?"

I take a deep breath and decide on the truth. At least part of it. "I decided to let you find out in your own time. I decided that I… didn't want you to find out any other way. I didn't want to tell you. I didn't want to lose that little, tiny bit of privacy I had left."

He doesn't speak but applies a lash with wicked precision. One smack after the other lands, and I want to cry. It burns and hurts, one wicked lash after the other building a wicked, consuming heat.

I feel like I want to cry. There's a lump in my throat, but I can't let it go. My back, my ass, my thighs, all burn from the pain of the lashing.

I try to gather my courage; I need to tell him something. I need to tell him the truth. I shake my head, trying to clear my brain, but I don't even know where to begin.

"Orlando…" My voice is shaky, and footsteps clatter at the doorway. He comes up behind me and rests his head on top of mine.

"You have to tell me the truth," he says in my ear. "I told you what would happen if you didn't. I told you the danger that you'd be in. Not just from me, Elise. There's a hierarchy of command here and not everything's within my control."

He's right. I'm in so much danger I don't even know how to begin to tell him the truth at this point. What would he do if he knew that I wasn't the woman I said I was? Even if he knew my motive? But if he finds out any other way… I have to tell him.

The door opens. "Orlando? You down there?" It's a woman's voice. There's no more hiding. I gather up what courage I have and face him. I have to tell him the truth. "I need a moment," I whisper to him. "I have to tell you."

He looks at me and holds my chin. "What is it that you have to tell me?"

"Orlando?"

"I'm down here, Rosa. I need a minute."

He stares into my eyes. "Will I have to punish you again when you tell me?" I look down at the floor, but he moves my chin back up so that he looks into my eyes.

"I'm..." I can't say it. My voice is clogged, my throat tight. I don't know how to say it. It requires courage I've only dreamed of having. The necklace feels like a collar, heavy and unyielding, but nowhere near as heavy as my heart.

"Orlando, I'm pregnant."

CHAPTER 15

"O time, thou must untangle this, not I.

It is too hard a knot for me t'untie." ~*Twelfth Night, Shakespeare*

ORLANDO

I stare at her, comprehension taking a few minutes to dawn on me.

"You're pregnant? I tied you up and used the flogger on you and you just now decide to tell me you're pregnant?"

I drop the flogger to the dungeon floor. It's a tame implement, one that sounds a lot harsher than it is, but still. If I knew she was pregnant, I wouldn't have brought her here, wouldn't have punished her at all.

She sags against my chest, her shoulders heaving. It seems a suitable reaction for what she's told me, what we've been through, but absolutely the first time I've ever given comfort to someone in the dark, windowless dungeon. For her, though...

I wrap my arms around her, pulling her to me, and my heart aches. I wouldn't consider myself a compassionate kind of guy, at least not anymore. But I love this woman. She's my wife. She was brought here without her consent, forced to marry me before we'd ever met. She gave me her virginity. She gave me everything.

I wanted to scare her. I wanted to put the fear of God into her for not telling me the truth, but she hasn't done anything worthy of a severe punishment. And the sadist in me revels in the chance of wielding my control over her.

Not telling me she had her phone's hardly a serious infraction. She should have told me, yeah. But I knew it'd be tapped, and what's she gonna do with a phone call anyway? It's tapped for her own protection above all.

But I don't want my *pregnant* wife in the dark, dank confines of the dungeon, where we convene in private and do unspeakable things.

"Upstairs. Now." I lift her in my arms, and she nestles her head against my chest.

"I don't want to see anyone." She sniffles. I hold her tighter.

"Of course not, *piccola*. I understand. Let's get you upstairs. I'm going to call the doctor immediately." I walk up the stairs with her tucked up against my chest, so sweet. A deep, abiding sense of the need to protect this woman and my child that she carries thrums through my veins with the heady insistence that this is it, this is what I've wanted. What I've waited for. I was born with the instinct to protect. Now I'll have a family of my very own.

When we get upstairs, my family mills about in the rooms adjacent to the war room. My brothers and sisters drink whiskey and wine in the study, and Nonna has everyone laughing around an open fire.

Rosa stands in the doorway.

My chest warms at seeing her. My big sister, come home. Natalia's by her side, and she runs to me.

"Please, Orlando," Elise whispers.

Rosa's eyes fall to Elise, tucked into my arms. "Ah," I tell Rosa, "so good to see you. I'm sorry, she doesn't feel well. I'm taking her upstairs."

"Oh, of course," Rosa says. "Good to see you. Good to see both of you."

Elise lifts her head, her hair falling all around her face, and waves at her, then collapses against my chest again. I hold her to me. Rosa grins.

"Aww, Lando. God, it's good to see you with her. I can't wait to catch up."

She turns and joins the others. My heart is filled to bursting. My sister's home, my family's safe. And my own family is going to grow. We've done what we were supposed to, married and now we're bringing children into our home. I never dreamed it would all happen so quickly.

"Thank you," Elise whispers. I hold her tighter.

"Why do you tremble, little one?" I whisper in her ear.

My wife.

My child.

"I'm just a little overwhelmed."

The overhead lighting glints on the necklace I gave her tonight, the *Riot of Flowers*. Worth every goddamn penny. It all was. My time in prison, the immediate joining with Elise.

A baby.

I wonder if Romeo will be jealous that we'll be the next who bring children into our fold. A cousin for little Natalia.

I take her upstairs, slide her to the floor, and undress her. "Bed for you. I'll call the doctor right now."

"Can we please call them in the morning?" She yawns widely. "I... I'm so tired."

I shake my head. "No, babe. I want you seen immediately. It's important that we make sure you're taken care of right away. You said you feel a little nauseous?"

She tucks the blanket up to her chin and pales. "A little," she whispers.

"I'll get them here right now. We'll take care of you." I sit beside the bed and hold her to me. I kiss the top of her head fiercely. I want to tell her that I love her. It feels like odd timing in our relationship to do that, but by normal standards we've done everything wrong from the beginning. "Rest, baby. I'll get you anything you need."

I leave her resting in that way that makes me swoon, her hands tucked under her chin. Goddamn adorable.

I call Romeo first. He answers on the first ring. "Yeah?"

"She's pregnant."

"Ah, brother. *Congratulazioni!* Aw, man, that's fantastic news." I can hear him turn away from his phone and share the news. He seems nothing but pleased, and my heart swells.

It would be a lie to call Romeo a good man. He's done things that many would never dream of, and has earned his right as head of this family because of it. But he is fiercely loyal to his family. To his wife. And one day, when he has children, to them as well.

He is not my father. Romeo doesn't share the thread of narcissism and insanity that drove my father to his death. But he is my brother, and that means everything. I hang up with him and walk to Elise.

"How do you know?" I ask her. But Elise doesn't respond. I walk over to her to see that she's fallen asleep. I look down at my beautiful bride who holds my child in her, and marvel at the miracle that the past few weeks have brought me. I've gone from fighting for my life in the bowels of hell to rebuilding a life of my own. I don't know what I've done to deserve such a chance, but I won't ever take it for granted.

Next, I call the doctor. But I don't want to wake Elise. She sleeps so soundly, and I remember Rosa telling me how exhausted she was in the first trimester of pregnancy. There will be time tomorrow for us to see the doctor, to find out what happens next. For me to take care of her.

Tomorrow, we start a new chapter of our life.

CHAPTER 16

"I was adored once, too." ~*Twelfth Night, Shakespeare*

"*ELISE*"

It was the second lie I told him, and I hate myself for it. *Hate.* I want to rip my hair and tear my skin for the crime of lying to my husband.

I have reasons, good damn reasons for what I've done. But I hate that I've taken two of the things that matter most to him in the world and lied about both of them.

I feel as if I've taken this beautiful necklace he's given me, this absolute masterpiece of perfection in jewels, and dipped it in tar. I feel that what I've done is irrevocable, and I hate that, because I really do love him. I do.

I hear him pacing the room while I pretend that I'm asleep. Maybe he's forgotten the phone in the excitement of what I told him just now.

I don't know if I'm pregnant or not, but I imagine that it's probably impossible. Well, not impossible. I haven't used birth control, and we fuck like damn rabbits. But I have nothing to show that I'm pregnant, and don't know what I'll tell him tomorrow when that doctor gives me a test, which I know he will, and it comes back negative.

I don't know what to do with myself. Rosa is here, and I thought I was going to die when she came up to say hello to us. I can't believe I escaped so easily. I can't believe it came that close to uncovering the truth.

First time since I came here, I hope that I am pregnant. If I am, it would be one tie to this family that I truly don't want to leave.

I wish I knew what would happen if they knew I'm not Elise. I wish I could predict what he would do. But I've seen that dungeon. I could almost hear the screams of the people he's tortured, and I'm not naïve enough to think it's only been men that he's punished. That any of them have. They may have taken me into the fold, but they aren't good people. They revel in organized crime, their wealth is built on crime, everything that they do is wrong.

At least this is what I tell myself. I have to, to talk myself out of wanting to stay here, to be welcomed into the fold. But more than anything...

To well and truly belong to Orlando.

He paces and paces, and I know that he's mulling everything over in his mind.

My heart aches for him. I came here to save my friend. I lied about being pregnant to save my life. And now...I want to save *him*, only I don't know how.

He gets another phone call, and when he put it up to his ear, he speaks in Italian. I don't know many words, but the tone of his voice is pleased. He hangs up the call.

I hear him rummaging around, and then scratching a note on a piece of paper. He slips it on the table beside me, then bends and kisses my head, before he heads for the door.

It's hard to pretend I'm asleep when I'm crying.

The door opens and closes behind him. I'm alone.

With trembling hands, I open the drawer.

Tomorrow, he'll remember I have this phone. He punished me for it tonight, and now I know what I have to do. I may be allowed my phone again, but I wouldn't be surprised if he punished me by taking it away.

For half a second, I fear it's gone, that they took it. But it still lies next to the black box he keeps in there for his kink games. I grab for it quickly, shaking in case he returns.

Would he punish a pregnant wife? I still feel the

sting from the falls of the flogger, but the memory's already become an erotic fantasy more than a punishment. What will he do when he finds out the real truth? All of it? There's no way I'll get away with this.

My phone buzzes. I almost drop it.

Bestie.

I answer the phone, my voice hoarse. "Hello?" I whisper.

On the other end of the phone, I only hear sobs.

"Hello? Hello? Elise?"

I hope and pray whoever taps this phone is confused by the name and doesn't suspect the truth. I sit up straighter in bed. "Are you okay?"

"They killed him. Oh, God, they killed him." She's in hysterics. Ice spears my chest, and I begin to shake.

"Who did?" I whisper. "My God. Who did?"

"My father found out the truth," she chokes. "Piero's friend ratted him out. He found us, oh *God*, he found us."

No.

"Where are you?" I ask. Tears of frustration and fear stream down my face, and the hand on my phone shakes so hard I grab it with my other hand to steady the shaking.

"I escaped," she whispers. "I can't tell you where I

am. They're tapping your phone, I know they are. I won't tell you where I am, but I'm safe now. I escaped." She sobs. "But he didn't. They shot him. He rescued me, and he gave his life for me. If he hadn't, I wouldn't be here." She sobs harder, gasping into the phone. "And they shot him."

I can't tell her what happened to me, I can't tell her what's happening now. She's got her own shit to deal with. I'm on my feet, shaking from the trauma of hearing this.

They'll go after her next.

And me. They'll come after me.

"Find a way to me," I tell her. "Please, honey. And we'll make this better." I fear for her life. Somehow, some way, I'll find a way to help her. We'll have to.

Footsteps sound in the hallway outside our door. "I can't talk," I whisper. "Stay in touch, *please*."

"Go," she says. "Stay safe. I'll call you tomorrow."

I drop the phone in the drawer just as the door to the room opens. I pretend I'm coughing, then bury my face in the pillow with the coughing fit as I try to stem my tears.

"Baby?"

The sound of his voice makes me all choked up. I have to face him. I have to face this all bravely and do what I must.

I have to find Elise, I have to save her, too.

How?

I roll over and face the door. Orlando's back with the doctor.

"Oh, good, you're up, Elise." I yawn widely, feeling like an absolute jerk. "I was gonna wait until tomorrow for you to see him, but he's heading to Tuscany tomorrow and was in the library with the family." He walks over to me and reaches a hand to my forehead. "You okay?"

"Ugh, I feel so sick," I whisper. A tear rolls down my cheek, and my heart aches so badly I feel as if it's going to splinter in two. "I don't feel good at all."

Orlando sits on the bed beside me and holds me. I sniffle into his chest, but it feels like a stolen moment. I'm not who he thinks I am. I don't deserve him. I don't deserve his comfort or protection or *any* of it.

"Can you help her?" The plaintive plea in his voice breaks my aching heart. He cares about me, really, truly *cares* about me, in a way that no one ever has before. Ever. "Elise, this is Dr. Cho. Dr. Cho, my wife Elise." For some reason, hearing him call me that name feels worse than it ever has before. I want him to call me by my real name. I want to be myself with him, the real me. But I want it all, and I know I can't have that.

I glance up at Dr. Cho, an older man who seems almost ready for retirement. He looks at me from the other side of his spectacles and smiles kindly.

"We'll start with a pregnancy test, just to be sure it isn't a false alarm. What makes you think you're pregnant?"

"I took an at-home test earlier today, and it said I was pregnant." *Lies upon lies upon lies, like a bed of snakes that will eventually strike.*

"Ah, okay. Please take mine to be sure. How late is your period?"

I knew it.

I give him all the details, then take the little plastic cup to pee in and head to the bathroom. Orlando comes with me.

"I can handle this part on my own," I tell him.

He hesitates, then finally concedes. "Fine, but we look at the test together." His eyes darken. "And don't you ever take a pregnancy test without me again, you understand me?"

I nod. Of course he'd feel that way. I wouldn't have, but the lies are piling up like logs in a woodpile. I'm so afraid that with a strike of a match, they'll ignite and burn me along with them.

Shaking, I do what I need to and come out to the doctor and Orlando. The doctor takes out a little strip of paper. I'm shaking with nerves, terrified of Orlando's reaction when he sees the negative test. Will I have to lie further? Tell him maybe it was a false positive or...or something.

I want this all over. I want to tell him the truth and face the consequences. I'm tired of living a life that's a lie. I want to live in the truth.

He told me he'd never lie to me.

It's all I've ever done to him.

I bury my head on his shoulder, savoring this one last moment of stolen comfort before the truth outs.

Dr. Cho smiles. "Congratulations, you two. You are indeed pregnant. It's obviously very early, and we can talk about the early symptoms of pregnancy and what the best course of prenatal care will be."

He drones on and on, but I hardly hear him.

Wait. What? *No.*

My mind is still fixated on that one word.

Pregnant.

Pregnant.

Pregnant.

How did that... How could he... He doesn't know that I need this right now. He doesn't know that he just complicated things so recklessly. Is he telling me the truth?

Orlando grins at me and hold me so close to him it hurts. "Easy," I tell him. "Please. That hurts."

He releases me as if I'm a hot potato, and Dr. Cho laughs out loud.

"You don't have to treat her with kid gloves. She's resilient. Lots of pregnant women are. But I know your family, and I know you'll take very good care of her. Tomorrow, we'll get her in with an OB in my practice, and she'll undergo the beginnings of prenatal care." He turns to me. "How do you feel right now?"

How do I feel? Stunned. Shocked. Relieved. Terrified.

I just shake my head. Orlando wraps his arm around my shoulders and holds me. A lump rises in my throat, but I swallow it down. Another moment of stolen comfort.

"She's tired, doctor. We had a very long day." Then he frowns and fiddles with the wedding band on his hand. "I was pretty hard on her earlier."

Dr. Cho waves at hand. "If you want to talk about sex, that's fine, I don't care. But I doubt there's anything you're going to do to her that's going to hurt the baby. I get these questions all the time."

Orlando looks at me. "Even if she gets spanked?" My cheeks flush. But I don't even care. I have bigger things on my mind than whether or not Dr. Cho knows that my husband is a kinky bastard.

"Nothing wrong with a little endorphin rush. I'm sure you're not going to strike her belly. Just use caution, Orlando. You should know that."

Orlando stands, gently sliding me down on the bed, and walks over to the doctor. They speak in hushed voices as they go to the door.

I wonder where Elise is. I want to rejoice in the sign of new life with my husband, but I don't know what he'll do when he finds out who I am.

The door shuts, and as soon as it is, there's another knock.

He opens the door. This time my heart races even faster.

Tavi's tapping my phone. They heard the tear-filled conversation, I know they did. And Rosa is in this house.

The gig is up.

I'm pregnant.

I sit up in bed, and I already know before I even look at the door who's there. Romeo stands in the doorway and the look he gives me is nothing short of terrifying. He's been polite to me. He's gentle with his wife, and good to his siblings, but when he looks at me, I see nothing but the ruthless leader of this family. The man who's earned his reputation as the most severe mafioso in all of New England.

He comes into the room and starts walking toward me. Orlando is bewildered, looking from me to Romeo and back again

"Brother." Orlando's hands are in his pockets, but as Romeo gets closer to me, Orlando's face looks concerned. He steps quickly between me and Romeo. "Why are you here? She's exhausted."

Romeo's eyes are thin like slits, his face a mask of fury. Behind him in the doorway, Tavi and Mario linger. All of them look at me as if I'm the enemy.

I guess in their eyes I am.

Romeo's hard voice fills the room, like the edict of a god from Mount Olympus. I shiver at the icy tone. "We need to talk."

"What's this all about?" Orlando says. "And back the fuck off, brother."

Romeo's only paces away from me now. He swings his gaze to mine. "Will you tell him, or will I?"

I open my mouth and will the words to come out. It seems as if my voice is caught, trapped in the tangle of lies, and as soon as one of them escapes, they'll flutter heavenward like a swarm of butterflies, all of them.

"I will." My voice isn't my own, as if I'm somehow possessed or enchanted. "I will," I whisper.

The look of fear that crosses Orlando's face makes fresh tears fall down my cheeks. "What is it?" he says.

I gather every ounce of courage I have and face him, bracing myself on the other side of the bed.

"My name is not Elise."

Romeo's face registers only fury, not a trace of surprise. He knows. They all do. And now my beloved husband does, too.

Orlando blinks, not processing any of this. "What?"

But now that I've shed the first layer of lies, it feels easier to speak, even if I face imminent punishment or exile. "I'm not Elise. I was in Tuscany when Elise was called by her bodyguard to catch a plane." I want to bury my face in the blanket so I don't have to face him, this fierce, loyal, bear of a man who's given me everything I needed and never knew that I did. "Elise Regazza is my best friend. We grew up together. That night, when you accused me of trying to escape? I was never meant to marry you. I—I was supposed to escape. You were supposed to think I was killed."

The silence in the room is deafening, along with the pounding of blood rushing in my ears.

I saw that dungeon. He fucked me in front of a prisoner before he killed him.

What will he do to me?

"You lied to me," he whispers. "It was all a lie. All of it."

I swipe at my eyes. "Not all of it."

"You betrayed me."

"I had to!"

It all happens so quickly I can hardly process any of it. Romeo steps toward me, his hand raised as if to strike me. Orlando's growl of fury as he stays his brother's hand. The next moment, Orlando tackles Romeo to the floor.

I scream, covering my mouth with my hands, when Romeo attacks. The two of them roll on the floor, hitting each other with such forceful blows it makes me sick. Orlando hits Romeo's jaw, snapping his neck back. Blood spurts from his mouth but it only makes Romeo angrier as he fights back. But Orlando's much bigger than Romeo. He's bigger than everyone.

"Orlando! No!"

The cold sound of several guns being cocked at once makes both of them freeze.

I can't breathe. I can't move. Mario and Tavi hold their guns to Orlando's temples, one on either side of him.

"Don't fucking make me," Tavi growls. "You know our code. You know our oaths. You know you've earned death by striking the Don. Get on your fucking feet and step away from him. Now."

Romeo shakes Orlando off. Mario keeps his gun trained on Orlando. I watch it all play out like a horror movie.

Orlando puts his hands in the air, palms out, in the universal gesture of surrender.

"She's pregnant, man," he says, his voice choked. "You can't hurt her." His eyes cut to me. "Leave that to me."

CHAPTER 17

"I'll be revenged on the whole pack of you."
~*Twelfth Night, Shakespeare*

Orlando

Romeo brushes his fingers along his jaw and shakes his head. "Jesus, man, you hit fucking good. Didn't waste any time in the big house, did you?"

The anger he showed just moments ago seems to have gone after a good hard fight. It's how we always settled shit as kids.

But that was before he was Don.

I feel sick to my stomach because I know the code. Right up with the Vow of Omertà is the vow we take to protect our Don, to defer to him in all circumstances, and to never, ever even speak disrespectfully to him. Before I went to prison, I gave a new soldier the beating of his life for talking back to Romeo. Even his wife speaks to him with nothing but respect, our own mother as well.

"I'm sorry," I say, but he's well within his right not to accept my apology. With one command, he could force me to my knees and tell one of my other brothers to pull the trigger. Execute me right then and there in front of my pregnant bride. I wouldn't even fight him. "Jesus, Romeo." I shake my head. "You went to hit her, and I saw red."

"As you should. She's your wife. I understand. Any of you bastards raised a hand to Vittoria, I'd kill you."

"So much for blood being thicker than water," Mario mutters, putting his gun away.

Romeo walks over to me and gives my shoulder a good-natured punch. "Put away your weapons." He sighs and looks at Elise. "I want her restrained or confined, though, brother. We don't know who she is or why she's here and we have questions to ask."

Fortunately, I've got a ready supply of restraints. She doesn't even fight me when I pull her arms together in front of her and cuff them.

"Nine months," I tell him. "She has nine months of pregnancy. I'll keep her here with me. We'll keep her prisoner. Make sure she brings the baby to term safely, has all her needs met. And then we'll deal with her after she has the baby."

She shifts on the bed and rests her hands on her stomach as if she's trying to protect the baby.

"The baby isn't going to be hurt." Jesus, as if I'd hurt my child.

Romeo walks around to her and crouches in front of her, his hands clasped. Squatting, he meets her gaze.

"Do you understand the severity of what you did?" he asks in that deadly tone he uses to interrogate our prisoners. I stand behind him, prepared to defend her and prepared to make her respond, whichever the case may be.

She nods. "I do. I know you could kill me. I knew that from the beginning."

He draws in a breath, then releases it slowly. "Where's the real Elise?" he asks. "Is she still alive?"

She blinks, and a tear rolls down her cheek. "I don't know, and I hope so."

Behind Romeo, Tavi nods. "She's telling the truth."

Romeo shakes his head from side to side. "You knew we'd find out the truth, didn't you? Eventually? Even Rosa knows the real Elise. You've been dodging bullets since you came here."

"Since I escaped the plane crash," she whispers. "Yes, I knew." She meets my gaze over his shoulder. "I did it to help my friend. She once saved my life, and it was only fair I save hers."

White-hot anger boils up in my belly. "She didn't come here to die. She came here to be married. I would've taken care of her. Protected her." I turn away with disgust. "Just like I have you."

She cries freely now, swiping at her tears. "I didn't know that. And she... she was in love with her bodyguard." A sob racks her shoulders. "But you killed him. You killed the only man she ever loved."

"We didn't kill him," I begin, but Tavi interrupts.

"I did. She had no right to love anyone," Tavi snaps. "I called that hit. I fucking knew it was a lie, all of it. I knew he betrayed our family and the Regazzas. I called Regazza and told him I'd end the traitor. He gave me his blessing. Told me to do what I had to." He shakes his head in disgust. "I hoped she'd come to you with the truth before we had to."

"I knew it," she says, shaking her head. "You're ruthless."

"You should know that by now," Tavi says, baring his teeth at her. I take a step toward him before I remember myself. I fist my hands.

Romeo stands and sighs. "Do you have any idea of the whereabouts of her friend?"

"She's somewhere outside of Italy," Tavi says. "But earlier tonight, she told her to come to her. Elise Regazza knows her friend is here." He turns to her. "Didn't you, Angelina?"

Angelina.

Angel.

Her real name is Angelina. The name fits her better than *Elise*.

It all makes sense now, it all clicks into place. The way she never knew Italian. The way she seemed too innocent to have been raised in the mob. The vague way she spoke of her family, and how so many times she didn't seem to fit the mold.

Romeo turns to me. "You'll keep her prisoner while we look for the real Elise. While she bears your child?"

My child.

My wife.

It feels so hollow now.

"Of course."

His eyes focus on mine for long moments, while he works his jaw. "The girls will want to interfere, you know."

"I know." Marialena and Vittoria won't like that she's prisoner. They'll fight us. "They'll have to be kept away."

"Punish me however you want after the baby's born," Angelina says. She lifts her chin bravely and meets my eyes while her own brim with tears. "I'm not sorry I took her place. My only regret is ever lying to you."

I cross the room and sigh. I cup her cheek with my hand. Her soft, sweet cheek, that fits perfectly in the palm of my hand. "Ah, sweetheart," I say with a note of sadness in my voice. "You'll have a lot more regrets than that before I'm through with you."

CHAPTER 18

"She sat like patience on a monument, Smiling at grief." ~*Twelfth Night, Shakespeare*

Angelina

I wanted the truth to be out, and now that it is, I don't regret it. I do have regrets, but telling the truth isn't one of them. If I had it to do over again, I would do it again for Elise. I only hope that none of it was in vain.

Everyone but Orlando leaves the room. There's a certain pall of silence that hangs in the air, and I don't know how to handle it. I squirm uncomfortably as he paces in front of me.

Orlando has always been very stern, my ass bears testament to that. In the short time I've been with him, I've learned what he likes. I've learned how to communicate with him. He has a sense of humor, and I can take some leeway, but he's a high-ranking member of the most dangerous mob in New England, and every day I don't forget that. I can't.

And now... I realize I almost have. Cuddling with him, showering with him, kissing him. Eating dinner with him, receiving gifts from him. Sitting on his lap. All of those sweet, precious moments I've had with him seem so far away now as I look at my angry, furious husband pacing in front of me.

He's told them that he will punish me. He asked for permission to be in charge of my punishment and imprisonment. He told me that I'd have regrets before he was done with me. And I didn't miss what he promised. He's going to keep me prisoner until I bear his child.

And then what? What happens with my child?

What happens when Elise finds her way here?

What if they find her first?

"What are they going to do?"

"Quiet." I freeze and clap my lips together. His anger vibrates in the room, a slithering snake about to strike. I don't want to be his victim.

Not that I blame him. I hate that there's a chasm of hurt between us, I hate that he's angry with me. But I did what I had to. And his family was the one that forced my hand. I never would've taken her place if she wasn't in danger.

But he told me he wouldn't have hurt her...

She was in love with Piero. But Tavi says she had no right to fall in love.

But if we ever had full control over who we fell in love with, would I be in love with the man in front of me now? Never.

I bury my face in my hands, and a wave of nausea ripples through me, making my mouth water. I swallow hard so I don't vomit.

"You go to bed. I'll deal with you in the morning. Tonight you're going to stay cuffed. Tomorrow I'll figure out what else to do with you."

When he walks to me, my voice is frail. Pleading. "Orlando."

A quick shake of his head silences me. I lay down on the pillow and go to put my hands under my cheek.

He pulls a blanket up over my shoulder. "Do you need anything to eat? Any water? How do you feel right now?" But I know his questions aren't because he's concerned about me. He's taking care of the baby. His baby.

I can't believe I'm pregnant.

"Did you truly know you were pregnant down in the dungeon?" he asks me. I will not tell another lie. I swallow and shake my head. "I didn't. I was only trying to buy time." He curses under his breath and turns away from me as if it pains him to look at me. He paces away. Then he turns back to me, his blue eyes blazing. "How much of what you've told me was a lie? All of it?"

"I told you I was Elise. I let you believe that I was a Regazza. But I'm not, obviously, you know that. But everything I told you about my family? True. Everything I told you about my father? True. Only, my father is not a Regazza. I know Elise's father, though, since I'm friends with her."

I turn away from him but can't turn too far away because I'm still restrained.

"I thought I loved you." His voice holds a hollow, cold tone that freezes my heart. I blink, hating that I shed tears I wish I couldn't. I wish I could freeze myself off from him, but it's useless. I sigh.

"Go to sleep. We'll deal with all of this in the morning."

I still feel the lash of the leather falls of the flogger from earlier. A strange part of me wishes he hadn't gone gentle, that he'd used something harsh and punishing. Then I could feel as if I'd paid my penance for the sins he hadn't known that I'd committed.

How was I to know I'd fall in love?

I watch in silence as he undresses and walks to the shower. The door shuts tight, and I hear when the water turns on. I want to be in there with him. I want to touch him, to feel him. Please him, even. I'd do anything now to make this right.

But I can't. God, I can't. I have to live with the consequences of the choices I made.

My phone buzzes in the bedside table. I try to reach for the drawer but can't open it with my wrists bound like this.

Where is she?

Elise is in more danger than she was before I took her place. Romeo said they would look for her, and Tavi put out a search party. He has records of our conversations and calls. He'll find her.

I told her to come to me.

She'll know I'm here. And when she comes... I close my eyes, suddenly so sleepy I can't keep them open any longer. I'm not dead yet, and that's the only plus so far in this terrible night. The only reason I'm not dead is because he did what he intended—impregnated me with his child. I used to hate the thought of bearing his child, but now it's the only thing that anchors me to him.

I wake in the middle of the night, immediately restless. I dreamed of being hidden in forests, running for my friend. And when I heard my husband calling my name, I turned to him. I open my eyes in the darkened room. I see Orlando, hunched over on the sofa. He twists and turns, and I know it isn't comfortable for a man his size to be squeezed onto a tiny little piece of furniture like that.

"Orlando?" He doesn't answer, but by the way his body goes still I know he heard me.

"Take the bed. You need it more than I do, and I can't sleep anyway." He doesn't respond at first, but he finally turns over and without opening his eyes mutters, "Go to sleep. If you think I'm such an asshole I would put my pregnant wife on a couch so I can take the bed, you don't know me at all."

So that's how it's going to be. I roll over but can't sleep. "Then get over here. So I fucked up. You know I did. You know I would do it again if I had to. And here I am, your prisoner, completely at your mercy. So get over here and lay down next to me and get a good night's sleep for God's sake."

To my surprise, he gets off the sofa, marches over to me, and lays down beside me, but only so he can turn me over and smack my ass so hard I gasp.

"Thought you knew," he says, "that you do not take that tone of voice with me and tell me what to do." He wraps his arm around me. I feel his hard length pressing against my butt. Just lying next to me he's hard. We've made love or had sex or fucked each other, whatever you wanna call it, every single night since we took our vows. Tonight might be the first time we don't.

"You're gonna break our cycle?"

I don't know why I am teasing him, why I am pushing him. If I was smart, I'd probably just shut my mouth and let him do his thing. Probably would be the right thing to do, considering I have no idea what's going to happen when Elise comes here. And

249

I don't know what it's going to be like being his prisoner.

"What are you talking about?" he says.

"This will be the first night you haven't fucked me."

He doesn't respond at first. Finally, he sighs. "I fucked you to put a baby in you. Now you have one. Mission accomplished. Now fucking go to sleep."

I hate the coldness in his voice, but he doesn't move away from me. In fact, it may be my imagination, but I think he moves even closer. Still, I close my eyes.

If I were him, I would imagine that I'd be pretty hurt right now. He fought Romeo for me, even though he knew full well that it was so against the rules that his own brothers drew weapons against him.

It's hard to fall asleep, with everything that's spinning in my mind, my fears above all. But finally, the trauma of the day and everything that's transpired wipes me out, and I fall into another troubled sleep.

I wake up the next morning with his hand between my legs. For a moment I forget who I am, who he is, and think that we're just a married couple that's enjoying honeymoon sex. But when I go to roll over, I feel my wrists restrained. And I remember…

Maybe he's the one that's forgotten, because his magic fingers work between my legs as if he can read my mind. He strokes me with the expert touches of his fingertips, and I already feel swollen and heated. Maybe it's pregnancy hormones, or more blood flowing down there than normal, but I'm immediately hot and bothered, panting as he strokes me harder and faster, dipping one finger lower between my legs to finger the edge of my channel. My legs part. And his hand stops. He rolls over and scoots away from me, tugs down his pajama bottoms and fists his cock.

"Let me..."

"No." He looks at me with cold, ruthless eyes as he jerks his cock, watching me the whole time. It takes long minutes before he nears release, gets to the end, throws his head back, and comes. I watch, mesmerized at the torturous look on his face. He's not doing this at all. He cleans himself up, then walks to the bathroom. I cry when the shower comes on. Try to reach my own fingers between my legs, but he's restrained me in such a way that I can't. He did this on purpose. The first stage of my punishment.

He won't whip me or hurt me in any way. He wouldn't, because his loyalty to the child within me is stronger than his loyalty to my punishment. But he'll find other ways, and I will regret what I've done.

Breakfast is a somber affair. I sit up in bed, and I don't know if it's the nerves I'm dealing with or the pregnancy hormones, but everything makes me queasy. He plies me with Nonna's scones and pastries, breakfast sausage and bacon, and it all turns my stomach.

"No, please. I'm going to be sick."

With a scowl, he holds up the wastebasket next to the bed. I lift my head just in time and vomit. I spit bile and spittle into the basket, then grimace and wipe my fingers—my wrists still fastened—across my mouth. Still scowling, he walks to the bathroom to clean out the basket and returns a few minutes later with a clean, damp washcloth, a towel, a toothbrush and a glass of water. With a tenderness belying the furious look in his eyes, he cleans my mouth, then dots my forehead with the towel.

He places his hand on my feverish cheek, then up to my forehead.

"You're burning up," he says angrily, as if I conjured a fever as part of the ruse.

"Probably just because I was sick," I say in a weak voice. I turn away from him. The pillow is cool, and now that the nausea's passed, it feels good. "I just need more sleep."

I close my eyes and sleep comes quickly.

The low murmur of voices drift from the doorway as I doze in and out of sleep, my stomach rumbling. I have a vague notion of lifting my head only to be sick, but every time Orlando's there to hold my hair then tuck me back into bed. I lose track of the time, and wake when the sun sets outside the window.

Have I slept all day?

Elise.

I sit up in a panic and reach for the bedside table, bound wrists and all.

"Did you really think I'd leave that there for you?"

Orlando sits in the dark recesses of a corner of the room, tucked into an overstuffed chair. He's got one ankle across his knee. I should've known.

I slump back in the bed and don't reply. If I speak, I'm going to cry.

"How are you feeling?"

I shrug. I still don't want to talk. I don't want to cry in front of him. I made the vow earlier on that I would never, and I've broken that now a few times.

No more.

"Answer me."

I jump at the harsh tone of his voice.

"I'm a little better," I whisper, still trying to prevent myself from crying. "Anything change today?"

"You mean are you still my prisoner? Yes. Are you still bound as my prisoner? Also, yes. Am I still staying Romeo's hand from ending your life? Of course, because you're pregnant with my child." I hate the feel of his anger, even though I earned it.

I don't look at him, I don't want to see him right now. I swipe my bound wrists at my eyes, dashing at my tears so he doesn't see.

"Why are you crying? We've taken it easy on you."

I don't know what to tell him.

Because I thought I loved you?

Because I fear for my friend's life?

Because I hate the thought of being nine months in a room with a man I love who no longer loves me back?

I just shake my head. He pushes himself to his feet and stalks over to me, his heat hitting me from across the room.

No, not now. I can't. Another wave of nausea hits and I sit up quickly, gesturing for the trash can which he brings to me just in time. There's nothing left in me. I haven't eaten all day, and I feel wrecked. My mouth tastes sour, and my stomach feels so empty it hurts.

He half-carries me to the bathroom where I freshen up, even as my eyes close from exhaustion. I brush my teeth and wash my face and use the facilities while he waits outside the door for me, then I take his arm as I walk unsteadily back to bed.

I crawl into bed and close my eyes.

I fall back asleep, and this time the only voices that stir in my dreams are my thoughts.

CHAPTER 19

"Whoe'er I woo, myself would be his wife." ~*Twelfth Night, Shakespeare*

ORLANDO

"Angelina." I try to keep the harsh tone of voice, but no matter how much I focus on what she's done and how she's earned what we're putting her through, all I see is the woman I fell in love with. The woman who gave herself to me to save her friend. The woman who carries my child.

She's so sick, she can't even hold water down at this point. By later that evening, I'm concerned. I call Mama.

She comes upstairs quickly, carrying a heated blanket, some tea bags, and a little bag of something I can't quite identify.

"How is she?" she asks.

I shake my head. Angelina stirs behind me.

"How much has Romeo told you?"

"Enough." My mother was wed to my father against her will, and her life was nothing but misery as a result. She knows we're bound by the rules of our brotherhood, that we've taken blood oaths of silence, obedience, and fidelity, at the very start of our promises to each other. She knows we walk a razor's edge when it comes to our safety among others, especially rival mafia. But her allegiance and sympathy will always be with the feminine species.

I don't think she could help it if she tried.

She walks to the side of the bed and sits beside Angelina.

It took me less time to adjust to her real name than I thought it would, but it suits her better. Mama's so small, so slight, the bed barely sags beneath her weight. Angelina rolls over and opens one eye.

"Hi," she says, her voice hoarse from being sick. "Don't know if you should be in here. I may be contagious."

My heart tightens. She's concerned for my mother, even when she's sick herself.

"Oh, I don't think I can catch what you have, I'm way too old," Mama laughs. "Here, sit up. Have some tea. It will help."

Angelina takes a sip from the mug and nods. "Thank you, that does. What is it?"

"Peppermint." Mama looks over her shoulder at me. "Go, Orlando. You've been here all day. Go take a walk, read a book. I'll sit with her."

I shake my head. "No, Mama. I'm staying here."

She rolls her eyes. "Even though Nonna made calzone tonight?"

Tempting. "Even then. Thanks for coming, Mama. I'll take it from here."

"Ah, so I'm dismissed, am I?"

I give her a tight smile and open the door.

When the door closes, Angelina's still sitting up in bed. "I do feel a bit better. I think." But her face looks a little green around the edges.

I get a phone call from Romeo and answer it quickly. "Hello?"

"I think we found her friend." I shake my head and turn away from Angelina. I don't want her to see or hear anything. It will only put her in a panic.

She stirs in the bed behind me, and releases a little moan. When I look over my shoulder at her, she has her hand on her belly. She's still sick.

"Where is she?"

"Looks like she stayed where she was. She hasn't made a move to come here at all."

"What are you going to do with her when you get to her?"

Romeo's quiet for long minutes. "The question is, is our deal with Regazza off the table now? He hasn't fulfilled his end of the bargain. He hasn't married to us. He hasn't given us a wife."

"He has, though. She's not our friend, I know. But the whole point of my marriage was that I would strengthen the family bond, bring a child to the table. And I've done that."

Romeo doesn't reply at first. "You married a woman who isn't mafia. She tricked you and deserves to be punished for that. If she wasn't pregnant, you know what would happen."

"And I *will* punish her." My voice is harsher than I intend. I did this very morning, when I made her watch me come, still teeming with her own arousal. One must be creative when punishing a pregnant woman.

I look over to see Angelina, but she's fallen asleep again.

He doesn't speak for a moment, but then when he does his voice is tight. "You know how I feel, Orlando. She's made our rules a mockery."

"For good reason."

No one talks back to Romeo. No one challenges the Don of the mafia. No one.

"Are you making an excuse for her?"

"Would you for Vittoria?"

He's quiet for another moment before he sighs.

"I'll do what I have to. You do what you have to. I'm working with Regazza to see where we stand after all this." He's actually letting this go. I breathe out a sigh of relief.

"No, thank you. I'll let you know if I hear anything else." I hang up the phone and go to her side of the bed.

I look at the woman lying there. Her cheeks are flushed pink, her lips parted and dry. Her hair is a tangled mess, but she's still absolutely beautiful, still the most beautiful woman I've ever seen. It hurts that she betrayed me. I hate that she's put me between her and my family, practically making me choose between the two of them. It isn't fair. After everything we've been through, both of us, to be in this position.

But Regazza promised us his daughter, and I'm not sure how much better off my family is than before she came here.

I know that I am, though. My entire world has tilted on its axis because of her, and not just because she's having my damn child.

I stand and walk away from her. I don't like being so close to her.

I want to touch her. Hold her.

I want to forgive her.

But forgiveness isn't in the Rossi code.

CHAPTER 20

"I shall crave of you your leave that I may bear my evils alone. It were a bad recompense for your love to lay any of them on you." ~ *Twelfth Night, Shakespeare*

Angelina

I lose track of how the days begin to blend into one another. I hope for something, anything, to end the miserable, torturous nausea and sickness and fever. Feverish dreams wake me from sound sleep, the sheets tangled and strangling me in the heat of the night, clinging to my sweat-drenched skin.

And all through it, Orlando takes care of me. Calls in a doctor to assess my condition and get me started on prenatal care. Brings me Nonna's good homemade soup and thick slices of bread with butter. The chicken broth tastes good, soothing my belly, and when I tell Orlando, he brings me steaming mugs of it to sip to ease my nausea.

I wake. Eat. Fall asleep, then begin it all again, all held hostage in my prison.

Will it ever end? Will I survive it?

I'm vaguely aware of him conducting business, but he speaks in low tones on the phone and rarely disturbs me. I wait for him to leave, half expecting him to station guards outside my door. He doesn't.

I'm always bound, even when bathing. He helps me, though.

A part of me wishes he wouldn't.

On the fourth day, my fever breaks. I sit up in bed and shiver. Orlando's in the shower, the heavy drone of the water like a thunderstorm in the background. I reach for my neck. I've never taken off the *Riot of Flowers*, my little diamond stars.

There's a slim silver laptop sitting on the bedside table within reach. With the water still running in the bathroom, I decide to risk it and dip my toes in the outside world. I take the laptop and tap in his password. I've watched him sign in and know it by heart.

I doubt he cares if I use it, though I know I'm not allowed on my phone.

I wonder about Elise. Is she coming here? Has she found a place to go?

Will she find me?

Or has someone else found her first?

I close my eyes with the thrum of heat that comes from fear, the prickling sensation along my neck that's not unlike the clenching of my belly. I haven't felt like myself in so long.

I tap on the laptop keyboard quickly. He didn't tell me I couldn't use it, but I definitely feel like I'm sneaking behind his back.

I want to look for Elise, see the latest news on her father, see if I can find out more about the Rossis. But instead... I find myself tapping out *Riot of Flowers Diamond Necklace*.

My cheeks heat, and my fingers come to rest on the lowest cluster of diamonds where it fits in the hollow of my neck.

Designed by the famous jewel smith James McAdams, the Riot of Flowers went for an amazing $5.1 million at a Christie's auction in Hong Kong. This exquisite masterpiece features twenty-six Burmese rubies and star-shaped diamonds with weights ranging from 1.27 to 5.38 carats. Each ruby is nestled beside a cluster of pear-shaped and white marquise diamonds. The diamonds and rubies are strategically placed to create a floral effect that makes the necklace resemble a riot of flowers. The precious gems are set in 18k white gold and precious platinum.

Five. Point. One. Million. Dollars.

This… this piece of jewelry right here could be my ticket to freedom. I could sell it to a dealer and live well for the rest of my days.

I close my eyes and stifle a sob. I know I could do that. I don't want to. It feels like utter theft to go from betraying the only man I've ever cared about to selling the only gift he ever gave me, this beautiful, symbolic piece of jewelry.

Five million dollars.

I quickly clear the browser history when I hear the shower turn off, then slide the computer back where it was.

A minute after the shower turns off, the door opens. His gaze immediately swings to me. "You behaving yourself?"

I don't want to lie anymore, and don't figure there's much that would get me in any worse trouble than I'm already in.

"Have you…" the words are hard to say. I draw in a breath then release it. "You haven't restricted my Internet use."

"I haven't. I knew you could access that laptop if you really wanted to."

I only nod. "That said, I… I looked up this necklace you gave me."

He turns away from me, as if the memory's too painful for him.

"It's too much, Orlando." I claw at the necklace, reaching for the clasp. "Even if things were good between us—"

"Don't say it. Don't you fucking say it." As he stalks my way, I can't help but let my gaze roam over his naked chest, the ink, his large biceps and defined abs. I turn away. I've never been attracted to anyone more in my entire life, and it pains me to think of what I've lost—not just the physical attraction but so much more.

So much more.

My hand rests on my abdomen, and I imagine what the next few months will be like. I swallow hard.

"You were worth it," he says, just before he reaches me. "You were fucking worth it."

Were.

I don't respond. A dull ache makes me feel listless. Even the bright sun outside the window seems dimmer.

I hate that he's talking as if it's in the past. I reach for the clasp and undo it, let it slither into my hand, and show it to him. "Here. I don't deserve this anymore." It doesn't feel right to keep it.

He only folds my fingers down over it. My body electrifies at the feel of his skin on mine, his large fingers with skulls encapsulating mine. He's barely touched me since this all went down. My throat burns from the pain of holding myself back from crying when he shakes his head. "It was a gift. I don't take back gifts."

"Orlando, a five million dollar—"

"Gift," he snaps, and his eyes flare with anger. The hurt in his voice makes tears spring to my own eyes. "I can't change any of this. If I could, I fucking would. Will you rob me of the one thing I can do? The only thing I can fucking give you?"

I wince. I didn't think of it that way.

"Thank you," I whisper. He doesn't respond at first. Finally, he stalks back over to the dresser and starts opening drawers.

"You look like you're feeling better." He drops the towel to the floor and stands there naked, picking through his clothes as if he doesn't have a care in the world, as if he doesn't even notice he's naked. He just doesn't care.

"Yeah, a little." The actual physical feeling of nausea and fever have passed, but I don't want to eat a thing. I stare listlessly out the window and finally push myself to standing.

Bad idea. My head spins and the room swirls around me. He catches me before I fall.

"What the hell happened?" I mutter. "What...?"

"Just get in bed," he says, supporting me with surprising gentleness. "You've hardly eaten a thing. Get some food in you."

"I don't want to eat."

He swings his hand and smacks my ass, hard. It's the first time he's spanked me since I told him I was pregnant, and it shocks me. I blink at him in surprise.

"Did I ask if you want to eat?" he snaps. I bite my lip and sit on the bed, then crawl to the pillows. It feels so good to rest again.

"Women have been doing this for millennia. *How*?"

He shrugs. "I think you were sick on top of everything."

When he turns back to his clothes, I rub my hand across my ass. It still stings. I bite my lip.

He's also turned me on.

I watch him dress in a sort of detached state of mind, like I'm out of my body and am not really here. When he's dressed, he pulls his phone out and goes to make a call.

"What do you want to eat?"

"I don't want to eat." The bed feels so comfortable. Dammit, I thought I was getting better but now my stomach feels hollow and achy.

"You're going to fucking eat."

"Of all the things to force me to—" I didn't realize he was right next to me, so close to me he could roll me over and silence me with his mouth on mine.

It isn't a kiss. A kiss is a word too gentle, too romantic for the way his lips abuse mine, like he brandishes his own body as a weapon of assault against me. I'm gasping for air when his tongue lashes mine. Fear and arousal spike my pulse. I knife up, flailing, but he only pins me beneath him and plunders my mouth.

When he finally releases me from the spellbinding assault, he grates in my ear, "Don't you fucking dare. I don't care if you're pregnant, don't you fucking dare push me right now. I will tie you to the bed and use the flogger on you until your whole body sings and throbs, then I will take you to the edge of climax and leave you there for fucking days."

A dry sob escapes me before I can stop it. He's edged me and spanked me and restrained me, but nothing punishes me worse than his simmering anger that I can't appease. I hate it. I hate it so much I want to claw at it and strangle it.

"And don't you fucking cry," he says, as his own voice breaks. "You took the only thing I've ever wanted and made a motherfucking mockery of it, a *mockery* of it!" I'm no longer constantly restrained, and he tangles my wrists in his fingers as he pins them above my head. "And I hate you, I fucking hate you for it."

I'm sobbing freely now as he holds me with his left hand and undresses me with his right. His thick, hard length presses to my belly.

"I hate you, too," I lie, knowing that his own words are lies of the highest order. A man like him would hate me by exiling me, not tying me to his bed and spoon-feeding me soup and holding my hair while I was sick, not by giving up every minute of his day to make sure I'm taken care of.

He kisses my tear-stained cheeks, and that's when I see his own tears shining in his eyes. My heart throbs in pain at seeing his.

"I hate you," he grates though his own misery and pain, as he pushes his cock to my entrance and thrusts, one perfect, agonizing burst of pleasure. And then his hands are on either side of my face while we move together, my hips rising to meet his thrusts, his cock filling me to perfection. He kisses me so fiercely I can't breathe. I'm suffocating under his heat and wrath, even as my body spasms with the first ripple of bliss. He's edged me for so long now, I'm about to combust.

I kiss him back. I lick his tongue and inhale his groan, I spread my legs and meet his strokes, I yield to his thrusts and kiss and utter domination.

"I hate you," he whispers, but his words are hollow and weak, a fading clang of a bell that's swallowed into the night. We roll over, me on top of him now as he tangles me in his limbs and continues his thrusting with perfect savagery. Tender lovemaking right now would slay me. I crave his fierceness to meet my pain.

My climax hits a crescendo as he screams his own rage and pleasure. We welcome the little death of self. I lay my hand on his cheek. He lets me.

"I love you," he whispers. "I fucking love you."

I lay my head on his chest and weep.

CHAPTER 21

"Alas, the frailty is to blame, not we, For such as we are made of, such we be." ~ *Twelfth Night, Shakespeare*

ORLANDO

Once, before my latest imprisonment, before Romeo met Vittoria and my father died, I was taken prisoner by rival mafia. I was chained and beaten, tortured and abused. I was left in my own filth for days on end and only kept alive with the bare minimum of food and water. And that... that torture is nothing compared to what I'm going through with Angelina.

How could I think I'd survive nine months as her warden? I fucking won't. She won't either.

Goddamn it.

Marialena and Vittoria try to visit, but Romeo puts an emphatic end to that. No way will he allow them to interfere with what has to be done.

That's on me. It's all on me.

Angelina is lonely, though. She misses the girls, misses the rest of my family. In the short time she had with them, they all got along so well, it was as if she were designed for this family herself.

She sits with a book, but it's fallen to the table, open.

"Book isn't any good?"

I watch her shrug her slender shoulder listlessly. "It just doesn't hold my interest."

"I could get you something else," I say but don't look at her when I do. "More books. I don't know. Knitting needles or whatever the fuck."

She gives me a withering look that's almost comical before turning away. "Not sure Romeo would approve of a hobby with a tool that could double as a weapon."

Yeah, she isn't the knitting type. Even in prison there are libraries and weight rooms, classes you can take. Chapel.

"Thanks anyway," she says in a hollow voice. "That's kind of you but I'm good."

I shouldn't feel the sympathy for her that I feel, I know I shouldn't, but I'd have to have a heart made of stone not to. She isn't like the prisoners who've had their punishment coming to them.

Sure, she fucked up. She *royally* fucked up, and we both know it, but I still feel myself softening toward her.

Romeo would kick my ass and assign someone else to her if he knew how I really feel. He probably thinks he's being merciful, allowing me time with her.

He has no idea. I didn't, either. It's fucking torture.

I wonder if she's sinking into a depression. After all that's happened, that wouldn't surprise me at all.

I shouldn't care. It doesn't matter how she feels. The woman means nothing to me. I'm only here to make sure she takes care of herself for our growing child, like a prison warden watching over a surrogate.

Christ.

My mind won't rest, as I move from one thought to the next. I'm here with her for a reason, to uphold my family's expectations and to follow through on her punishment. I know why I'm holding her here, I know it in my head... but in my heart, this is so wrong it's painful. It's the worst job I've ever had.

Romeo's come to me and offered to station another guard with her, or an army of guards if I want them. Our men are trained well and bound by loyalty to defend and protect unto death. She'd be safe under their watchful eyes, and I'd get the space I need to begin to heal from all of this. But I won't ever let anyone take my place. Never.

I married Angelina. That's my child she's carrying within her. I'm the one that will guard her, even if it kills me.

But now that she's going to have my child, the question remains... how will we continue to strengthen the Rossi family? A child without a mother leaves a gaping hole in our plan for fortification.

And the thought of raising a child of Angelina's without her...

"We can't stay up here forever, Orlando," she says on a whisper. "We can't. We both know that."

I turn away from her. I can't listen to her plaintive whispers or reason with her. If I do, then it feels like we're a couple again, and we can't go there.

"What if..." her voice trails off as she worries her lip. She sits in nothing but a little tank top and shorts, staring out the window that overlooks the ocean. Here in Gloucester, apart from everyone and everything, we're practically on an island. The exact opposite of what it's like at our home in Boston. A part of me wishes that wasn't the case, that we could be among the hustle and bustle of the city as a form of distraction.

She's safer here, though. At least I tell myself that.

"What if what?"

"What if we escaped?" she whispers. She won't look at my eyes, but I won't allow her to make suggestions like this without owning them fully. I walk over to her and reach for her face, dragging her gaze to mine.

"I'm not the prisoner here."

She doesn't look away or even blink. "Aren't you, though?"

"Angelina..." I love her real name. It feels real and authentic and fitting, like honey on my lips.

It's the first time I've ever considered the fact that she may have a point, but it makes me angry.

"What the fuck are you talking about?"

"Do you have free will?" she says in that steely voice that doesn't waver, doesn't back down in the face of her own safety. "You didn't marry who you wanted to. You don't behave the way you want to. You don't stay here because you choose it but because you feel you have no choice."

Rage boils within me, hot and furious. My hands clench harder on either side of her face, and she winces but doesn't push me away, doesn't even blink. I release her because I don't trust myself not to hurt her.

"You don't know what you're talking about." She doesn't. She wasn't raised in the mafia. She doesn't know the vital connection of family that runs through me like blood through my veins. I live, breathe, and die by the conviction to love them, to protect them, and turning my back on them to pursue my own relationship would be the height of narcissism and selfishness. I saw what that did to my father. I wouldn't do it to anyone. I couldn't.

"Orlando," she says gently. "You have your own family now. Me. Our baby." Her voice cracks at the end, breaking my heart.

"I know," I whisper. "I know. But I have family here, too. My brothers, my sisters, my mother. We all took oaths, Angelina." I draw in a deep breath. "Look at me."

Her eyes come to mine, and they're filled with tears. She knew when she asked me this what I would say. She knew what my answer would be. It doesn't make it hurt any less.

She put me in this position. It's because of her that we're here to begin with.

I turn my back on her and walk away.

"We can't leave. You know that, and so do I. And even if I could, I don't want to."

She nods sadly and rests her fingers in her lap.

"But we can leave this room. You may be my prisoner, but that doesn't mean we don't have some freedom within the confines of our home." I'll have guards at every door, and I won't let her out of my sight. "Get dressed and we'll go to the library."

She blinks in surprise before she leaps to her feet and hurries to dress. I watch her tug on leggings and an oversized sweatshirt, my heart aching. I love watching her dress. I love her simplicity and whole-someness. Even now, her excitement over heading to the library makes me want to hold her to me and kiss her cheeks until she blushes.

Guards flank us on either side as we head down-stairs. Romeo is talking with Tavi in the Great Hall. They pause their conversation as he notices us but it's barely noticeable, and he quickly nods his head before talking again. He trusts me. I won't forget that.

"Ah, Angelina!" Rosa meets us at the dining room. "It's a pleasure to meet you." She reaches for her hand and clasps it with both of hers before she tugs her in to kiss each cheek.

"Thank you," Angelina says. "And you must be Rosa."

Rosa, my eldest sister, as always is dressed as if ready for a runway, complete with stiletto heels and a form-fitting dress that was likely custom-made. The scent of decadent perfume enrobes us, cloaking her like a veil.

"Natalia speaks so highly of you," she says. "And congratulations! I am so excited for you and Orlando."

I'm losing my patience, my voice a low growl. "Rosa."

"I know, I know." She waves her hand at me. "I've heard what Romeo said. I was at dinner when he filled us all in. But don't take this away from me, Orlando. I gained a sister when you married, whether she is who she was supposed to be or not."

As she turns to leave, Marialena comes downstairs.

"Ah, there she is, and there's her *prison warden*." Her words are laced with venom as she stabs her finger at me. "I don't know who you guys think you are with your swagger, like you know everything there is to know and you're the god Zeus himself."

"Marialena, *enough*."

She opens her mouth then clamps it shut again, as if thinking better of what she was about to say. She silently fumes, then shakes her head.

"No. *No*, Orlando, this is wrong. So she isn't Elise Regazza, and thank God because that girl is boring as fuck compared to Angelina."

"Hey!" Angelina protests but her eyes are shining. "That's not fair."

"I didn't say I didn't like Elise, just that you're way better," Marialena says, waving her hand as if to dismiss Angelina. "She's got your baby in her, so obviously, you know, *ew*, but still. You've gone there."

"Marialena, for the love of God—"

"What's going on over here?" Romeo strolls casually over, his hands in his pockets. "Is there a problem?"

"I think you men are archaic idiots," Marilena snaps. "To hold a woman prisoner. Who is having *his child*. After she gave her entire life for her friend? Ha!" she scoffs. Her furious eyes swing to mine. "You know what? You don't deserve a woman like her. Uh uh. You want a brainless idiot like those Campanelles marry? Hmm? You could've had your pick of them. How many women are willing and able to give you a pretty little virgin pussy in exchange for being a mafia princess? Brainless idiots, that's who."

Even Rosa gasps. My father would've slapped her face right in front of everyone before he dragged her upstairs and exiled her to her room for a month.

But Romeo is not my father. "Do you think Vittoria a brainless idiot?" he asks mildly, a tone that we all know spells danger.

"Of course not," she says. "But if you think, for one minute, that I'm going to stay here and allow you men to treat her this way, you're wrong." She shakes with the intensity of her anger, vibrating with it while everyone, including staff, watches. A door opens at the top of the stairs and Santo stands scowling, his hands in his pockets. Rosa looks up at him, then back to Marialena.

"You know better than this," I scold her, shocked at her audacity. She knows how we function. She knows our rules. Unlike Angelina, she's been raised to respect our family from the cradle.

"Ah, I know you won't," Romeo says, leaning up against the banister. "You made that clear, didn't you?"

Everyone stands silent. We've accepted Romeo as Don from the moment he took my father's place. He makes difficult decisions, but decisions we respect nonetheless. We've never seen his authority questioned so boldly. I want to shake Marialena for it.

"Which is why you'll spend the rest of the time during Angelina's confinement in Tuscany." He looks up at Santo. "You'll take her, Santo?"

Santo nods. "Of course." He knows it isn't a question, but a command phrased politely.

Romeo looks back to Marialena. "You have one hour."

"Romeo." Marialena's face blanches. "No, I can't —"

"You can and will," he says with an air of final authority that we all know is immovable. "One hour, Marialena. One more word from you, and we leave now." He turns to Rosa. "Will you question this as well?"

Santo speaks up. "You know she won't, Rome."

Rosa shakes her head. "No. I trust you."

She has opinions of her own, as she should, but she's not one to question authority or to upset things as they are. She's grown jaded to the ways of

The Family while Marialena still holds a candle for justice.

Marialena mutters under her breath as she stomps upstairs to pack.

Romeo turns to me. "Where are you taking Angelina?"

"The library."

He nods, giving us permission. "Go."

When we enter the library, so quiet, so removed from every other part of the house, Angelina sighs.

"Ugh, I feel terrible about this. Terrible. I can't believe Marialena's being sent away because of *me*." She slumps into a chair and closes her eyes as if to staunch the flow of emotion.

I shrug. "It's not because of you. She took that on herself. And believe me when I tell you, she's hardly imprisoned in Tuscany." She's got friends galore, an entire suite to herself, and even a part-time job at the Tuscan springs. "She doesn't want to go because he's making her, not because she dislikes it." I wave my hand at the tables, chairs, and books that fill the library. She opens her eyes. "Now go. Find something to read."

I busy myself doing business on my phone. I hear insistent voices down the hall, rising and falling, and put my phone down to listen harder. The dogs bark to warn us that guests have arrived. From the library, I can't see anything.

I wonder who it is. Guests rarely come here unbidden.

Romeo calls me.

"Yeah?"

"Get over here, Orlando. Regazza's come."

CHAPTER 22

"Journeys end in lovers meeting." ~*Twelfth Night, Shakespeare*

Angelina

"Regazza?" Orlando scowls, staring at me but not seeing me.

I'm on my feet, my fists by my sides.

Elise Regazza? Did she make it here after all?

What did I think would happen, that she'd show up and we'd have a welcome party? She betrayed this family right along with me, and we both are suffering the effects of that choice. Only I have a talisman with the child I carry.

Elise has no such luck. They'll kill her when they see her.

Orlando makes a gesture for me to sit, but I couldn't sit now if he held a gun to my head. I shake my head at him, frantic, and take a step toward him.

"Just a minute, Romeo," he says. With a scowl, he puts the phone on mute and places it in his pocket. He grabs my arm, swings his out in an arc, and cracks his hand against my ass. "Sit your ass down. It's never been more crucial for you to do exactly what I fucking say. Sit. *Down.*" He punctuates each word with another stinging slap of his palm.

Should've gotten the doctor to lie to him and tell him to be more careful with a pregnant woman. Jesus.

I sit on my stinging ass, my heartbeat skipping erratically.

"I'll be right down."

He hangs up the call and faces me.

"What the fuck came over you just now?" He stands wearing a T-shirt and jeans, his feet apart and planted in his boots, but it's the look in his eyes that makes him scarier than I've ever seen him. "You've been a model fucking prisoner and now you openly defy me? You saw what happened to Marialena just now."

When he takes a step toward me, my pulse races. "Is she here? Elise?"

It would be the biggest mistake of all if she showed up here openly. My coming here and taking her place would've been in vain, if she isn't safe, if I didn't protect her.

Orlando shakes his head. "You thought when I said Regazza I meant your friend? No. It isn't her." He curses in Italian, faint splotches of red coloring his cheeks. "It's her fucking father."

Some might say Romeo's a scary Don, and I'm sure if I heard stories of what he's done, I might agree. And he is scary. He basically issued an edict for his sister's exile from the country for questioning his choices, and I know he's no stranger to murder. He scares me. I have a feeling a good discussion with Orlando about what Romeo's done would only make that worse.

But he's *nothing* like Elise's father.

I spent my days as a child with Elise in the Catholic Church, attending every sacrament with her and her father as if he wasn't a full-fledged criminal. We went to mass every Sunday. And I distinctly remember one sermon the pastor gave about Satan and his wicked ways. I stared at the statue of St. Michael, his beautiful wings on full display as he raised his sword and crushed the demon under his foot. I imagined myself under his protection, but that isn't why I think of him now.

The demon reminded me of Elise's father.

No.

My voice is a strangled cry. "Why? Why is he here?"

Orlando gives me a withering look. "Why is he here? Because he owes us his life because of what you and Elise did. He's probably come to grovel at Romeo's fucking feet and throw his daughter under a bus, isn't he? We'll see. I have to go deal with him." But something troubles him. He doesn't trust Regazza, I'm sure of it.

I wouldn't either.

Orlando reaches the door and then shakes his head. "Jesus, I don't trust you in here."

I'm on my feet, pacing a few feet behind him. "I'm not going to do anything, I—"

He tosses a palm up to stop me. "No, Angelina. I don't trust that you're safe here." He scowls at the uniformed men outside the door, armed to the teeth. "Not when Regazza's here." Without warning, he spins on his heel and reaches for me.

He tangles his fingers in my hair and yanks me over to him. "I'm sorry," he says. "I'm so sorry for all of this."

It's the last thing I expect him to say. I rest my head in the hollow of his neck and force myself not to cry, not again.

"Me, too," I whisper.

His mouth is on mine, hot and insistent. My head falls back and my knees buckle, but he holds me upright against him. I love this man so much it makes me ache inside. His tongue plunders my mouth, and I taste the wet saltiness of tears, his or mine I don't know.

"I'll do whatever I have to, Angelina. I'm going to bargain with Romeo. We have hard and fast rules, but I've given everything for my family. It's time I asked them to give back."

Hope blooms in my heart. Does he...does he think he can make this work?

"What do you mean?" I whisper.

"I don't know yet," he whispers back. "But I know I'm not going to let this go." He holds me so fiercely it hurts, but it's just what I need.

"We'll have rules, Angelina. We'll have to start from the very beginning."

"We will." I close my eyes and hold him tighter. "I can do that."

I want to show him the real me, not the half-hearted version of me pretending to be someone else. And I want to know the real him—the one unencumbered with the demands of making me his. The one who *chose* me to be his wife.

Will they even allow it? Or will he, like so many others, be exiled from everyone he's known and loved?

I know I'm not the only one he's obligated to. I know this.

"Go upstairs with me. And you do exactly what I say. This is not the time to step even one tiny little toe out of line."

I nod. My heart feels as if it's going to burst, my pulse races so fast. Elise's father made me quake before I had reason to fear him.

"Quickly, Angelina. Tell me about Elise."

I don't expect the question. "What?"

"Was she really raised mafia?"

"She was. She hated it because her father's ruthless and as an only child she had the full force of his attention. She's a little spoiled, likes to shop. But she's loyal and kind and hardworking."

He nods. "Good to know."

I can't imagine what bargaining chip he has up his sleeve.

I gather up my courage and draw in a deep breath, then let it out slowly. I can do this. We can do this. It isn't just me; it isn't just Orlando. I'm having his baby. We're a family now, and no matter what happens, I'm going to do whatever it takes to take care of my family.

CHAPTER 23

"Love sought is good, but giv'n unsought is better."
~ *Twelfth Night, Shakespeare*

ORLANDO

THERE COMES a time in a man's life when he has to make the right decision—for himself, for his family, for the course of the rest of his life. And I know in my heart I've made the right decision.

I've given my whole life to The Family. I'd lay down my life for my brothers. But I'm not going to turn my back on the woman I love for the sake of rules and codes that were written before I was even born. Before Romeo was, even. Rules were meant to be broken, and sometimes laws need to change.

We've never married for love, it's only happened accidentally. But this time...this time I choose love.

This time I choose Angelina. If I'd been in her position, would I have even had the courage to do what she did?

But first, we deal with Regazza. Together.

Romeo's arranged it so Regazza sits in the reception room at the entrance to The Castle, the room where he hosts all our guests, which means Angelina and I have to walk the entirety of The Castle to get to them. Through the library, past the kitchen and pantry, through the sun room, then past the courtyard and Great Hall I hold Angelina's hand.

My wife is safe here, my family is safe. Staff roams through the majestic home, the home I grew up in, a structure of such massive fortitude it's hard to imagine it not withstanding any natural or man-made disaster. Past the coat room and one of the spiral staircases that lead upstairs, we finally reach the main lobby and reception room.

The reception room is outfitted for hosting, with an imposing fireplace flanked with bricks, sturdy furniture, and an opulent display of our best wines, whiskeys, and liquors. Romeo's had high-ranking officials here, politicians, mafia Dons from all over the world. Tonight, the tension in the air hangs like velvet drapes, smothering and oppressive.

"There he is," Angelina whispers to me in the doorway. "Luigi Regazza." I look in surprise to see a small, slight man sitting beside Romeo on the sofa by the fireplace. Thin, wiry gray hair and a scant beard make him look older than he is. His large, bland eyes reminiscent of an ancient barn owl barely focus as he sips a whiskey. If I didn't know what he was capable of, I'd think he could barely tie his own fucking shoelaces. It's only a ruse, though. Convenient to give an air of frailty when it couldn't be further from the truth.

He rises when we enter, bowing to us, but I don't miss the wicked glint of hatred in his eyes.

"Ah, the newlyweds. Welcome and congratulations."

"Thank you." I look to Romeo for guidance, but he only stares at me, unblinking, before giving me a short nod. He trusts me but does not trust the man who sits across from him.

It's hard to imagine a man so small even wields the power that he does, but Romeo has told me the story of his deeds. They read like a textbook on crime one might read when studying criminal justice in college. If there were felonies he could've committed to rise to the top of power among Italian mafia families, he checked off every damn one.

"Angelina. Orlando," Romeo says. "Have a seat, please. Drink?"

A member of staff walks over with a tray of wine-glasses. Angelina frowns when she looks at them.

"Ah, no wine for me," she says, but she seems distracted and thoughtful.

"Tea, then, Miss?" one of the staff members asks. I don't recognize any of them, but I've been away so long I don't think much of it. Still, Angelina's uneasy. She looks as if she wants to say something, then shakes her head.

"Tea would be lovely, thank you."

She stares hard at the staff who bows in front of her and leaves to prepare her drink. I bend my mouth to her ear. "Everything okay?"

She shrugs. "I think so?" she whispers.

It isn't, though, we both know it. Regazza is as ruthless as they come, and if I wasn't sitting right here beside her, if she wasn't sitting in the presence of my brothers and guarded on all sides by my staff, she'd be dead.

It's because of her that his plan to escape retribution from my family went sideways. In his eyes, that's worthy of death.

"You have a traitor among you, Romeo," Regazza says, leaning back in his chair. "And yet she wanders free without any mark of punishment on her."

My blood begins to boil.

"You mean my wife?" I ask, tossing the gauntlet into the ring. "It seems your daughter is the one who betrayed us, Luigi. For shame." My body vibrates with the need to hurt him. I gesture for staff to bring me a glass of wine, hold the stem between my fingers, and drink heartily.

A vein pulses in his temple. "How dare you," he growls.

Romeo clears his throat. Unlike others who bluster and swagger, Romeo grows deadly when his temper ignites, like a poisonous snake coiling before he strikes. When he speaks to Regazza, his voice is so low I can hardly make out the words.

"He's right, Luigi," Romeo says. "And you know it. Angelina is under the protection of my family now."

She stiffens by my side. She's under the protection of my family only for the length of her pregnancy, as far as Romeo's concerned, but Regazza doesn't need to know that, and I'm doing everything in my power to change that.

"On what grounds?" Luigi has the audacity to snap.

"She's pregnant with my child." I place my wine-glass on the coffee table. My fingertips tighten around the glass, steadying my shaking hand.

Regazza rises in seconds, but before he's even on his feet, I've drawn my gun and cocked it. Pride swells in my chest to see not just mine, but the gun of every one of my brothers trained on Regazza. All but Romeo, who sits back, crosses one leg over one knee, and laces his fingers together.

"You were saying, Luigi?" On instinct, Regazza looks to his bodyguards, but they've been immobilized several paces behind him. He won't be allowed protection, not here.

Regazza scowls but doesn't sit. "You think you're so much better than me, don't you?"

Romeo smiles. "I don't think it, Luigi."

A vein pulses in Regazza's temple and he twitches. The man has more nervous habits than a dealer, tapping his foot, yanking down his sleeves. Waiting for his next hit?

I step over to him, casually tap the back of his knee with my foot, and he collapses on the couch behind him. "Have a seat," I say amiably. Angelina's eyes dance. This man has been someone she's feared likely her entire life.

Not anymore.

Romeo speaks as pleasantly as if we were having lunch in the garden. "Why don't we chat like friends, Luigi?"

The door to the Great Hall opens, and Mama walks in in stilettos, as poised and majestic as ever. She smiles, but it's the type of smile that doesn't quite reach her eyes. "Luigi, how are you? How is Anna?"

Regazza scowls. "She's fine," he lies. We all know they live on separate continents for reasons we don't care to know.

"Now, back to business," Romeo says. "Stay seated, Regazza, or the next words out of your mouth will find you restrained. And we don't want that, now, do we?"

As Don of the Regazza family mob, Luigi Regazza isn't used to not getting his way. He's got a reputation for being savage, ruling like the tyrant that he is. I wonder how he's plotting his revenge for Romeo for taking control and putting him in his place. And he will get his revenge, but only after we've bargained for exactly what we want.

"Of course not," Luigi says with mock repentance. "But you understand that Angelina's life is under my control now. I'm sure we can agree to that. Children or pregnancies or no, she betrayed my family by negating the agreement we had."

"Actually," Tavi says coolly, pausing to take a sip of wine, "I believe it was your daughter who did that." His merciless gaze lingers on Angelina for a fraction of a second before swinging back to Regazza's. "And we have a proposal involving your daughter and me."

Regazza sits back in his chair, white with fury. "I have no daughter." He contorts his face as if to spit, but Mama speaks up.

"Oh, Luigi, I wouldn't do that if I were you. These rugs were a gift, and if you spoil my home, my sons will not look kindly upon you." She yawns as if bored and inspects her cuticles. "In fact, if my husband were here, I think he'd agree with me that they've already granted you far more grace than you actually deserve."

Luigi opens his mouth as if to say something scathing to Mama. I have a vague recollection that the man Mama had an affair with was an archrival to Regazza, but I haven't bothered with the details. Mario, however, casually shifts his suit coat to reveal his gun, which he lovingly strokes in front of Regazza. Disrespect to any female member of my household would earn swift and severe punishment or death, and Regazza knows this. He chooses instead to continue the façade of pleasantries.

"And for that I'm so grateful, Tosca. We've all been granted grace we don't deserve, haven't we?"

Her gaze grows cold.

"As I was saying," Tavi continues, as if Mama and Regazza haven't been hurling sugarcoated insults at each other. "Romeo and I are willing to excuse your betrayal and allow Angelina to live, seeing as she's taken vows to my brother and carries his child, under one condition."

"Oh?" Regazza says, but his eyes gleam with keen interest. He knows his life is forfeit to us and we're granting him a second chance at life. I watch as he shifts restlessly in his seat and tugs down his suit coat jacket. Odd.

"Give us your daughter. Your actual daughter this time."

Angelina gasps and raises her hand to her mouth, her eyes meeting mine. I nod at her, encouraging her to trust Romeo, to trust Tavi. To trust me. My brothers would lay down their lives for each other, any of them, and I know beyond a shadow of a doubt that they would do anything for me.

"I don't even know where she is," Regazza begins, his beady, watery eyes pleading for mercy where he'll get none.

"Under normal circumstances, that would be a problem," Tavi says with a frown. "But fortunately for you, I know exactly where she is."

I reach for Angelina's hand and give her a gentle squeeze. Regazza stares at me, then her, and shakes his head. "I was set up. You set me up to play me for a fool so you'd gain two women instead of one."

Romeo casually nods to our guards to come closer. Silently, they obey. Mario removes his gun and holds it by his side. Killing the Don of another family without starting a war of massive proportions will be excused only under certain conditions. He has to raise a weapon to us first or issue a threat against one of the inner circle or their loved ones.

He's fucking close.

Angelina looks to me, and I give her a nod. I know she wants permission to speak. I want to gather her to me and kiss every inch of her. I'm proud of her for waiting, for not setting foot into the lion's den unaware.

"Yes, baby?" I ask. Our affection for each other seems to infuriate Regazza even more, but he has no way to hurt us without risking his own life.

"We didn't try to play you at all," she says, shaking her head. "I promise. I only tried to help my friend escape a life she didn't want to lead." Her voice shakes, but she continues nonetheless. "A life that… a life that you chose for her."

Regazza's watery eyes narrow on my wife. I hope he does pull a weapon. I'd slice his throat right here, right now, gleefully.

Mama's rugs are replaceable.

"You filthy liar," he growls. "I always thought you weren't good enough for my daughter. I always thought—"

"Right," Tavi says when I brandish my own weapon, cutting Regazza off mid-sentence. "Back to your daughter? She was promised in marriage to my brother, and she did not show at that altar. She'll be punished for that, but we'll grant her life if she fulfills her end of the agreement belatedly."

"Where is she?" Regazza says. "I'll punish her myself before you lay your hands on her."

Tavi laughs. "Ah, no, you won't. I've got her secured. I've been tracking her now for quite some time."

Son of a bitch. Brilliant, ruthless son of a bitch. Romeo doesn't register surprise. None of this is news to him.

"Take my daughter if it will get you off my back," he says, shifting restlessly. "Fine. Take her."

"Ah, Luigi." Romeo shakes his head. "We've granted you impunity for infractions that would bring severe consequences to anyone else. I believe a thank you is in order."

Luigi's lips thin. "Thank you," he says, shaking his head.

"A few conditions, before you go," Tavi says. Regazza doesn't bother to hide his hatred.

"You will not set foot on our property again for the remainder of your life, nor will anyone from the Regazza family."

"Fine. A done deal." Regazza looks bored as his eyes dart around the room. I've convinced myself he's a user. I look him over and see the classic signs of an addict — persistant sniffling, scratching at his arm and tugging down his sleeves.

Angelina watches all of this with wide-eyed shock. I, on the other hand, love this plan. It is the very one I was going to propose to Romeo, and why I asked Angelina about her friend.

She'll need time. Tavi is the one responsible for the death of Elise Regazza's bodyguard. But we'll spare her life in the process. And honestly, we all need time to recover from what's happened.

As we discuss details and arrangements, staff enters the room with trays of coffee and tea. One hands Angelina a cup.

Angelina reaches for it, but she's staring at the woman who serves it to her.

The woman turns from her and meets Regazza's gaze. His lips tip up, a conspiratorial look if ever I've seen one.

It's a fatal mistake.

As soon as his eyes meet hers, I know. They know each other. Vicious, savage fury boils in my veins. I can hardly control my voice.

"Put that down, Angelina." She freezes with the drink to her lips. I smack it from her hands and she screams when it smashes on the bricks by the fireplace, at the very same second someone—Marialena?—screams in the hallway. Regazza wastes no time. He draws his weapon, but he's old and unused to fighting for himself. I grab my wineglass, smash the fluted top on the coffee table, and lunge at him with the ragged glass stem.

My mother screams as Marialena runs into the room and straight to Mario. Regazza lunges for Angelina, but I swipe at his throat with my makeshift weapon. Seconds after I slice his throat, Tavi and Santo's guns are drawn. Regazza's grasping at his throat, scarlet blood coating his hands, gurgling for his life as they pull the triggers.

Romeo scowls but misses nothing. "Mario!" he shouts, as the woman who served Angelina her drink runs. Mario tackles her to the floor, and quickly restrains her.

Mama pours herself a scotch and shakes her head.

"Maya, it's Maya," Marialena says. "I found her in the pantry..."

Maya, one of the most loyal of our staff. I shake my head, but Romeo stands tall and begins to issue commands.

"Santo, secure Regazza's body. Tavi, you have it all recorded?"

"Of course, brother," Tavi says with a nod.

I hold Angelina to my side as Romeo looks at us. "Good call, Orlando." He smiles at Angelina. "He saved your life, sweetheart. Remember that."

Angelina looks up at me in shock. "She was the flight attendant. She flew me over here from Tuscany." Even Tavi, who seems to be one step ahead of everyone else, blinks in surprise.

"Who?"

Angelina nods to the staff member restrained by Mario. "Her."

"No shit," he mutters. "Want me to kill her?"

"Not yet," Romeo says with a sigh. "Take her to the dungeon."

"She looked vaguely familiar," Angelina says, shaking her head. "But I couldn't place her."

Mario yanks his captive's hair. "Tell the truth. Who are you?"

She doesn't even try to fight him. "If I tell you the truth, will you spare my life?"

Mario shrugs. "There's a small chance."

The woman only sighs, as if she knew it would come to this. "Regazza paid me well. I knew Angelina wasn't his daughter, and I went to him and told him."

"He knew?" Romeo says in surprise.

Restrained, her face pressed up against the hardwood floor by the exit, she nods. "Yes. He paid me well to come here, to poison Angelina."

I cock my pistol, but Romeo stays my hand. "No, brother. Not tonight. We've had enough bloodshed for tonight. All who've betrayed us and threatened the lives of our family will pay." He nods to Mario. "Now bring her to the dungeon with Elise."

Angelina's eyes widen, but she doesn't speak. If Elise is in the dungeon, she's still alive. For now, that's all that matters.

Santo moves quickly to remove Regazza's body as Romeo continues to give orders. "Tavi, you'll deal with our prisoners after dinner. And Orlando..." He looks to me and Angelina. "You wanted to talk to me about a plan you had." His eyes twinkle at me. "She's yours, brother. Do you still want to talk?"

I nod my head. "Yeah, we have a lot to talk about."

Mama polishes off her drink and extends her arms. "Now, my loves, Nonna's cooked us a standing rib roast with those potatoes you all love. Let's eat, shall we?"

Angelina looks at me, a little stunned, but with relief shining in her eyes. "Your family's crazy," she whispers. "Like, certifiable. You know that, don't you?"

I yank her over to me and kiss her head fiercely. "Welcome to the family, baby."

CHAPTER 24

"How does he love me? With adoration, with fertile tears, With groans that thunder love, with sighs of fire." ~ *Twelfth Night, Shakespeare*

Angelina

ORLANDO KEEPS me by his side through it all. Through every grueling, gritty detail as the rest of the day unfolds. I watch it in a sort of stupor, half regretting the nausea had passed so I didn't have an excuse to go lay down and not emerge from the bedroom until the dust had settled.

First, Romeo took the big, beefy guards by the door and personally swept The Castle grounds for any remaining traitors or Regazza family. He found none.

"They were pretty confident, weren't they," he says to his brothers when they return to the Great Hall, the huge room in the center of The Castle where it seems all real business and gatherings take place.

"Jesus, you could say that again," Mario says. "What kind of a fucking lunatic comes here when his life is forfeit and behaves the way he did?"

I can still see Orlando's cool decision as he swiped the broken wineglass at Elise's father. I can still see the way the broken glass swept through his skin like a hot knife through butter, splitting him wide open and spilling blood onto the pretty carpet Tosca hoped to save.

"It's of no consequence," Tosca says, leaning back in her chair with an aperitif after the good dinner her mother made. "My husband was more attached to that carpet than I am. I just wanted an excuse to tell that bastard Luigi what to do."

I think I might love this woman.

Mario comes into the room with a grim expression on his face, accompanied by Marialena. "I'll let you tell her story," he says, taking a large platter of food the kitchen held for him. He eyes the tray of fresh-baked bread with only a few slices left and scowls at his brothers.

"I bake five loaves," Nonna says, waving her hand at him to settle down. "Go on, tell story." She waddles off to the kitchen to fetch more food for Mario and gives me a wink. "This why I no watch TV."

I think I might love her, too.

"I came down to get some food to take with me to

Tuscany," Marialena begins, giving Romeo a sniff before she continues. He only shakes his head at her and sprinkles salad dressing on his salad, tucking into what must be his fifth plate of food. I have never in my life seen anyone eat like these guys do.

"You can stay," he says. "But only because you were the one who blew the whistle."

I'll have to remember not to talk back to Romeo or give him shit about anything. It's all archaic, but here I am, a member of this fierce, loyal, crazy family I don't want to part from.

She sighs and raises her eyes heavenward before continuing her story. "I wanted to pack some snacks because the staff in Tuscany doesn't cook as well as Nonna and Mama, you know that. And when I opened the pantry door, I saw a trail of blood." Her eyes grow wide, like she's telling a ghost story by the fire. She isn't afraid of any of this. None of it is new to her. "I followed it, and that's when I found her." She makes a face of disgust. "She was naked, stripped of her uniform, so I knew immediately someone had taken her place."

"And that's when you screamed?" Mario says, spearing a piece of roast that's as big as my forearm with his fork.

Marialena nods triumphantly. "Exactly." She turns to me. "Orlando knew, too."

He nods, and gently eases his hand along my lower back. I move closer to him.

My friend, my best friend in the entire world, is being kept prisoner. But I know if she's to marry Tavi, they'll take care of her. It isn't what I hoped for her. It isn't what we planned. But even though this family may be terrifying in the eyes of the world, I feel as if Elise will get along just fine.

I look at Tavi, easily the sternest in the bunch, and that's saying something next to Romeo. He watches over everyone with a cool, detached look, then glances at his phone. I wonder what he's looking at. From here it looks like camera footage, though it's too dark to see. Just when I get a glimpse, he puts it away again. I'd bet good money he has a camera trained on Elise so he can watch her.

I want to go to my friend. I want to see her. But I know I can go only when Orlando allows it, and it's too soon to push my luck. I've only been released from imprisonment myself within hours.

I'm distracted, though, and Orlando knows it. "You've been through so much, babe," he says while the staff clears our meal. I can't believe after everything they've been through, they actually ate that meal.

I'll admit I did, too, though. Maybe I've been affected by being in this crazy family already. But damn, I was starving.

Nonna walks over to us, a tray of pastries in each hand. "Mangia," she says, holding a tray out to me. "One for you, one for bambino."

I take a pastry in each hand and slide them onto my plate in front of me.

"Italiano," she says with a laugh. "Eat like one, though."

Orlando laughs out loud, this deep, sexy, booming laugh that makes my belly dip and my heart beat faster. I turn to him and stare, hardly believing that the nightmare has almost passed.

"What's on your mind, baby?" he says gently, swiping a finger through my pastry and stealing a dollop of frosting.

I draw in a deep breath as I think about where I am, all that's happened. He's my husband, and I'm his wife. I'm carrying his child, and I've been accepted, no question, into his intense, crazy Italian family.

"Angelina Rossi," I say with a little smile. "There's a certain ring to it, isn't there?"

"It sounds like music," he says. "But that's not what's on your mind."

I bite my lip and look away. It may be too soon to push my luck, and my own nerves are fraught after everything we've been through today. But before I can articulate my concerns, he leans in and takes my hand. "You want to see Elise?"

I feel odd about it, admitting that I want to see the woman he was supposed to marry. But I nod. It doesn't feel right to sit here with my hot husband, after he killed my best friend's father, stuffing my face with pastry. Though that is, I now know , what the Rossi family does.

"Let's go upstairs," he says. "I can assure you, if Elise is to be Tavi's wife, he's taking good care of her. She's done us wrong, and you know that. She won't have an easy go of it, not right away anyway."

I nod. I know. That they've spared her life after this is nothing short of a miracle. "Yeah."

"But he won't hurt her. Let's give them the night together. I don't want to interfere. Then tomorrow, I'll talk to Romeo and Tavi and see what I can do."

I nod. Agreeing seems like the most intelligent choice right now.

"It's definitely a luxury pushing back from a delicious dinner with no dishes to wash, no kitchen to clean," I say to Orlando. "I could get used to this."

"Good," he says with a tired smile. "Let's just say it's one of the perks."

His hand comes to my lower back in a possessive move that I love and crave. Romeo watches us from where he sits beside Vittoria. He crooks a finger at us, and we walk over to him wordlessly. Orlando gives my fingers a little warning squeeze.

I nod. "I know, I know. Believe me, I am not stepping one toe out of line right now."

"Let's try yes, sir," he whispers in my ear.

My cheeks flush pink. "Yes, sir." He has kinky plans for me tonight, I know it.

Romeo has his arm resting casually behind Vittoria's seat. She's so lovely, sitting straight as an arrow with her hands folded in her lap. Her eyes gentle when she sees me and she slowly nods.

"You've been through a lot, Angelina."

I nod, not sure where she's going with this.

Holding my gaze, her brows draw together in a look of concern. "How are you holding up?"

I wait for Romeo to censor her, or tell her not to interfere, or something. He's so in everyone's business, I'm surprised he doesn't interfere at all.

"I'm okay," I say in a little voice. "Thank you."

"You're one of us now," she says. "I've heard all that happened. Whatever you need, you come to me or any of us. You have brothers who will defend you to the death, even if they'll swipe the scones right off your plate and go all caveman bossy about your safety. And sisters who have been in your very shoes." She smiles sadly. "Well, except for the baby part. But we'll get there."

"Thank you," I tell her warmly, a little choked up. God but it's been a day. "And you will."

"Orlando." Romeo looks straight past me to his brother.

Orlando nods.

"Take her upstairs. You two have had a long day. We all have. And tomorrow, we meet to discuss what happens next." Though Romeo's implacable features are stern and unyielding, there's a ferocity in his eyes that tells me he's loyal to his family. He'd take a bullet for my husband, and I can't help but love him for that.

Orlando swallows hard. "Thank you." His voice is all husky. I wonder why.

We go upstairs hand in hand. The house is strangely quiet, the only sound the voices rising and falling in the dining room.

"Where is everyone?" I ask.

"Romeo's dismissed the rest of the staff for tonight."

Ah. They've suffered a loss of one of their peers. I imagine it's sobering.

"Is he sure that everyone's safe here?"

"Absolutely. We have cameras trained on every inch of this property."

"And yet... someone was able to get in here and overtake your staff."

He nods. "She had inside help. The other reason Orlando dismissed staff for the night. We'll see who returns to work tomorrow and take it from there."

I feel as if they're all playing a game of chess and I'm still playing checkers. I'm looking ahead to the next move, and they're making moves that will result in the ultimate checkmate.

I think about Elise... Orlando says she's safe. She's probably safer than I am, anyway, and that's one thought that consoles me.

The baby within me is safe.

And somehow, despite all the odds...so am I.

CHAPTER 25

"If music be the food of love, play on." ~ *Twelfth Night, Shakespeare*

Orlando

A FEW DAYS pass before I take Angelina to Elise. I feel strange about seeing the woman I was supposed to marry, the one who's now betrothed to Tavi. And I want to be sure things are safe for Angelina before I do. Elise may have been her childhood friend, but she's being kept prisoner against her will, I murdered her father, and Tavi had her bodyguard murdered. She'll have to be watched very closely.

Tavi and Romeo have her stationed in a guest room in the most remote part of The Castle.

"At least she isn't in the dungeon anymore," Angelina says as we make our way to see her.

"For now." I have no idea what Tavi and Romeo have planned, and I will not interfere. She's escaped with her life, and that's what matters for now.

Angelina walks beside me and holds my hand. Her cheeks are flushed pink with the pregnancy glow I've heard about, and her belly's gently rounded. My chest swells with pride walking the corridor with her.

She sighs. I don't ask her why. I know it will take some time for her to get used to our ways. She may accept them for herself, but fear for her friend. Sometimes there are no good choices. Sometimes, you pick up the pieces after tragedy and make the most of what's left.

I'm hopeful, though. So hopeful. My brother, as Don, has made better choices and led our family more confidently than my father did for decades.

"Are there… like, rules or restrictions for what I can say?" she asks when we reach the door where uniformed, armed guards stand by.

"I wouldn't mention anything about the wedding just yet. Not sure she knows."

"Ah."

She stands closer to me when the guards step forward. "Sir, are you going in?" Romeo's actually taken one of our capos off his job to stand guard. I doubt it's Elise himself he fears, but repercussions from the Regazza family. Mario's working on communication about what's happened, and so far, so good.

"Yeah, we're going in. The Don's given us his blessing."

One nods to the other, confirming this, but they'd likely take my word for it as well. They stand back and open the door.

Elise Regazza stands by the window, staring out of the large frame. Sunlight shines in her hair, illuminating it. From here, she actually does look like Angelina, the same shade of hair and skin tone. But when she turns to me, she looks nothing like her at all. She's pretty, but she isn't my radiant wife.

Elise looks as if she's been crying, her eyes red and swollen, but when she sees Angelina, her whole face lights up. "No. No! You came!"

Angelina runs to her. She goes to clasp her friend's hands but finds them secured in handcuffs.

"Ah," she says with a wry smile. "So they've given you the gilded cage, have they?"

Elise's widened eyes swing to mine in alarm as if expecting my wrath. Angelina only laughs. "Oh, he has a temper alright, but won't get angry for me stating the truth." Elise only watches me warily.

"I'm just glad you're okay," she says to Angelina. "I can't—"

Her eyes fall to Angelina's swollen abdomen, and she gives an audible gasp, bringing her cuffed hands to her mouth. "Are you…"

"Pregnant with a little mobster baby? Oh yeah."

I give her a teasing smack to the ass. Fucking adorable.

Angelina sits on the edge of the bed, the only place to sit in the small confines of the room. I stand by the window, giving them a little space.

"I suppose privacy isn't gonna happen," Elise mutters.

"Yeah, no," Angelina agrees. "But he's my husband, Elise. And you can trust Orlando."

Elise snorts. "Trust? We can't use the words trust when we talk of any of the Rossis. Angelina, have they brainwashed you?"

Oh, Tavi will have some fun with this one.

They talk about what happened, at length. Elise wants to make sure Angelina's really alright, and it warms my heart to hear Angelina assuring her that she is. They talk of Elise's escape, and both cry when they talk about her bodyguard Piero's death. Elise stares out the window mournfully. "He died for me," she whispers.

Angelina reaches for her hand and gives her a little squeeze. "I know. I'm so sorry."

I wonder if she'll ever hold a candle for my brother, knowing that he was responsible for Piero's death. I wonder if that matters.

It amuses me to hear Angelina talking to Elise about our family, what's expected, what she's learned. "They're nothing like your father, Elise. Nothing."

Elise seems unmoved.

Finally, I tell Angelina we need to go now. They've talked at length, and I won't trespass on Tavi's need to confine and punish his prisoner. He won't wait long to take vows. He'll want to move quickly to solidify our treaty with the Regazzas. And he, along with me, will want to fortify our own family with the bond of marriage and children.

The women embrace as we take our leave. Angelina bows her head and holds my hand.

"It's an end of an era, isn't it?" she asks quietly.

"Ah, I don't know about an era." My father's death was an end of an era. "But I guess you could say another chapter's begun."

We walk hand in hand, the two of us bearing the painful wounds of love, loss, and tragedy, but finding solace and comfort in each other.

"Let's make it a good one, Orlando," she says with that confidence and conviction that make me love her so. "Our story. Our chapter. Let's make it a good one."

I kiss her cheek. "Once upon a time..."

EPILOGUE

"Be not afraid of greatness." ~*Twelfth Night,* *Shakespeare*

Orlando

"Shhh," Angelina says when I open the door to the nursery. Unlike other women in our extended family, Angelina has forgone any help from a nanny or maid. She says she's waited long enough for a child of her own, and she'll relish every minute.

And even though sometimes she's tired and weary from keeping up with the late-night feedings and around-the-clock diaper changes, I know she wouldn't have it any other way.

With a large, bustling family like ours, we've decided to stay at The Castle for the first few months anyway. I'll take her to Tuscany and we'll spend time in Boston proper as well. But for now, it's nice having dozens of sets of arms that will gladly take a turn with the endless rocking and soothing.

Nicolo Lorenzo Rossi came into this world screaming, making his presence known, and even as an infant, my son is a force to be reckoned with.

My son.

"You ready?" She wears a gorgeous champagne-colored dress that accents her curves, silver heels completing her look.

"I am." She turns to me and raises her eyebrows. "And you look pretty damn good yourself." She whistles low so she doesn't wake the baby. "Hubba hubba."

It's the day of our son's baptism, a Rossi family tradition that spans the ages, and our entire extended family has come to celebrate. It's the first time many of them will meet my son and wife. My chest might burst from pride.

Elise Regazza is still a prisoner, though she spends so much time with Angelina and the baby it hardly feels like it. Tavi keeps a watchful eye on her. I was surprised at first he was so insistent on her being held captive as long as he has, but he's a patient sort, and unyielding as fuck. "I won't have a wife who doesn't know her place," he said to me one day. My father would be proud.

They marry next month. Angelina and I will be their witnesses, and the rest of our family will attend.

They'll have the lavish Italian wedding Nonna and Mama dream of.

The Regazzas have made their peace. A smaller group than ours, they moved fully to Tuscany after the death of Luigi Regazza. Elise doesn't seem bothered at all. Probably grateful she has fewer reminders of Piero to haunt her.

Romeo and Tavi, despite their strongest efforts, could not find the traitor who aided Regazza. Romeo fired every last one of them, from the gardener to housekeeping. A new start, as it were.

Nonna sits at the front of the church in her traditional formal black dress, beaming at all of us. Mama sits beside her, her gaze cooler but still pleased, and when she sees me, she gives me a wink. Romeo holds my son against his shoulder, dressed in the white satin baptismal gown passed down from generation to generation.

"Why does he wear a dress?" Natalia asks Rosa, who smiles and shushes her.

"It's tradition," Rosa tells her then gives me a wink.

Tradition. It's the very foundation on which we're built, the rock that sustains us. Some may call them pointless rituals, but I know better.

My brothers take vows upon their initiation to the Rossi brotherhood, woven in the customs that bind us. Oaths that weave our family from threads to tapestry, a seamless bond that outlasts the ages.

Romeo smiles at me when he hands me my son. I

tuck the sleeping child against my shoulder and draw Angelina to me. She looks up at me, with her eyes shining. I bend and kiss her, my beautiful wife. All around us, cameras flash like we've been captured by paparazzi, but I know why they encapsulate this moment. Life is fleeting and the days pass quickly, but love... love is eternal.

FROM THE AUTHOR:

Thank you for reading Oath of Obedience! *I hope you're loving the Rossi family saga. If you haven't yet read book one, you can read* Oath of Silence HERE. *Ready for more Rossi family?* Pre-order Oath of Fidelity HERE!

PREVIEW

OATH OF FIDELITY: A DARK MAFIA ROMANCE

CHAPTER ONE

Tavi

I STARE at the cracked tile that leads to the altar of Saint Anthony's and remember how it broke. I wonder if anyone else here does. Not everyone can say they remember the way their father body slammed the alter server on their first communion day.

Why? Who the hell knows. Probably looked at him funny or showed my father what he thought was a form of disrespect.

I can still see the way my mother's face grew cold and impassive, her typical response to my father's fits of rage. Unless his fury was aimed at one of *us*. Then, we saw another Tosca Rossi, one whose own face and body bore the brunt of his fury and anger when she came between him and us. My father was, after all, a psychopath. He bled out over a year ago on the very property I was born.

We didn't try to save him. It was time.

I wonder sometimes if mental illness is genetic. I wonder if it knocks on my own door, but I refuse to answer it. It's the age-old question I think most men ask themselves at one point in their lives.

Will I become my father?

I fold my hands and listen to the gospel readings, chosen for today by my sister-in-law Angelina for the special occasion of her son's baptism. My niece Natalia fidgets uncomfortably in her seat, and when she looks at me, I put my finger to my lips to remind her to be quiet and soften the correction with a wink to show her I'm as bored as she is. With a sigh, she turns around and obeys.

Elise, my betrothed, catches my eye. I feel my body go rigid, a coldness suffusing my limbs. She blinks and starts as if struck, then turns to Angelina and whispers something. Angelina hands her the sleeping baby dressed in the traditional white gown used for every Rossi family baptism.

Elise and I didn't choose this. Few of us in The Family ever do.

I think of every sacrament we endured within the walls of this church. While I was way too young to remember my own baptism, I remember Mario and Marialena's, my younger brother's and sister's. I remember how Mama bought us small, matching tuxedos, and how my father made us polish our shoes. I remember Romeo making me and Orlando sit still when we fidgeted. I remember First Communions, a few of my cousins' weddings, and the somber funeral for my father, probably the only funeral I've attended where not one person shed a tear. Romeo ordered champagne for the funeral brunch.

As I remember the Sacraments we've celebrated here... I know why that broken tile's never been replaced. Romeo himself probably ordered it kept there, since he's the church's largest benefactor and has a say in all repairs and projects. But that tile... it's a stark yet subtle reminder of the power the Rossi family holds. We singlehandedly support this church. I've looked over my family's bookkeeping for years. There's a reason why Saint Anthony's is the most affluent in all of Massachusetts.

My brother Orlando clears his throat and wiggles his eyebrows at me. The whole church is silent, expectant, even the organ still as he waits for me. I'm baby Nicolo's godfather. It's time.

I stand and join Orlando, who beams as he walks to the altar beside his beautiful wife Angelina. They both smile at me, but I don't share their joy.

Angelina nearly threw my family into ruin. She forced my hand in ordering the execution of a man I never wanted to kill. It's because of her I'm marrying the woman beside her.

"Come, godfather," my future wife murmurs. "You're supposed to stand beside me." I don't like her telling me what to do in even the most innocuous way, so when I give her a look that seems to startle her, she softens her tone. "Please."

She bends her head toward the baby and nuzzles Nicolo's soft, fuzzy head. His matching white satin hat has fallen to the side, attached loosely to the traditional gown with a matching satin ribbon. I watch as she kisses the baby and still doesn't meet my eyes.

I look at the beautiful and proud Elise Regazza, the woman betrothed to me, and walk to her side. We're the chosen godparents for Orlando and Angelina's baby, so we take our place where we belong.

Elise Regazza may be many things — spoiled, head-strong, and materialistic, to name just a few — but the woman is beautiful. Stunning, really. Shorter than me by about six inches, she still stands tall in chunky heels. She has the same light brown hair as Angelina, the one character trait that allowed them to pull a temporary identity switch at one time. Now, however, Angelina's highlighted her hair lighter, making Elise's look slightly darker in comparison.

Her hair is long and straight, and hangs well past her shoulders. Her beautiful, pale blue eyes framed in thick lashes, catch my attention. I know she wears contacts but occasionally glasses, though she's never let me see them.

I know everything about her. It's my job.

Her gently rounded face would make her look almost girlish, if not for the wild defiance in her eyes, eyes as deep and amber as a shot of amaretto. A gentle smattering of freckles and a dimple in her chin complete the fetching, nearly girlish look, but her full, light pink lips, and curvy, hourglass figure are *all woman.*

What my family knows, that no one else likely does, is that Elise Regazza is my prisoner.

I allow her some freedom, at Orlando's suggestion, because his wife Angelina is her best friend. But I don't trust either of them. Those two were, after all, guilty of conspiring against my family.

They've paid their due diligence, some would say — Angelina is now married to my brother, after a lengthy imprisonment of her own. Because of their marriage, she's now a full-fledged member of our family. And Elise has been kept under lock and key for months.

She's allowed to walk, and allowed to travel to the shops within ten miles of here, but I track her every move and insist she have three high-ranking bodyguards on her at all times. It's nothing short of walking confinement. I don't regret it.

I don't think she's dangerous. She'd like to think I do. But no, I don't keep a tight leash on her because I fear her escape. I want her to remember she's my prisoner and will be until we take our vows and consummate our marriage.

There's an embedded gps tracker under the skin of her left upper arm, the exact place where one would implant birth control. Not that *that* will never happen. I know wherever she is when she's not directly in my line of vision.

She also wears a thick, gold cuff bracelet fitted with GPS as well, one connected to the apps on my phone. It heats and generates a warming sensation across her wrist, when I want to issue her a warning. It also shows me her constant whereabouts, as well as her vital signs — her heartbeat, her body temperature, and even when she's waking or sleeping.

I know when she's doing yoga, when she's jogging, or when she's resting. I watch her more closely than most wardens monitor prisoners.

But Elise has behaved herself. She's comported herself with the dignity befitting a mafia princess— as she was raised, and as she'll soon learn to become once more.

"Welcome," Father Richard says, smiling benevolently at the large, well-dressed group of family members that have come after mass to witness Nicolo's baptism. Nonna and Mama sit up front, Mama dressed in a form-fitting black dress, and

Nonna wearing her own traditional black dress and sensible shoes as well. But among those in the congregation are my sisters, my brothers, the sworn brothers of The Family and their own loved ones, as well as my cousins, aunts, and uncles. Nearly ever bench in the church is occupied with someone dressed in black or gold, like an Italian mafia photo shoot for a travel guide.

"We've come to witness the sacred ritual of baptism," the priest continues. "What name have you given your child?"

"Nicolo Lorenzo Rossi," Orlando says without hesitation, his chest nearly swelling with pride. Angelina beams at the baby, and as the baby begins to sniff and fuss, Elise automatically begins to sway from side to side to soothe him.

The priest begins the ritual of anointing, first making the sign of the cross on the baby's forehead, then leading Elise and the baby to the solid marble baptismal font that stands in front of our semi-circle. He lifts a small golden cup, Elise holds the baby over the font, and with the ritualistic prayers, Father Richard pours water over Nicolo's head.

The baby starts, opens his mouth, and wails so loudly you'd think he was being tortured. Undeterred, Elise smiles and holds him steady while Father completes the baptism. Her pretty, dainty hand, adorned with several slender gold rings, her nails manicured and painted a bold, vivid red, cups the baby's head gently.

"Here, Uncle," she says, handing me the baby after the last sprinkling of water. I reach for him, gathering him up in the miles of satin, while he continues to wail his heart out. "Why don't you hold your godson?"

I hold him up to my shoulder and tuck one hand against his bottom, and imitate her swaying from side to side. I have lots of younger siblings and a niece, as well as tons of cousins, so I'm not new to this. The baby nuzzles my shoulder and begins to quiet.

Elise's lips gently part and her eyes widen as she watches me, but the look only lasts a few seconds before her gaze shutters and she looks away.

I don't know what the look means. I don't much care, either. We're following the steps laid out to us from our fathers before us and their fathers before them, from generation to generation.

"Come, Elise. Follow me."

She mutters something under her breath that sounds like *as if I have a choice*. She's right. She knows I've set her bracelet to close proximity, and if she's more than ten feet away from me her wrist will begin to heat. It won't heat to burning, but it won't be pleasant.

"What was that?" I ask in a low voice out of the side of my mouth, still smiling for the flashing cameras all around the church. The smell of incense envelopes us so strong it's nearly cloying.

"Oh, nothing," she says in a voice as sickly sweet as the incense. "I said exactly what you want to hear. *Yes, Tavi.* That's what you want to hear, isn't it?"

Ah, so she's decided to toy with being smug. We'll see if she's still smiling tonight, after I show her the new present I got her.

"Good girl," I say, in a tone as mocking as hers. "That's exactly what I want to hear."

Among other things. We'll get there.

Four weeks. Four weeks until we take our own place by the altar, when we both take vows to each other. Orlando and Angelina will be our only witnesses, but we've caved and allowed Mama and Nonna to plan the huge, lavish wedding that's our custom, the wedding Romeo and Orlando never had. They've waited long enough. It's our turn now.

Four more weeks until we consummate our marriage. When we do our duty and become a couple.

In theory, anyway.

I've watched my brothers grow soft with marriage and a bride, allowing their wives to basically do what they want. They think they're in charge, that their the heads of their houses, but I've seen how lenient they've become.

That won't happen with me. I won't have a wife that doesn't know her place. And even though Elise has been kept prisoner, she's nowhere near done paying the price for what she's done.

Elise will be my wife, and she'll learn exactly what that means.

READ MORE

USA Today bestselling author Jane Henry pens stern but loving alpha heroes, feisty heroines, and emotion-driven happily-ever-afters. She writes what she loves to read: kink with a tender touch. Jane is a hopeless romantic who lives on the East Coast with a houseful of children and her very own Prince Charming.

You can find Jane here:

Jane Henry's Newsletter

Jane Henry's Facebook Reader Group

https://www.janehenryromance.com

BB bookbub.com/profile/jane-henry

f facebook.com/janehenryromance

O instagram.com/janehenryauthor

a amazon.com/Jane-Henry/e/B01BYAQYYK

Made in the USA
Columbia, SC
05 March 2022

57239329R00185